George Bush

Also by Fitzhugh Green:

A Change in the Weather
American Propaganda Abroad

George Bush

An Intimate Portrait

FITZHUGH GREEN

HIPPOCRENE BOOKS
New York

For information address:
Hippocrene Books, Inc.
171 Madison Avenue
New York, NY 10016

ISBN 0-87052-783-5

Printed in the United States of America

To Barbara Bush: Her 45-year alliance with George Bush has yielded triumph in many realms, survived some sadness; and made a marital union that inspires a nation.

Contents

Acknowledgments

To prepare for this book I interviewed some 400 individuals, a number of them several times. Tapes and notes have captured their thoughts. I am grateful to them all and am listing a few of those who were most helpful:

Richard V. Allen, John Allin, John S. Andrews, Thomas Ludlow Ashley, Mr. and Mrs. John Ashmun, Judith Ayers, Gregg Baise, James A. Baker III, Charles L. Bartlett, Fitzgerald Bemiss, W. Tapley Bennett Jr., Francis S. Blake, Tom Boyer, Paul Boynton, John A. Bross, L. Dean Brown, Mrs. David Bruce, Josiah Bunting, Dean Burch, Barbara Bush, Dorothy Bush, Fred Bush, George Bush Jr., Marvin Bush, Mrs. Prescott S. Bush, Mr. and Mrs. Prescott S. Bush Jr., William T. Bush, Samuel Campiche, Rudolph Carter, Henry B. Catto, C. Fred Chambers, John Chancellor, John H. Chafee, John E. Chapoton, Chester V. Clifton, Ray Cline, Derek Crandall, Walter J.P. Curley, Mrs. Edwin Dale, Mr. and Mrs. Robert W. Duemling, Anthony D. Duke, Linda C. Durkee, Mrs. Alexander Ellis Jr., Rowland Evans Jr., Richard Fairbanks, Andrew Falkiewicz, Seymour M. Finger, Laurie Green Firestone, John C. Fitch, Marlin Fitzwater, Clayton Fritchey, Bruce Gelb, David Gergen, Frederick A. Godley, Vic Gold, Louis Grab, C. Boyden Gray, Penelope Green, Arthur T. Hadley, Mrs. Ferris Hamilton, Elizabeth W. Hamilton, Jay Hass, Richard M. Helms, Palmer Hill, Toby Hilliard, James L. Holloway III, Sonny Hutchins, Robert L. Ireland, Jonathan T. Isham, Ardon Judd, Michael Judd, David A. Keene, Nicholas King, George Lauder, Eugene K. Lawson, John M. Laxalt, Bill Liedtke, J. Hugh Liedtke, John V. Lindsay, George deF. Lord, Richard B. McAdoo, Allan McHale, Grace Moe, Richard A. Moore, Jonathan Moore, Daniel J. Murphy, Edmund S. Muskie, Donald D. Notman, Michael J. O'Bannon, Jim Oberwetter, John Overbey, Maureen O'Ryan, Charles H. Percy, Roswell B. Perkins, Elizabeth Pfau, James Pierce, Steuart L. Pittman, Christopher H. Phillips, Walter Pincus, Charles Powell, Martha Rafferty, Thomas F. Railsback, Kenneth Raynor, Albert J. Redway Jr., Don Rhodes, Mr. and Mrs. James M.C. Ritchie, Paul Robinson, Debbie Romash, Susan Porter Rose, Lou Rotterman, Peter Roussel, William D. Ruckelshaus, Arthur M. Schlesinger Jr., Daniel L. Schorr, Jonathan W. Sloat, John J. Slocum, Mary Louise Smith, Aleene Smith, Jack Steel, Andrew Steigman, John R. Stevenson, Mrs. Potter Stewart, Richard Taggs, Nancy Thawley, Mr. and Mrs. Harry E.T. Thayer, Richard Thaxton, Anthony J. Thompson, Timothy L. Towell, Jim Joseph Tozzi, Margaret Tutweiler, Chase Untermeyer, Brian Urquhart, Henry Vadnais, Jorge Vargas, Mrs. Alexander Vietor, Paul Wagner, Diana Walker, Charles S. Whitehouse, Deborah Wince, Jing Xianfe, Rose Zamaria and Fred M. Zeder.

My thanks are due to Catherine Pitts and Katherine Guthmiller for organizing, duplicating and understanding the output of word processors used for the manuscript; and to Nancy Ganahl and Kimberley Spain for their skilled research help.

Vital to this enterprise have been three people: George Blagowidow, my publisher, whose idea the book was in the first place and whose enthusiasm has kept it moving at flank speed; Marie Arana-Ward, whose editorial brilliance has continuously kept the author from the twin sloughs of banality and vagueness; and General Chester V. Clifton, whose wise counsel has maintained reality in the project throughout its evolution. All three of these individuals have the author's profound gratitude.

Writing is thought to be a solitary occupation. Yet this biography has been a joint venture involving the ideas and memories of many people.

Preface

WALK THE STREETS OF GRAND RAPIDS, MICHIGAN, and with a little fine tuning of the imagination one can hear the exuberant shouts of Eagle Scout Gerald Ford. Stand in the seared streets of Yorba Linda, California, and gaze at the tiny boyhood home of Richard Nixon, and suddenly there is a tug to move on. Journey to the grass and stand along the ocean's edge at Hyannisport, Massachusetts, and you can hear, as John Kennedy did, the distant calls of warriors and ship captains. Squint from the front porch of Lyndon Johnson's early Texas home and there is the huge sky and the hard weather waiting beyond to temper and shape a man. Loiter on the hill above the Rock River in Dixon, Illinois, as the summer light fades and Ronald Reagan and a gang of kids will come out of the shadows and tussle on the green lawns, trusting and believing in their code and their country.

Where to find George Bush? Along the rocky shore of Kennebunkport, Maine, or on the manicured lawns of Greenwich, Connecticut? Maybe in the windowless Skull and Bones clubhouse of Yale University, or at the Petroleum Club of Midland,

Texas? Though he may be the mildest, the most unassuming, the least self-centered of the modern presidents, Bush may prove to be the most illusive when examined by today's legion of presidential analysts.

He is, if we may borrow from Bush's own political lexicon, a million points of light, and some shadow too. How they play on each other and what they will mean for us will ultimately constitute the Bush adventure, the 41st chapter in the American presidency. Given the natural vigor and growth of the modern media, it probably is not a great stretch to suggest that already more has been written and broadcast about George Bush early on the job than any other recent president. He has been in public life so long—23 years through seven assignments. And yet there is the vague feeling that we know him less, only dimly understanding what makes him function. He has been so many places, done so much—but so politely and quietly.

Presidents, like other striving humans, resemble complex geologic formations. They are created over the years as the various strata are deposited by heritage, by experience. They do not suddenly leap into full power. There is no manual on how to be president. They do not appear overnight at center stage, nudging nations this way and that. They are gentled by mothers, challenged by fathers, inspired by teachers, humbled by failure and assembled finally in the forge of continuous exposure to the world's realities.

George Bush is the most blessed of the presidents of this century. He was born with wealth (but not too much), given health, intelligence, talent, good looks, family love, discipline and the confidence that follows all of the above. He observed the great depression but was never scarred by it. He was called to war and his courage was summoned in combat, but he was not maimed by battle, either in mind or body. His political defeats were never of such magnitude to discourage him. His victories were not so great that they bred arrogance.

What now to expect? The presidency is a challenge far beyond anything else that Bush has undertaken. It is impossible to chart the way ahead. The world is so capricious, the problems too intractable, even this privileged man—so carefully shaped and burnished by Providence—will need a kind of magic to claim success. What moves in Bush's heart and mind? From whence did it come? We can at least get some hints.

Fitzhugh Green writes here of the intimacies of George Bush's formation, the little things that are the glue of the human soul. In his way, Green offers us some of the best glimpses yet caught of Bush, especially the early Bush where the building blocks of character were laid down. In the flashes of insight one can see courage and concern, in the crevices of family experience there are calls to honor and duty, in the narrative of his adult life there are the marks of hard work and ambition. Collect all of them and they make up the mosaic which is George Bush, they are the reasons why he is president of the United States.

—Hugh Sidey
June 1989
Washington, D.C.

George Bush

CHAPTER 1

Heir to Excellence

THE BOY IS FATHER TO THE MAN, AND GEORGE BUSH is no exception. But the father of the boy was such a paramount figure in George's life, that Prescott Bush's story comes first.

For George and his siblings, Prescott stood tall, an imposing father in the small enclave of Greenwich, Connecticut. In their eyes he must have seemed invincible. He not only was a strict and loving father, but he also was a hardworking and successful businessman who disappeared into Manhattan for nearly twelve hours daily, a community leader who spent long evenings on the Greenwich town council and hospital board, a champion golfer who brought home silver cups as often as some garnered groceries, and a stern church-goer and a singer with a booming bass voice.

He was built to match these accomplishments. Prescott was six-foot-four; weighed two hundred pounds; had a physique of well-conditioned muscle; and was blessed with a handsome, craggy face topped with thick charcoal-black hair and prominent brows.

He bore no nonsense from the boys: Prescott Jr. (born in

1

1922), George (1924), Jonathan (1931), and William T. ("Bucky," 1938). He was a bit more gentle with his third child and only daughter, Nancy. But the children revered him. He was warm and affectionate with them, although they knew he could mete out firm discipline if necessary. Friends of the family over the years found him dignified, courtly and never really hard on anyone. With all his talents and accomplishments, he clearly liked people, had a twinkle in his eye, and made them feel at ease.

Prescott Bush was a theatrical fellow, a man who held center stage naturally, regardless of what was happening. Perhaps he had been influenced by the famous actor Douglas Fairbanks, who took an interest in young Prescott when the boy caddied for him in the family resort at Watch Hill, Rhode Island. At the time Prescott was the schoolboy golf champion of Ohio. Fairbanks electrified young Bush when he was at Yale by sending him free tickets to see one of his plays on Broadway. There also was Prescott Bush's gift for singing, which gave him the timing and technique of a public figure even before he became one.

The children were raised not to be like him, but to accept the values that he and their mother, Dorothy, laid down for them: honesty, modesty, neatness and an unwillingness to talk about money. Yes, their father made enough money for them to be comfortable, but he had to work hard to do so. Therefore, it was wrong to leave one's bicycle out in the rain.

To Prescott's satisfaction, all of his boys (except for George) had good voices too, and he spent many hours teaching them how to sing together, in quartets, the way he had learned at Yale. They were well aware that he had sung on the nationally known Whiffenpoofs and Yale Glee Club; that he had been so good that he almost was a musical legend there. One spinoff of all this was the "Silver Dollar Quartet," a popular amateur group of which he was a part that was asked to sing in various cities on the East Coast.

The children enjoyed hearing how he had met their pretty and athletic mother in St. Louis and how the two had fallen in love and married and were in the process of living happily ever after with their adored progeny. It was a secure upbringing with these parents who did everything right and expected the same from people around them. The children learned about the night when their father and mother were at a soiree celebrating an event with toasts and songs. One of the speakers used the four-letter S word in a joke he was telling. Immediately, but without fanfare, the Bushes excused themselves and went home. Their son Jonathan has been quoted as saying he never heard his father break wind; as a fact that may not make Prescott Bush unique, but, as a report from his child, it bespeaks an attitude, more along the lines of not that he didn't, but that he wouldn't! Curiously, George Bush's youngest son, Marvin, has specified that he wouldn't commit that faux pas in front of his grandfather.

Prescott Bush's children steadily picked up more information about him. His war experience was of great interest to them. He had fought in the Meuse-Argonne offensive in France and actually had found the adventure of it all exciting. He had become a captain in the army and was decorated. He also was well thought of not only by his fellow officers but also by soldiers in general with whom he was said to have enjoyed swapping yarns.

From the unbending requirement that they attend church every Sunday, the children were not surprised to find out that when Prescott was a student at St. George's boarding school, he had briefly considered becoming an Episcopalian minister, like his grandfather. They also were proud to discover that he had been an outstanding athlete and senior prefect of his school.

It was more complicated to understand how he had reached the happy and lucrative business heights with Brown Brothers, Harriman where he was a partner in New York. They knew that it had to do with investing money. They did grasp that it involved their grandfather, George Herbert Walker, a hero in their lexicon, since he had held the amateur heavyweight boxing crown in Missouri. Now he was head of his son-in-law's company. Another key person there was Roland Har-

riman, who had been at Yale with their father. They had both
been members of the exclusive and mysterious Skull and
Bones Club.

It wasn't like Prescott Bush to boast about himself to his
children. Gradually, though, by listening to their parents and
their friends converse and questing elsewhere for information,
the elder boys pieced together their father's climb to success.
Details were skimpy, but they became aware that he had found
his first job after the war by talking to a fellow Yale alumnus at
a reunion in New Haven. Then he worked in numerous places
in the Midwest, South and Northeast, under several nationally
known industrial names like Simmons, Winchester Arms and
U.S. Rubber Company.

After these switches he settled on an affiliation that would
endure for the rest of his life. How he was hired was certainly a
useful lesson for his boys. The investment banking house of W.
A. Harriman brought him in as the first young (he was then 31)
college graduate in their organization. They thought his time
with U.S. Rubber was useful, and that his varied industrial
experience most likely would enhance his judgment on security values. They also looked favorably on his wide acquaintance through his education and military service. In
short, they felt he had a lot of contacts for a young man; that he
could attract business.

The Harriman firm had begun just a few years earlier. It was
owned mainly by W. Averell Harriman, who would later hold
many top diplomatic and other positions in Washington. He
was chairman of the board; Prescott's father-in-law, G. H.
Walker, had become president. Walker and Averell's brother,
Roland, also owned a substantial share of the business.

The next step was only vaguely clear to Bush's children as
they heard about it in succeeding years. This was the 1931
merger of the Harriman company with Brown Brothers, who
were respected veterans in investment and commercial banking both in the United States and overseas. The deal gave an
infusion of prestige to the Harrimans and much-needed capital
to the Browns, who still suffered financial strain from the 1929
crash.

The resulting firm was a model of cooperation. All the men at the top were convivial, most of them close friends of many years. The young Bush boys surely were affected by the easy nature of their father's success. What a pleasant way to make money! Brown Brothers, Harriman did increase business and profits despite the lingering economic slump in America, which ended only with the onset of World War II.

As Brown Brothers, Harriman prospered, Prescott Bush again found himself, as he had at St. George's, among the "favored few." He wasted little time living up to his earlier resolve to plough his good fortune back into the system that provided it. Soon he devoted himself to this aim via numerous volunteer routes.

As time went on, the Bush children saw their father grow in importance. He was president of the U.S. Golf Association and managed to change a silly rule about stymies. Until Prescott Bush changed it, the stymie allowed one player to use his ball to block his opponent's ball from a free shot at the hole.

During World War II Prescott was made head of the United Service Organization (USO), which provided recreation for soldiers and sailors both at home and abroad.

As an investor in companies that became successful, like Pan American Airways, Columbia Broadcasting System and Dresser Industries, Prescott Bush built his fortune. He also joined their boards, thus helping produce employment for Pres Jr. in Pan Am and later for George in Dresser Industries.

While his kids were emerging into the competitive postwar world, their father's career kept on its rising trajectory. In the late 1940s he began to advance from his community service activities, which had included raising money for the Republican Party of Connecticut, toward elective office. Soon he had an opening to run for the U.S. House of Representatives.

His partners at Brown Brothers, Harriman balked at the idea of this political move. They thought he was too important to them to leave just to become a congressman. But when he had the chance to go for a Senate seat, they acquiesced. His race for the Senate and his service there is covered later since it coincides with George Bush's career.

This review of Prescott Bush's excellence would not be complete without sufficient emphasis on his supreme talent: music. His children were aware that it was in Bush Senior's musical side that his soul thrived. They well knew that his singing companions were legion, like John Holmes, fifteen years his junior, former president of the Yale Glee Club and a Whiffenpoof. One sunny spring afternoon in 1950, Holmes encountered Bush walking up Fifth Avenue in New York. Holmes introduced the attractive lady at his side to Bush, who immediately recognized her name. "I believe you are a fine singer. Is that right?" asked Bush. Holmes affirmed that indeed she was. Whereupon Bush threw an arm around her shoulders and said, "Well, why don't we have a little song?" At that, he led the other two into the nearest bar on a side street and, as Holmes recalls, "We sang one number after another for the next two hours. We two were in awe of him, he was such a distinguished fellow, and his music was pure gold. Yet he was so pleasant to us more youthful types. It wasn't that his voice was so outstanding, but it was his ear, his enthusiasm and his concept of a second bass part in a quartet which revolutionized barbershop singing," Holmes said. "Also he had an incredible repertoire of old songs that we had never heard before. He taught us some that day."

One story about their dad was kept quiet until the children were adults. Evidently he had an inner office in Brown Brothers, Harriman, and when he was in there his secretary would tell callers that he was in conference. That room had a little piano in it, and if his secretary said "Mr. Bush is busy," he probably was puzzling out a new arrangement with Chuck Spofford, one of his partners in the Silver Dollar Quartet.

Also in awe of Prescott Bush were three young Washingtonians who sang with him from about 1962 to 1968, after he quit the Senate. These were Joyce Barrett (daughter of Clark Clifford, lawyer and advisor to presidents since Harry Truman), her husband Richard D. Barrett (a banker), and Wesley M. Oler, (a physician). When I told Barrett about the meeting on Fifth Avenue, he said he was surprised that Bush didn't burst into singing right on the spot since he loved to do it so much.

This threesome were all thirty years or so junior to the senator, actually of his children's generation, but they enjoyed each others' singing company so much that they met for dinner and song a half-dozen times per year. Usually they sang at Bush's house in the Georgetown section of Washington. He called them the Kensington Four, named for the city suburb in which the Barretts lived. Dick Barrett described Bush in those days as still handsome and fit-looking, with his black hair turned to salt and pepper.

Dr. Oler feels that he probably already had been stricken with the cancer that he suffered until his death in 1972. He had left the Senate because he said his arthritis limited his strength somewhat. Often thereafter, Bush sorrowed that he had not run again. He missed being a senator; it appeared to him and others that he could have carried the state easily.

The Kensington Four helped ease this disappointment. They also met sometimes in Bush's Greenwich house, or the one in Hobe Sound, Florida. Barrett remembers that at Greenwich they would sit around the swimming pool on summer evenings while Dorothy Bush would listen. "We would join him wherever he asked us to go," says Barrett. George and Barbara were only present at one of these occasions, in Washington, and then only for dinner. Son Jonathan Bush would sometimes come from New York to join in along with Jonathan ("Jack") Sloat.

The Alibi Club in Washington was another rendezvous for these evenings of dinner and song. The Alibi has only about 50 members, with very few of them politicians. It is so named, according to unverifiable sources, because if a member's wife calls him at the club, the head waiter says he isn't there even if he is.

"We would take over the entire club, just the four of us," says Barrett. "First we would have food and drink in that dark wood-paneled dining room," which has the skull of a sabre-toothed tiger, heads of African wildlife, quaint eighteenth-

century pictures and trinkets from everywhere. The club has
very few rooms; it is housed in a small building now squeezed
on both sides by modern structures in downtown Washington.
The late Senator Leverett Saltonstall of Massachusetts and
Senator Bush would lunch there on Fridays while they were in
the Senate together.

"Then we would stand up and sing for hours," Barrett goes
on. "He was just full of singing reminiscences. He would teach
us all his old Silver Dollar Quartet songs. He was the bass,
Joyce was the first tenor, I was baritone, and Wes Oler the lead
tenor."

He usually came to these get-togethers dressed in a blue
blazer, with a Senate tie that carried the Great Seal of the
United States, and a white handkerchief bunched roughly into
the pocket. Asked what they talked about at dinner, Barrett
said he couldn't remember, but it seemed to be mostly music.
What about his family? "No, he didn't talk about them," was
the reply.

A similar recollection comes from Edward K. Wheeler, who
as a young lawyer in the 1950s would be invited to join
Senator Bush for a round of golf. Those were the years that
Bush often played with President Eisenhower at the Burning
Tree Club. Wheeler was good enough to be club champion and
found Bush fully competitive in the best levels of golf.

"What did you talk about?" I asked Wheeler recently.
"Mostly golf or politics," said Wheeler, whose father was Senator Burton K. Wheeler of Montana. "What about family?" I
pursued. "No, he never mentioned his family," returned
Wheeler.

Wheeler brings to mind Jack Kennedy's father, Joe. The day
Kennedy was elected president, Senator Wheeler called Joe
Kennedy to congratulate him. It is well known that Joe had
groomed his first son, Joe Jr., to be president some day. After he
died when his plane was shot down over a Nazi submarine pen
in World War II, Joe concentrated on preparing Jack for the
presidency. Now, according to Wheeler, old Joe's response was
"Yeah, thanks, Burt. Jack's all right. But keep an eye on Bobby,
he's got a future; he's the one with the brains!" Sure enough,

Robert F. Kennedy entered the Senate and ran for the presidency as soon as he could after JFK's death.

Prescott Bush never tried to prepare his sons for anything but good citizenry. Much has been made of Joe Kennedy's coming home infrequently to conduct issue-oriented talks among his children at the dinner table. Bush's daughter, Nancy, points out that he dined at home regularly but did not force political discussions on his children.

Although Prescott Bush was busy on multiple business and public service fronts, he never tried to push his way of life on his kids, nor did he give advice unless they asked for it.

This is the Prescott Bush his children knew: He was a man who won recognition in a number of arenas. He made money and friends. He gave back to mankind through charitable activity and national public service. He was collegial, warm, dignified—many say he had a presidential presence. Yet what was his legacy? He left a set of values; money; memories of his devotion to wife, children and grandchildren. Yet he changed little in government. He introduced no landmark legislation. He fought moderately hard for civil rights and other social causes, but he never seemed to feel strongly enough about anything to make enemies. He challenged Joe McCarthy the senator but maintained civility with McCarthy the man. He was respected widely and believed in principles, but left no substantive footprints. He offered no particular vision, except that of a life of rectitude and of music—always music, shared with the young.

How did Prescott Bush's life of excellence influence his children, especially George? Did Bush's prominence and universal approbation inspire or overwhelm George? Did George always seek his father's approval, both during his life and even afterwards, like so many boys with famous fathers? Or did he develop a quiet, persistent ambition to beat his old man at his own game: to make his own money, be even more popular, at least as religious, as kind to the unfortunate, as fine a public servant—in the end, perhaps a more prominent, more powerful man?

CHAPTER 2

New England Youth

ON JUNE 12, 1924, GEORGE BUSH BEGAN HIS LIFE AT Milton, Massachusetts, a temporary dwelling place of his parents.* They christened him George Herbert Walker Bush. His mother couldn't decide which of her father's names to pick, so she used them all. Since his uncles called their father "Pop," they took to calling him "Little Pop," or "Poppy." His father recognized after a while that this was a sobriquet the boy would want to shed later. It was acceptable for a child, but wouldn't do for an adult who one day might become prominent. I sympathize with that situation; my school label was "Popeye." Both Bush and I eventually unloaded these little burdens, but not without effort.

In his siblings' eyes George Bush was a happy, generous and loving brother. Right from the start he had a pal to play with, firstborn Prescott Jr., two years his senior. They got on so well they became inseparable. To save space their mother bedded them in the same room. As they grew she decided a nice

---

*This is only about nine miles from Brookline, where Bush's 1988 Democratic presidential opponent, Michael Dukakis, was born.

Christmas present would be to install a dividing wall to give them more privacy. When the holiday came, they asked her for the present they really wanted: to remove that wall!

After the Bush's full complement of five children had arrived, they all seemed to get on as well as the first two. George was the most giving individual, offering to share anything and everything—from food, to toys, to clothes—with the others. They nicknamed him "Have Half" for this trait. Though he tended to be the best in sports, he never lorded it over Pres Jr., Nancy, Jonathan and Bucky. According to Nancy he was totally modest.

When Pres Jr. went into the first grade at Greenwich Country Day School, George was miserable being left without him. So their father decided to let George go a year early, although Pres Jr. says he was somewhat fragile in those days. George was not sickly, he stresses, just smaller and less strong since he was younger than his classmates. He adds that

"George always was coordinated, even as a little guy. He had a good pair of eyes, good hands, natural reactions, and he caught and hit the ball well. He's always been quick and bright. I used to get so furious I'd want to pound him when we were kids. He was smart and a terrible tease."

"With practical jokes, or things he said?" I ask Pres as we discuss his brother at his Greenwich house in 1988, near the site of his and George's boyhood home.

"Mostly just barbs, verbal barbs, but not malicious, just tweaky," he answers.

At Greenwich Country Day the teachers liked George's outgoing and friendly manner. He was a favorite of theirs, though never a "teacher's pet."

From early youth July and August was one endless party for the Bush children. Their parents would pile them into the family station wagon along with baggage and dogs and trundle them to Walker's Point in Kennebunkport, Maine.

Washed clean by sun, wind and sea, Kennebunkport gleams like a jewel on Maine's coast. In the pre-spring days before the tourist hordes begin their trek to the area, the tiny town of less than a thousand differs little from when it was discovered by summer colonists, except for the cars, paved streets, power yachts and modern fishing trawlers. Kennebunkport and nearby Cape Porpoise form a kind of social unit.

One veteran year-round inhabitant laughed to me that if Bush were running for sainthood in this area he'd make it unopposed. They've known the man since boyhood. As I walked in and out of stores and talked to people of all levels and professions in the spring of 1988, that rather extreme opinion went unchallenged.

Some sage has observed that for a growing boy home is where you spend the summer. Home is where you catch your frogs, swim, canoe, fish, camp, hike, go bicycling, play tennis, have your picnics, play parlor games, see movies, first become aware of girls as a different breed.

For George Bush all this meant Kennebunkport. More specifically it meant Walker's Point, a ten-acre spit of rocks and soil reaching into the Atlantic Ocean. There, on the edge of the sea, sits a large, ten-bedroom house. Bush's maternal grandfather, George Herbert Walker, and his father, David, had bought that house together for summer vacations.

For his daughter, Dorothy, and her husband, Prescott Bush, George Walker added a simple, unpainted wood bungalow a hundred yards shoreward. At first their stays were peaceful and private. They grew increasingly hectic as the children started coming, one after the other, until there were five.

But there was respite for all seven: During the week, the kids' father would return to his New York office and their mother would eat supper with her parents in the great house. This arrangement afforded the five youngsters welcome freedom from parental discipline for at least part of every day. It also helped to weld sibling bonds that remain close even today. George Bush is the quintessential family man, one who enjoys spending time with his family above all else. His summers at Kennebunkport did much to make him that way.

Like some of the better-known East Coast watering spas, Kennebunkport began attracting city dwellers from the south around the turn of the century. Escaping the summer heat, those who could afford the costs of travel came mostly by train, since neither good roads nor automobiles were available in those early years.

The year-round residents welcomed these "economic royalists," as FDR later would call them. They spent money on food and services and domestic helpers from the town. The different cultural strata of those days tended to separate people along income lines, so the summer visitors and the "natives" didn't mingle much.

Still, Kennebunkport was more democratic than other more elaborate resorts like Bar Harbor, Marblehead, Nahant, Newport and Southampton. It also drew more of the intelligentsia. Nationally known sea and landscape artists, for example, Abbot Graves, Louis Norton and Prosper Senat, came to absorb and recreate its natural beauties. Famous authors like Booth Tarkington and Kenneth Roberts rested and wrote there. Summer theatre in the Kennebunkport Playhouse attracted popular actors like the late Edward Everett Horton. Russell Nype comes there currently, but the Playhouse, adjacent to the town's Cape Arundel Golf Club, burned down many years ago.

By the 1930s, when the young Bushes were reveling in their Kennebunkport vacations, the natives and the well-to-do summer colonists got on tolerably, although they kept their distance during mealtimes. In other words, they didn't go to each others' houses to dine.

Unaware of these socio-economic inequities, the growing Bush offspring would spend idyllic summers fishing, learning tennis, swimming and running free with their friends. These included people like Billy Truesdale from Greenwich; Fitzgerald (Jerry) Bemiss from Richmond, Virginia; Billy Richardson from Philadelphia; Bill Collin from Pittsburgh and other children whose families took up summer residence. Many have remained in touch to this day.

Their sports center was the River Club, whose members were mostly from the seasonal colony. The club comprised a modest enough tennis pavilion about a hundred yards across the road from the sea; opposite it, standing on long uprights stuck in the mud under the water, was the boat house which served as a kind of primitive yacht club. The club still exists, about a mile or so from Walker's Point, on the outskirts of Kennebunkport. In 1989 it celebrates its 100th anniversary.

The tides going up the Kennebunk River nearby vary as much as ten feet, making the river very dramatic to watch, and useful. A skipper can tie his boat to the public pier at high tide and when the ebb is complete, he and his crew can climb down to the sea bottom and scrape barnacles from the hull. If they hurry they can repaint the hull before the boat refloats. Young Bush observed such goings on and if he'd wished could doubtless have become a fine lobsterman or trawler pilot. He did catch the fishing bug for life.

At the River Club he also sharpened his tennis game and became a fine player. Jerry Bemiss says that the other Bushes and chums like himself who had been eliminated would cheer George on as he wound up each summer in the club's finals. He usually went home with the silver.

Bemiss said his style was to get everything back. Being ambidextrous, he could make some astonishing retrieval shots. He played to win. But Bemiss points out that he didn't try to overpower the ball. Unlike many teenage players he wouldn't lose his temper and throw his racquet when he double-faulted or hit one out.

Grandfather Walker indulged the boys from an early age with outings on his seaworthy lobster boat. He allowed them turns in operating the craft on their own. They became expert at boathandling, particularly Pres Jr. and George, and they took a special pride in rescuing less "salty" amateurs who over-turned their skiffs or little sailboats in the windy sea.

As Vice President, Bush still was delighting in his visits to Kennebunkport. He has been known to race about in the ocean at the wheel of his 28-foot high-speed, noisy Cigarette class motorboat named "Fidelity." He will challenge the roughest weather, exulting in the fresh Atlantic breezes. His land-bound security guards sometimes struggle in their slower craft to keep the pace up and their lunches down.

At both Kennebunkport and Greenwich, Mrs. Prescott Bush maintained her strong presence as a mother and teacher of her brood of five. Dorothy Bush inculcated her offspring with a competitive edge as much or more than her imposing husband. She was with them day after day, playing tennis and swimming with them, even engaging in foot races, which she would win until well into the boys' teens. Even today, as she completes her ninth decade, her eyes and manner are alive with determination. George Bush's durable will-to-win certainly reflects this remarkable role model.

She made a difference in the lives of her children, often curbing their egos as only a marine drill instructor can. Once when her adolescent George lost a tennis match, he explained to her that he had been off his game that morning. She retorted, "You don't have a game."

She didn't abandon her corrective ways even after George grew up. When he touted his war record in a campaign spiel, she berated him for boasting. I asked her as we talked at Walker's Point in 1988 if she was joshing him when she did that.

"No, I was serious," she replied.

"But surely your husband must have had to toot his own horn when running for the Senate," I suggested.

"No. He never talked about himself in glowing terms," she said.

Her only daughter, Nancy, inherited the drive and style of her gifted parents. She has a charisma all her own, and bubbles with warmth and wit. When her brother George followed their father's lead into politics years later, she spoke on the stump for her candidate brother before all types of audiences. They applauded her, and many have told her that she ought to be running. Some flatter her that she would make a better candidate. She takes her popularity in stride and is devoted to George.

Nancy (now Mrs. Alexander Ellis) reminisces about their youth together, as she and I lunch on the porch of her shingled frame house across the road from the Atlantic Ocean in July 1988. It is situated precisely eight-tenths of a mile from Walker's Point. She has prepared a salad with lobster doubtless pulled out from one of the pots next to the Point. It is so fresh and sweet it melts on our tongues.

"What did you eat when you were kids?" I ask.

Without hesitation she responds. "Cereal. Hot cereal in the winter. Sausages and hominy and pancakes on Sunday. Big wonderful spaghetti dishes and salad and french bread for Saturday lunch. For Sunday we'd have roast beef and roast potatoes, and vanilla ice cream and chocolate sauce. Then they [the parents] would lie down on the sofa in the library and listen to the Philharmonic. Mother would read and knit. The kids would all go do whatever. I'd go make fudge, to try to please the brothers and make them notice me."

"It was a very ordinary life," Nancy continues. "The press tries to build up all this Greenwich estate and everything. Have you seen the house? It's a nice brown-shingled house, kind of like this one. Couple of acres, max. My brothers Pres and George were thick as thieves. They were a twosome. Always shared the same room, and always together and shared friends. I was in the middle. Then came Johnny in 1931; then Bucky [William] in 1938 or so. We did a lot of things as a group. We played a lot of family tennis together. In the winter our parents sometimes would take us to the theater in New York. I'm sure we did exactly what you did.* We'd go in and see *Life with Father*, *Louisiana Purchase*, the *White Horse Inn*, with Kitty Carlisle. . . ."

Nancy added that when she reached her teens her father would take her—but not the boys—to the opera; they were happy to be left out of that excursion.

His children remember that their father was set in his judgments. They insist he in no way bullied them. He ran a taut ship at home but was fair in dispensing corrective measures.

He was confident in his own opinion about things, whether it was people or ideas. Nancy remembers coming down from Vassar, where she was taking Economics 105 with Mabel Newcomb, who had briefly served in the New Deal for Roosevelt. After this dose of partisanship, Nancy told her father how wonderful the New Deal was.

*This refers to the fact that the author grew up in Harrison, N.Y., three station stops nearer New York from Greenwich. Our parents did just what Nancy described, once per winter.

"He took it pretty well," she laughs. "He didn't let me have it. He might have, if I'd been one of the boys."

This chat took place at breakfast, and he asked if she would make some coffee.

"I don't know how to make coffee, Dad."

He declared, "My lord, a Vassar education, all this economics and you don't even know how to make coffee!"

He was conscientious about his responsibilities to the community, Nancy says, and chose a house on Grove Lane in Greenwich very near downtown, and very near the Greenwich Hospital. He thought that more appropriate than being over in the more fashionable Round Hill area, which would have made a much longer drive to his pro bono jobs in town.

Their weekday morning routine was for the whole family to have breakfast together, with the *New York Times* on one end of the table, and the now-defunct *Herald Tribune* on the other, which were passed back and forth.

The family cars were a Ford station wagon and a Chevrolet. A hired man, Alec, who was a Pole from the Russian part of Poland, would drive Mr. Bush to the station and then come back and deliver the children to school. Their father was a non-car man, says Nancy. The only car he ever had for himself was a second-hand Rover which had a lot of headroom; he was six feet four, she stresses.

Religion always was a factor in their lives. Father would read a lesson from the Bible before breakfast on weekdays. On Sunday the family reflected its ecclesiastic forebears with regular trips to church. The children sometimes could get excused for a tennis game. They were not bound by all the rules. The story of Grandfather Walker was strong in their memories. He had been sent to study in England because his mother and father thought there wasn't a good enough Catholic school in Missouri. When he came back he decided to marry the "most beautiful girl in America," according to Nancy. The trouble was, according to the Walker family priest, she was Presbyterian.

He told George Walker, "If you marry her in a Presbyterian church, you'll go straight to hell."

Walker looked him in the eye and replied, "I'll tell you one thing. I'll go straight to hell if I don't marry her."

The couple had two weddings, one in each church. It's not clear what actually happened. From then on, though, Walker let his Presbyterian wife handle the spiritual side of their marriage. Some say he never went to any church after the incident with the priest.

"So my grandmother had her way with church twice a day, no cards on Sunday, no movies. We didn't have that in the summer at Walker's Point, either, while growing up. No dice on Sundays. We could play checkers, but not backgammon. We could play anagrams, but not '21.' No chips; we couldn't play poker," recalls Nancy.

George Bush never fought against these requirements, and may have picked up the deeper sense of Christian teachings. Witness his reaction one day at the Greenwich Country Day School. He was nearly 12. With his parents and brothers and sister he was watching visitors' day activities. When the obstacle race got under way, all at once everyone started to laugh at a fat youngster who got caught trying to crawl through a barrel; everybody except George Bush. His mother looked at him and saw he was crying. George walked out onto the field, pulled the trapped lad out of the barrel and ran the rest of the race at his side.

In the fall of 1936, at the age of 12, George Bush left home. In fact, his mother took him away to Andover, Massachusetts, and installed him in Phillips Academy. Known as "Andover," this was one of the country's largest all-male college preparatory schools.

Founded in 1775 and somewhat more catholic in its selection of students than neighboring prep schools, Andover was highly regarded then as now. Its seal, designed by Paul Revere, carries the motto "Non Sibi" (Not for Self) and the reminder "Finis Origine Pendet" (The End Depends on the Beginning). About 900 boys were enrolled at that time with some 90 teachers—a rich ratio that provided large amounts of teacher time per student. In George's day it had its share of "Mr. Chips" types. He remembers Mike Sides, the math teacher who checked boys into morning assembly, and Horace Pointer, a colorful Latin "master," as teachers then were called.

The physical plant of Andover is imposing. I visited it on a cold winter morning with my daughter in our search for the right school. She found it as big as a small college, but ugly and lacking character. Going in from the outside, as young George did, the first impression is rather impersonal.

The campus of some 50 acres sits on a hill, indeed commands it, a few miles from the town of Andover. State highway route 28 splits the grounds. The first buildings one notices are Samuel Phillips Hall (named for the founder, one of the Phillips brothers, the other having founded Exeter), a long rectagon, the Addison Art Gallery, the handsome chapel and a carillon. These and the three-story dormitories all are constructed of red brick.

Culturally, the school ranked high. Students were required to take short courses in music and art appreciation. The art gallery was well equipped for this purpose, containing originals of famous artists such as Homer, Aikens and Pendergast. Boys who studied the classics were excused from these forced infusions of culture. The Samuel Morse Science Hall boasted the latest laboratory tools in those days and could offer good grounding for boys who aimed to be scientists, doctors or engineers. The Oliver Holmes Library housed probably one of the finest school collections of books available.

Andover was (and is) a well-endowed institution, and the boys lived in simple but ample one- or two-bedroom suites. Far more luxurious living than the British "public schools" on which American prep schools are modeled.

For early morning assemblies the boys tumbled from their beds into George Washington Hall. With Mr. Sides's checkmark their day began. Claude Fuess, a brilliant scholar known as the "Bald Doctor," was the headmaster, and he would appear for this daily ceremony.

New England is well-named, at least for its adoption of the British mold of private school that offered rich and privileged boys moral, physical and intellectual training. Graduates during Britain's great empire days more often than not became leaders in British military, political and commercial circles. The Duke of Wellington paid them their most famous tribute when he stated that the Battle of Waterloo was won on the playing fields of Eton.

These institutions were called "public schools" because they were open to anyone who could afford them. They dated back to King Henry VII in the fourteenth century. The most influential schools have been and still are Eton, Harrow, Rugby and Winchester.

In New England there are two types of prep schools. The first includes the church schools known familiarly as "St. Grottlesex," grouping St. Paul's, St. Mark's, St. George's, Middlesex, and Groton; the second numbers the more secular "academies," of which the most notable is Andover.

New England prep schools are meant to be learning institutions away from the temptations and interruptions of city life. Schools were established in rural settings as self-contained utopias where boys were taught to live cleanly. Emphasis was on Christian teachings. Scholastic excellence was expected of the pupils; they were given study hall times and tough tests on a regular basis. Privileges were granted to those with good marks. The curricula stressed the classics and mathematics. Boys were required to participate in athletics, particularly contact sports, and physical fitness was a way of life.

But no matter how fierce the competition to win, boys were reminded of the injunction to strive mightily, but eat and drink as friends. Dirty play was unacceptable, especially among friends. One night, before World War I, the legendary St. Paul's hockey star Hobey Baker deliberately was tripped. His team lost. Afterwards, a teammate found him weeping. He said, "Forget it Hobe, we'll take 'em next time."

Hobey shook his head. "It's not the game; it's that a friend should do such a thing!"[1]

In his history of St. Paul's, August Heckscher dwelt on the purpose of these schools: "From providing rural surroundings for children of the urban rich to importing the civilized customs of British education."[2] What he didn't spell out was that, like military academies, they tended to graduate homogeneous boys with no more originality than the products of a cookie cutter.

Good attitude was honored more than creativity. Etonian Cyril Connolly wrote that public schools may cause permanent adolescence because their influence is so strong it arrests development.[3] Did he mean that their graduates talk and act like "preppies" for the rest of their lives?

Woodrow Wilson also implied that these schools for the sons of the rich might stifle individuality. He was addressing the students and parents at St. Paul's on Anniversary Day 1909. As president of Princeton at the time, his remarks created a public stir. He said: "I am sorry for the lad who is going to inherit money; the object of college is to make young gentlemen as unlike their fathers as possible."[4]

The preparatory school system at its best, despite criticism that will accrue to any elitist movement in a democracy, breeds idealism and sound work and play habits. Graduates have distinguished themselves in public service both in Britain and the United States. They are accepted in the choice universities of the country and often go on to positions of leadership.

Although only a few boys had scholarships to Andover when George Bush was there, and even fewer blacks and other nonwhites had scholarships, the present day finds this changed dramatically. All of these schools have raised their sights to offer free education to as many as 25 percent of their students.

Young George Bush plunged into the regimens of Andover with gusto. From the outset he displayed good attitude. He was a good sport, topflight athlete, industrious student, and friendly and accepted by teachers and schoolmates alike. His only real misfortune at Andover struck while he was a senior; it proved to be a plus in the end. He developed a staph infection in his right arm, and it turned into a brush with death. With no sulfa to repel the germs, he languished in Massachusetts General Hospital for weeks.

When he recovered he and his family arranged to have him take an extra year to make up for lost study time. This resulted in a bonanza of honors and successes. He was no longer a bit young for his class. He matured and excelled scholastically, athletically and in extracurricular activities. He became, as his sister put it, the head of everything. Still, according to one English teacher, his studies reflected more industry than brilliance.

Nevertheless, the details of his achievements are manifold. Some examples from the Andover Yearbook of 1942 for George "Poppy" Bush are: President of Senior Class, Chairman of Student Deacons, President of Greeks, Captain of Baseball and Soccer, Johns Hopkins Prize as well as member of Varsity Basketball Team, Editorial board of "The Phillipian," Society of Inquiry, Business Board of the "Pot Pourri," Manager of Basketball, Deputy Housemaster, and so on.

There is considerably more, but the natural leadership he acquired at Andover was most important in terms of his career to come. Unlike the usual ambitious people in any organization, Bush never electioneered; he simply let relations with others take their course. This inevitably rendered him the man they wanted to be their chief.

He never asked for credit and as a result earned it, according to Class of 1934's Colonel John Hill. Hill remembers the school's ethos was to be laid back about what you were accomplishing. You would try to give the impression that you weren't really doing much—a direct translation of British understatement. Hill recounts an event that Bush never mentioned to anybody. One afternoon an Andover senior was roughing up a scrawny, homesick new boy—Bruce Gelb. He tells the story. His brother Dick Gelb had been in Andover ahead of him. At the start of a school year Dick was confined to a wheel chair due to an injury. A schoolmate took advantage of Dick, badgering and tormenting him. When Dick recovered his health he got his revenge by beating hell out of the bully, says Bruce.

By the time Bruce arrived at Andover, the bully was still there—in his final year—and he bore a family grudge against the Gelbs. To get even, he soon began to pick on Bruce. One day he told him to move a big stuffed arm chair. Bruce tried, but could carry it only a few feet. At that moment, Bruce recalled the time his best friend in an earlier school was being hazed by older boys, and he, Gelb, had bitten the hand of the toughest one. Encouraged by the memory, Bruce stoutly told the Andover bully that he just couldn't lift that chair any more.

Whereupon the bully put a hammerlock on him. Suddenly, Bruce heard a voice say, "Leave the kid alone!" The bully promptly released Gelb and slunk off.

Gelb asked some boys who had witnessed the scene, "Who was that guy?"

"Oh," chorused the others, "That was Poppy Bush. He's the finest guy in the school. He's a great athlete and everybody loves him."

"At that point," Gelb recalls now, "he became my hero and has been ever since. Nothing makes me a more willing loyalist than a guy who sticks up for a little kid and puts a bully down. Bush has friends like me all over the U.S. and the world," says Gelb. "The reason we stay his friends is that he is still George Bush. He knows who he is. Some people forget where they come from and all the people they have known along the way."

In the midst of his final, triumphant year at Andover, Bush was looking ahead from the comfortable campus life. December 7, 1941, the day the Japanese bombed Pearl Harbor, George made up his mind to serve his country at war. He met the practical requirements first by earning his diploma from Andover and reaching the legal enlistment age of 18. By June 12, 1942, he had done both.

He also had fallen in love. It happened at a "Get Together" dance at the Greenwich Country Club during the Christmas holidays. This was one of the rituals for young people in the Rye/Greenwich social axis. Boys and girls would return from three months of boarding school confinement and mingle at festive parties, mostly at country clubs.

Now that the country was at war, these occasions seemed all the more romantic and bittersweet—the lively orchestras playing Glenn Miller tunes, the rustle of crepe de chine and satin, the occasional military uniform. Bush entered this atmosphere having already determined to join the navy. He was ripe for the plucking, if he found the right girl.

As he circled the dance floor, George grabbed the elbow of a friend and asked who was the vision in the red and green dress.

"Want to meet her?" laughed his friend.

"That's the general idea," said Bush.

The tall, handsome athlete was led over to the girl with lustrous brown hair. After an introduction and the requisite self-conscious preppy funnies, the two stepped off to dance. Barbara was an accomplished dancing school product, whereas he was less practiced. They danced until the orchestra struck up a waltz. Unacquainted with this step, George suggested they sit and talk. So began a dialogue that continues to this day.

The couple doesn't talk very much about their romance. Nancy Bush (Ellis) had observed them however. She culls up thoughts about him that year.

"His friends told us he was becoming a sort of god [at Andover]. I think he began to become an enormously well-regarded person in a huge school. And he was always dreamy-looking, so my friends were all crazy about coming and spending the night because of my brother. But he already was falling in love with Barbara, so their quest was in vain. . . . He was sort of tall, and thin and graceful, and handsome and funny. He was quick-witted and had a million friends."

George and Barbara were little more than children at that Christmastime party, just 17 and 16, yet the sparks evidently flew. It appeared to be love at first look. The fact that they are the children of substantial marriages may explain their 44-plus years together. Unlike so many failed marriages in America today, they had solid role models in their parents.

As their neighbor, I remember Mr. and Mrs. Marvin Pierce. He chaired the McCall Corporation, which published women's magazines like McCall's. They lived in Rye, New York, the town next to Greenwich. To us youthful observers they seemed to be important and distinguished. He was a dark-haired and barrel-chested fellow who took the time to speak to the young. She was better-looking than most mothers, as we saw her.

Their children, Martha, Jimmy, Barbara and Scott, were lively and popular. Another neighbor, Fred Godley, used to play with Martha, Jerry Knapp, and Cammie Peake in their preteens. He remembers now that Mrs. Pierce would complain at the end of the day, "Martha, why are you always even muddier than the boys?"

Within a couple of years, Martha grew so beautiful her face began to show up on magazine covers. When Martha came to supper at our house, everyone was excited. She and Barbara were sought after by many of us young swains.

Barbara and George remain decorously guarded on specifics of their courtship, but they concede it proceeded apace after the mating dance. We have to assume that letters passed weekly between Andover and Ashley Hall, her prep school. We presume a passionate reunion at Easter vacation, cemented by the secret engagement. They are extra quiet on that point. Barbara says she can't pinpoint how or where he proposed, because, she smiles, he never actually did ask her to marry him. By summertime, George had signed up with the navy, but on his minileaves, the young lovers engineered visits in Rye and Kennebunkport with each others' respective parents—a giant pace toward matrimony.

By the time George was shipped overseas, wedding bells seemed certain, guaranteed by a public engagement. To some people commitment to marriage means the official end of youth. Perhaps so, but Bush's youthfulness still lingers in personality and attitude.

CHAPTER 3

Fighter for America

Onward Christian soldiers
Marching as to war
With the cross of Jesus
Going on before!

DURING AND AFTER THE VIETNAM WAR, THIS STIR-
ring hymn had a hollow ring. But it reflected America's
spirit when George Bush joined the United States Navy in June
of 1942. President Franklin D. Roosevelt had prepared the
country's psyche. Americans were ready to fight the Axis
powers, despite the counter-efforts of "America Firsters," who
wanted the country to stay out of the European conflagration.
Japan's attack on Pearl Harbor conveniently angered the citizenry into wholeheartedly backing the declaration of war
against Japan and Germany. From then on anyone of military
age who didn't join up risked harassment from those who did.

For George Bush America's entry into World War II meant his

first serious challenge. An enthusiastic eighteen year old, he volunteered immediately upon graduation from secondary school. Despite his young age the navy snapped him up for its air arm as he had hoped they would from the day after Pearl Harbor.

The story of George Bush's military career began, in a sense, on graduation day at Phillips Academy in Andover in June 1942. Secretary of War Henry L. Stimson delivered the official address. He advised the students to stick with their education and go on to college, indicating that Uncle Sam could come and pry them out for military service when the need arose.

Bush recalls that his father, "an imposing presence, six feet four, with deep-set blue-gray eyes and a resonant voice," asked him if the secretary's speech had changed his mind. Bush replied, "No, I'm going in," and his dad acquiesced with a handshake.

One wonders if the secretary's attendance at this rather small school had anything to do with the influence of the well-known Prescott S. Bush, George's father. Possibly it was only because Secretary Stimson was a distinguished graduate himself. The question also arises as to whether the young man wasn't trying already to step free of his father's sway as much as to fight for his country. Without indulging in psychobiography, it is probably safe to say young Bush's decision encompassed both motives.

One wonders why the navy relaxed its two years of college requirement for flight training in George Bush's case. He had built an outstanding record at school as a scholar, athlete and campus leader, but so had countless thousands of other youths.

Yet it was George Bush who appeared to be the only beneficiary of this rule-waiving, and thus he eventually emerged as the youngest pilot in the navy—a fact that he still can boast about and because of which he enjoyed a certain celebrity during the war.

Bush modestly acknowledges his youth at that time, saying that "Even then I got the impression that my instructor thought I was still too fuzz-faced to trust with an expensive piece of navy equipment. . . . To make matters worse I looked younger than I actually was—enough to make me self-conscious." Indeed when his fiance visited him during his days at pilot school he asked her to pretend she was 18 instead of 17.

He went smoothly through preflight exercises in Chapel Hill, North Carolina, to flying school in Corpus Christi, Texas, and elsewhere to finish his polishing as a pilot at the Naval Air Station in Charlestown, Rhode Island. It was June 1943 before he won his wings as the youngest naval aviator.

Stationed briefly at the navy base in nearby Quonset Point during that period, I remember seeing those youngsters from Charlestown. From my great age of 25 it seemed as if the government were indeed robbing the junior high schools to man our armed services.

In the fall of 1943, George Bush was one of the flyers sent to practice torpedoing a target destroyer escort (DE) in Cape Cod Bay. By then I was part of the encampment at Hyannis, on the Cape, which provided this instruction. Each pilot had to drop four live torpedoes, in sequence, against the DE.

The plane used was an Avenger Torpedo Bomber designed by Grumman Aviation and built by General Motors. It was called TBM, Torpedo Bomber, with M designating it as a General Motors product. It carried a crew of three: the pilot in the forward seat; the turret gunner behind him; and below, facing aft, sat the radioman/tail gunner, known as the "stinger."

This machine performed well in releasing bombs, depth charges and torpedoes against stationary installations, surface ships and submarines. It was effective but fat, ugly and slow. Critics among the crews said it could fall faster than it could fly. It made an easy target for antiaircraft guns, as Bush was to discover soon enough. He said he liked the plane and found it forgiving in the precarious carrier landings at sea.

I harbor a personal resentment against the TBM. One day that fall I offered to take notes for a decorated veteran of Guadalcanal while he taught the junior flyers how to launch torpedoes. His plane would stay aloft for the whole morning. The visiting students would join us one after the other. Each would make a run at the target vessel under the watchful eye of the teacher, who would radio by TBS (talk between ships) instructions during the exercise. The notes I kept were to help the teacher remember details of the morning's classes, how each student pilot performed, with suggestions to give them when we reassembled back at the Hyannis airfield.

He seated me in the gunner's turret just abaft of the pilot's space. Shortly after takeoff, as we headed across Cape Cod Bay, the escape hatch next to me broke loose and flew off, falling into the water below. I told the pilot; he uttered an expletive and called our base to find a replacement for the hatch.

Meanwhile I sat in the open air at 25 degrees fahrenheit. In its whooshing exit, the hatch had nicked my hand and I was bleeding freely. I wore only a pair of summer khakis and shirt—normally the engine would have generated enough warmth for the interior. We flew back and forth with different student pilots for four hours that day, while I shivered and entered blood-spattered remarks in the record book.

When we finally landed, there on the tarmac stood the entire crew of our unit, some 40 people, at attention. A bugle blew and the officer in charge awarded me a freshly cut tin medal which the medical corpsman pinned on my shaking chest for "heroism beyond the call of duty in bombing a United States destroyer escort target vessel with a TBM escape hatch." Laughter broke up the ceremony.

That was one of the days that prepared George Bush for actions that later won him a Distinguished Flying Cross and three air medals. His squadron underwent our Hyannis torpedo course during that period. Although I already knew his future wife, Barbara Pierce, for some reason I don't remember meeting him at Hyannis. He survived that omission very well.

Despite Secretary Stimson's remarks at Andover, the navy was short of pilots, and Bush was hurried through the training process in a mere ten months. In the fall of 1943, commissioned Ensign Bush was assigned to Torpedo Bomber Squadron VT 51 aboard a newly commissioned ship, the *San Jacinto*. Set on the hull of a 10,000-ton light cruiser, the "San Jack," as she was promptly nicknamed, became a light aircraft carrier. She was narrow for a carrier and difficult to land on.

Together with 24 F6F "Hellcat" fighters, the nine TBMs of VT 51 and their crews took their shakedown cruise aboard the *San Jacinto* in the balmy Caribbean. The resort area lent an ominous feeling to the exercise. There they were in one of the most beautiful spots on earth, drilling on how to destroy other humans and their machinery.

The *San Jacinto* didn't dally. Soon she headed west through the Panama Canal, stopping at San Diego and Pearl Harbor. Then she sailed toward the Marshall Islands in the western Pacific. There she joined Vice Admiral Marc A. Mitscher's Task Force 58/38 in the early spring of 1944. This was the fast carrier group of the Pacific Fleet. The American offensive was beginning to move inexorably toward Japan.

The United States had suffered heavy naval losses during 1942 and 1943, principally from the Pearl Harbor attack and the great air-sea fights around the Solomon Islands, as well as attrition from submarines. Now a plethora of American shipyards poured forth hundreds of warships. They steadily replenished the weakened navy. Ultimately they provided much of the muscle needed to drive the Japanese back to their home islands.

The *San Jacinto* was part of this "New Construction," as the veterans of the Pacific battles called the quantities of naval craft arriving in ever-increasing numbers. I remember reporting to the Seventh Fleet at about this time and hearing shipmates talk hungrily about the opportunity to go home for "New Construction." This meant leave, a billet on some new warship and long delays until it would be ready for the fighting zone.

Still the United States was short of enough vessels for a knockout punch. To make his forces seem stronger, the American commander for the Pacific, Fleet Admiral Chester W. Nimitz, called one fleet by two names: the Third and Fifth, depending on who was in charge.

This "cover up" was well managed. I learned about it only by chance just after the war at a small dinner with two of the major players: former Secretary of the Navy James A. Forrestal and Admiral Raymond A. Spruance. We were guests in a New-

port, Rhode Island, house perched by the sea. Admiral
Spruance left early. Rain and wind roared through the front
door as it opened to let him out. The autumn storm mo-
mentarily silenced the four of us still there.

Then Mr. Forrestal began to reminisce about the Pacific campaign. He beamed in the firelight, reliving the recent great
victories at sea. An ex-boxer with a flattened nose and heavy
brows, his pugnacious demeanor helped recreate for us the
drama in which he had starred.

Spruance was one of the navy's big guns, he reminded us—
not as well known as (Admiral William F.) Halsey (Jr.)—but at
least as capable. To confuse the enemy, he told us Nimitz's
Pacific command decided to alternate these two men in running the one fleet.

"When we put Spruance in charge," he said, "we called it
the Fifth Fleet, and his tactics and strategy came into play as
the classic naval warrior that he was. By the time the Japanese
would begin to learn what to expect from Spruance, we would
abruptly switch to Halsey and call it the Third Fleet. 'Bull'
Halsey, bold and unpredictable, presented the enemy with
troubles they had not yet imagined. As soon as the Japanese
showed signs of adapting to Halsey, we would replace him
again with Spruance."

When George Bush plunged into the campaign from the *San
Jacinto*, it didn't matter whether Spruance or Halsey was in
command. From then on the San Jack's role was relentlessly
aggressive. She and her planes steadily pounded enemy bases,
ships, subs and planes.

By now VT 51 was finely tuned and entered the fray with
well-earned confidence. Their first foray was a raid on Wake
Island, held by the Japanese since the United States Marines
had made their heroic stand there in 1942.

Then a major action began. Task Force 58 (Fifth Fleet), of
which the San Jack was part, attacked the Mariana Islands in
preparation for the invasion of Saipan. The Japanese reacted
violently, sending up 400 fighters to repel the massive assault.
American planes and ships had a field day, downing some 300

enemy aircraft. Reporters termed this one-sided operation the "Marianas Turkey Shoot."

In the midst of it, George Bush and other flyers were ordered to get their TBMs off the *San Jacinto's* flight deck to avoid the Japanese strafers and divebombers. Because of their heavy load of ordnance the TBMs were to be catapulted rather than to take off unassisted. This meant the carrier had to be headed into the wind. In the midst of battle maneuvers, she couldn't do this right away. So for a half hour or so the flight crews, including Bush, had to wait, their planes lashed to the deck with their motors idling as hostile fire arched over them from all directions. Armed with TNT-filled depth charges, the TBMs constituted a danger not only to the personnel manning them, but also to the carrier itself. One hit and everyone aboard the "San Jack" would be atomized. It was essential to remove the planes, and fast.

Bush sat in "Barbie," his TBM nicknamed for fiance Barbara Pierce, and hoped the fusillades would miss them. At last the San Jack swung upwind and shot Barbie into the relative safety of the sky. The escape from the dangers of the flight deck was short-lived. In minutes either enemy or American fire hit the TBM's oil system; the pressure plummetted and Bush announced to his crew that they would have to ditch.

Turret gunner Leo Nadeau has commented glowingly on the skill with which Bush slid the disabled TBM into a rough sea. He recalls that Bush coolly wrenched the life raft free of the sinking plane. The two uninjured crewmen had exited by the escape hatch, a duplicate of the one that had cut my hand over Cape Cod Bay in 1943. The three then rowed feverishly to avoid the explosion of the antisubmarine charges which would occur when the plane reached the depth set on their fuses. Sure enough the sea soon erupted like a volcano, but at a safe distance.

At this point his two crew members, Ordnanceman Second Class Nadeau and Radioman Second Class John L. Delaney, started singing "Over the Bounding Main." Nadeau recounts that "Mr. Bush turned around and said, 'You guys had better shut up or they're going to think we're having too good a time out here.'"

An American destroyer picked up the three survivors within a half hour. Some days later Bush was swung by breeches buoy from the destroyer to another carrier. This is a traditional navy rescue device that consists of a buoyant canvas ring that a man can step into, like a pair of pants. It works simply: A rope is thrown and secured either from a ship to another ship or to shore. Then the breeches buoy is attached to the rope on a pulley. Now it can be drawn by another line, with its passenger, in the desired direction. Once aboard the carrier Bush was issued a new Avenger (TBM) which he flew back to the *San Jacinto*.

While being fished out of the water, Bush and his crewmen missed a strange event aboard San Jack only a few miles distant. As the battle was winding down after dark, a lone Japanese airman tried twice to land on the *San Jacinto*. Her flight deck personnel waved him off each time since his tail-hook wasn't down. On his second pass he flew only about 50 feet over the entire flight deck. Then the Americans saw the red meatball marking his plane as Japanese. He made no hostile moves, and neither did the Americans. The ship's radar tracked his blip about 50 miles until it disappeared mystically into the blackness. Was this a Japanese Rudolph Hess who had decided on his own to contact the *San Jacinto* and sue for peace? The Americans never found out.

The fighting ground on for George Bush and millions of others for another year. Bush saw his share of its horrors. One day he watched a Hellcat fighter plane crash on the *San Jacinto's* landing deck. He stood in shock as the machine smashed into a gun mount and killed four men.

Even today he remembers vividly the sight just yards away: a leg cleanly severed, still twitching with the shoe on its foot. Specific glimpses of gory scenes do linger in veterans' minds. They serve as good mental seatbelts against future hawkishness, good guidance if the veteran has become a politician. George Bush often has said as much.

His own TBM encountered numerous close calls in the

course of bombing Wake Island, Palau, Guam and Saipan. Within a few months his luck was destined to run out, as it had for nine out of the 14 original pilots of VT 51. The most harrowing adventure lay ahead.

The date was September 2, 1944. By now the tide had turned in the Pacific. The Japanese grand plan for an "East Asia Co. Prosperity Sphere" had deteriorated into a desperate defensive struggle to save their original archipelago. As George Bush himself has noted, however, the closer the Americans got to Japan, the tougher the fighting grew.

VT 51's task at hand on that day was to take out a radio installation in Chichi Jima, one of the Bonin Islands, where the protracted and bloody battle for Iwo Jima soon would thunder. From Chichi Jima the Japanese were reporting the American bombers that they observed en route to target areas. This warning ensured hot anti-aircraft reception for the Americans on arrival.

On September 1, the day before, Bush and his fellow squadron members had raided the island and found the ack-ack thick. So on the second, they steeled themselves for another tough defense from the ground. Their fears were well-founded. When George Bush approached Chichi Jima, his TBM pregnant with 500-pound bombs, he could see the black puffs blossoming. The weather was clear and he had no trouble identifying the radio station below. Despite a lethal hail rising from underneath him, he dove his plane at a 60-degree angle.

For his two crew members, life was about to end. Lt. (JG) William G. White, the squadron's gunnery officer, had asked and gotten permission from Bush and the squadron commander to come along as an observer. He took the place of Leo Nadeau, Bush's regular turret gunner. Radioman John L. Delaney, as usual, was in the stinger seat below.

George Bush was about to face one of man's most critical tests: to stay steady under threat of combat death. Halfway through Bush's dive, the enemy found his range with one or more shells. Smoke filled his cabin; his plane controls weakened; the engine began coughing, and still he wasn't close enough to the target. He presumed the TBM to be terminally damaged. Fighting to stay on course, eyes smarting, Bush managed to launch his bombs at the last possible moment. He couldn't discern the result through the black fumes. But a companion pilot affirmed later that the installation blew up, along with two other buildings. The navy would decorate Bush for literally sticking to his guns until he completed his mission under ferocious enemy fire.

Good! Now the trick was to keep the plane aloft long enough to accomplish two objectives: first, get far enough away from the island to allow rescue from the sea before capture or killing by the enemy; second, give his planemates time to parachute out of the burning aircraft.

The TBM sputtered on its last few hundred yards. Unbeknownst to Bush, one man freed himself. Neither fellow squadron pilots nor Bush ever were sure which crewmember this was. As he jumped, however, his parachute snarled and failed to open.

The plane's altimeter now registered barely 1,000 feet. Bush forced himself to open his canopy, lurch up, and out. Instantaneously he felt his forehead bang on the TBM's tail. The airplane was not forgiving, he would concede later, for emergency inflight bailouts.

In the next moments Bush's navy schooling paid off. He deftly decoupled himself from the parachute at the moment he splashed into the sea. VT 51's skipper, Lt. Cdr. Donald J. Melvin, who had led the attack on the radio tower, made a pass over Bush and saw that he was struggling to stay afloat. Bush was dizzy from the smoke as well as the deep gash in his head suffered from hitting the plane's tail. From his TBM Melvin pointed to Bush's rubber boat which had automatically inflated. Bush swam to it and hauled himself aboard.

He now took stock of the situation. His crew had disappeared. One of them, White, was a boyhood friend. Leo Nadeau lamented afterwards that he was more familiar with the machine than Lt. White. Had he been on board that day, he might have been able to insure that both he and Delaney could leave the aircraft safely. As it was, Delaney, who had shared many flights and other actions with Bush, evidently went down with the bomber. The loss of the two men numbed Bush.

The wind and sea rapidly set his raft back toward Chichi Jima, less than ten miles away. He checked his supplies and found a pistol in good working order. *Not too useful,* he thought grimly. What he needed was some oars. He knew the Japanese would be headed his way shortly. Like a dog in an undertow, he paddled gamely away from the island, stopping now and then as nausea gripped him. His wound, the polluted air of the TBM cockpit, and a stomach full of seawater had taken their toll.

Sure enough, the Japanese dispatched boats in his direction, but Lt. (JG) Doug West, who was on the mission with Bush, strafed the small craft and, according to accounts, sank two of them and stopped the others.

Bush's predicament was now slightly eased, but his puny handstrokes scarcely slowed his drift toward the enemy shore. The Japanese eventually would be sure to find him. Yet if the wind and current did shift, he might be wafted to an unknown and more dire fate, like myriad shipwrecked sailors since man first took to the sea.

What Bush really thought during the hours that followed can only be surmised. He is characteristically silent on most of it, saying merely that the experience changed his view of life.

His gloomy ruminations ended abruptly some hours later when he saw a miracle bubble to the surface nearby. Startled, he wasn't sure the emerging periscope and then the hull of the submarine were friendly. But he soon perceived that they were. A modern deus ex machina! A man with a camera appeared on deck and began to crank pictures of the raft and its bloody occupant.

Melvin had radioed Bush's position, and the *U.S.S. Finback,* on lifeguard duty in the area, had responded.

Within minutes the *Finback's* men hauled Bush on board, ushered him below and dove the "boat," as submariners call their vessel. From death or a living hell on the open ocean, Bush found himself magically moved to the snug wardroom of the *Finback*. Quiet phonograph music played in the background as his good Samaritans surrounded him with warm fellowship.

Thus began a remarkable odyssey for an airman. Bush and four other downed, rescued flyers were welcomed as temporary members of the submarine's crew. They were detailed to stand watch on deck at night when the sub recharged its batteries and freshened the air below. Bush liked that duty. The star-filled nights and bright phosphorous in the ship's bow wave transported him from the raging war in the Pacific.

Bush and his fellow refugees remained aboard for 30 days while the *Finback* hunted and sank enemy ships of all descriptions. She was depth bombed and shot at by her prey and its protectors—aircraft and destroyers. The passenger aviators found the experience harrowing, and admitted to their hosts that, on the whole, they would prefer fighting from the air.

The *Finback*'s executive officer, Lieutenant Commander Dean Spratin, remembers that Bush and the other aviators really entered the spirit of battle on the large, 292-foot submarine. "Every time an enemy plane would force us down, they'd curse it just like we did."[1] The bonds of camaraderie proved to be lasting ones; George Bush began friendships aboard the sub that he keeps to this day.

Bush's dismay over the loss of his two crewmates on the TBM stayed with him throughout the cruise on the *Finback*. When he was eventually brought to Pearl Harbor for a month's rest and recreation, he cut his leave short. He says that he felt honor-bound to return to the San Jack and complete his tour with VT 51.

The squadron remained a dynamic unit of the American armada as it steadily closed in on Japan. Bush took part in bombing raids for another month or so until VT 51 was ordered back to the states in November. The official history notes that during his 58 missions, Lt. (JG) Bush shared credit for sinking a small Japanese AK (cargo vessel) near Palau. Again on November 13 in Manila and Subic Bay, he and several other squadron pilots scored four torpedo hits, destroyed a floating dry dock, and made bomb and torpedo hits on three AKs.

Life at sea fighting for a cause suited George Bush. He was noted for industriousness and bravery. In his 1979 biography of Bush, Nicholas King, a USIA colleague of mine, cites the squadron's executive officer, Legare R. Hole as saying that people didn't realize Bush was so young. Hole declared that "he never shirked his duty and shone as the leader of the group of younger squadron men. His natural interest in people made him popular. And he certainly wasn't the man to be in front of when there was a volleyball game going on on top of the hangar elevator."[2]

Later, Hole added, "He was an exceptionally good pilot. He was a smart fellow who had his head screwed on tight . . . very serious for his age. Never got in trouble like some of us did."[3]

King quotes another squadron member, Jack O. Guy: "We looked up to George automatically. There just didn't seem to be any question about our confidence in his leadership."[4]

Now an Atlanta businessman, Guy adds, "he was fun to be with. You could depend on him. He was one of the boys. Practical joker and excellent pilot."[5]

Lt. (JG) Louis Grab, another VT 51 veteran who has moved to Sacramento, California, says, "He had a lot of character . . . was reliable. Very intelligent. Very capable. Excellent pilot. He was likeable. Had a sense of humor and perseverance."[6] Bush's nickname, according to Grab, was his full name: George Herbert Walker Bush. With this "weapon" his shipmates kidded him unmercifully.

Others speak of his religious devotion. One says he was always asking somebody to go to church with him, referring evidently to Bush's behavior when on shore duty after returning to the United States.

Forty years later, on September 1, 1984, Navy Secretary John Lehman staged a reunion at Norfolk, Virginia, to celebrate Bush's wartime rescue by the *Finback*. Navy historian John Vadnais created a teak plaque from the "cigarette deck" of the scrapped *Finback*—this was where the watch standers could smoke while the sub was steaming on the surface. Admiral John Kane wrote a message for the brass plate on the plaque recalling the *Finback* as "your home away from home Septem-

ber 2–October 2 1944." Tied up at the end of dock where the
ceremony took place lay the brand-new *U.S.S. Finback*, a nu-
clear submarine.

For George Bush the war ended tidily. The navy delivered
him home on Christmas Eve, 1944, and he celebrated the
holidays with his family and Barbara Pierce—whom he married two weeks later in Greenwich, Connecticut.

Mr. and Mrs. Prescott Bush gave a prenuptial dinner the
night before at the Greenwich Field Club. Nancy Bush Ellis
remembers the joyous occasion. What a pleasant respite from
the brutal global conflict that still roared on overseas.

Fitzgerald Bemiss, one of George's Kennebunkport boyhood
pals, still feels the dramatic, poignant sense of that wartime
wedding. Like others of the half-dozen ushers, Bemiss had
hurried in from his own military duties. Outside the Presbyterian church in Rye, the roads were slippery with frozen
snow, the air crisp.

"I was rushed up the aisle, just ahead of the bride and her
father, and put in place near the altar."

George was waiting in his navy blues (with only his gold
pilot's insignia on his chest—he had come back so fast he
hadn't purchased his medals for valor yet). Barbara stepped
along at the elbow of her tall, solidly built, dark-haired dad.

Prescott Jr. was best man; Nancy Bush (George's sister) and
Martha Rafferty (Barbara's sister) were respectively maid of
honor and matron of honor. Nancy recalls the bridesmaids
wore green velvet. There were six bridemaids: Lucille School-
field, Roseanne Morgan, Shaun Robinson, Bess Rafferty, Sally
Parker and Margaret Merrick.

The ceremony spun off like clockwork. No one misbehaved
or faltered or dropped bouquets or giggled uncontrollably.
Only a few tears of happiness. The omens were favorable.

The 300-or-so guests then drove to the reception at the
nearby Apawamis Country Club. Immediately thereafter most
everyone scattered back to their duties, military or otherwise,
hastened by the warpace still gripping their lives.

But despite the hectic atmosphere of the country, those who

witnessed the solemnification of Barbara and George's union felt their marriage would last. It was what the French call a *marie ton voisin* affair. The families approved, and the wide circle of friends saw its logic. Nancy Ellis says she was impressed by how quickly George knew at only 17 that Barbara was the right girl for him. These two shared ideals, social and economic backgrounds, and church orientation along with their superb and glowing health. Their future would tax all these qualities.

But for the golden days just ahead lay the promise of unalloyed rapture. First the honeymoon. They spent it at the Cloisters on Sea Island, Georgia. This quiet, flat land by the Atlantic drew many newlyweds then as now. Swimming and tennis and golf and great food of the Cloisters, still a five-star hotel, were the attractions—perhaps a bit irrelevant at that point. While there, George wrote to Nancy: "Married life exceeds all expectations. Barbara is a fine wife!"

Then the navy assigned him to train younger pilots. So their first stop as Lieutenant Junior Grade and Mrs. Bush was the Naval Air Station, Norfolk, Virginia. The small M.O.Q. (Married Officers Quarters) demanded only light housekeeping, except for the cooking.

George's duty also was light. As for other young marrieds whose husbands were between warzone tours, this was kind of an extended (and paid) honeymoon.

On the night of August 15, 1945, he and his wife were enjoying themselves with other young navy couples at the officers' club, when word circulated that the Japanese had surrendered. Bush and his bride disappeared quietly and slipped off to church. They returned to the party without mentioning where they had been.

Now with only a couple of months left in the navy, it was time to assess George's accomplishments. The navy gave its answer: For his courageous completion of the bomb raid on Chichi Jima in spite of being shot down, George was awarded the Distinguished Flying Cross. His subsequent heroics resulted in three air medals. So solid was his war record, that the

slings and arrows of 25 years of political campaigning never
called it into question until August of 1988.

During a *Washington Post* series on Bush, just before the
Republican convention in New Orleans, Squadron 51 officer
Louis Grab told me that the *Post* researcher had quizzed him
for two hours trying to get him to say that Bush could have
saved the two crewmen who lost their lives over Chichi Jima.
Shortly after that, another squadron airman, Chester Mierze-
jewski, indicated in an "eyewitness" account in the *New York
Post* that he didn't agree with Bush's version of the shootdown.
He posited that Bush's plane wasn't as seriously hurt as he
claimed it was, and that he needlessly lost his two crewmates.
Why did Mierzejewski keep silent for 44 years and then make
such a claim during an election? Whatever his motivation,
Mierzejewski was soon forgotten by the public.

Some day it may be possible to examine the actual wreckage
of Bush's plane. On September 12, 1988, *Time* magazine carried a report that some businessmen were determined to find
Bush's TBM on the ocean floor, just as the *S.S. Titanic* had
been located. They planned to televise the salvaging, said
Time. If so, more light can be thrown on the exact nature of the
damage.

How was Bush the man affected by the war? He was moved
by the loss of friends, marked by memories of combat. Repeatedly he has averred the war gave him a realism about governing
for which there is no substitute.

With more firsthand acquaintance of the world and its dangers than most men collect in a lifetime, George Bush now
became a college freshman.

CHAPTER 4

Yale Star

WHEN GEORGE BUSH ENTERED YALE IN THE FALL OF
1945, the United States was in the throes of joyful read-
justment to peace.

For years the country's young men had been overseas fighting the world's greatest war. At home the young ladies had
been lamenting the meager choice of available males.

> They're either too young or too old!
> They're either too gray, or too grassy green.
> The pickins are poor and the crop is lean;
> What's good is in the army—
> What's left can never harm me.
> They're either too old or too young!

Barbara Pierce had ended this distress earlier in the year, on
January 6, as she and George marched up the aisle. They had
married only two weeks after Prescott Jr.'s wedding. Prescott
had been working for Pan American Airways and had met and
married Elizabeth Louise Kauffman, another childhood friend
of my family. Indeed, I later became aide and flag lieutenant to
her father, Admiral James L. Kauffman, in the Pacific.

43

George's shipmates in the Pacific recounted that while in the navy he didn't chase after women like them. He always had Barbara. He cared for her and made no bones about it. With her it was a two-way street: She had quit her sophomore year at Smith College that fall to marry him. Jeane McBride sat next to her in a class on the history of American economics. Jeane remembers they were both bored, and that she was jealous of Barbara's escaping for such a romantic purpose. She has kept in touch off and on. Now both she and Barbara live in Washington, and have seen each other a bit. She says Barbara still has her wonderful wry sense of humor.

Postwar Yale, like colleges all over the country, had been hungry for students since 1942. Now it presented a rare opportunity for veterans like George Bush, who was in a hurry to finish his formal education. It made arrangements whereby they could complete a four-year course in just about two-and-one-half years.

Not surprisingly, when George Bush entered in November 1945, his was reportedly the biggest freshman class (over 8,000) in the history of the college. He selected economics as his major.

This was a practical choice. He intended to engage in commerce of some kind and needed to understand the foundations and dynamics of the American system. Business school would have been even better, but time, he felt, was important. An undergraduate degree in economics was all he needed.

Presumably his father, the high-powered investment banker in Brown Brothers, Harriman, had whetted his appetite for the opportunities in business at that time. In becoming the "Arsenal for Democracy," in Roosevelt's phrase, America's industrial machine had deferred making the washing machines, automobiles and a myriad other consumer products until peacetime. Now the country would commence a buying frenzy that would extend into the 1950s.

To comprehend this promising phenomenon, George Bush tackled his studies singlemindedly. As a newlywed he would not be distracted by the joys of the campus bachelor.

There were many other married scholars in 1945. Fred God-

ley (Frederick A., who had known the Pierce family in Rye),
was at Yale then, in the engineering school. His father had
been a professor of architecture. He was speaking, therefore,
from long familiarity with the college, when he said that there
was a whole different attitude during those immediate postwar
years. In place of the usual predilection with collegiate pleasures like proms, football games and house parties, there was
an almost feverish concentration on schoolwork—particularly
among the war veterans. There were so many of them they
outnumbered the younger students. They had missed several
years of education; they were behind in the competitive race to
get somewhere in private life. They were anxious to put college
behind him. Getting good marks meant getting good job offers.

Godley recalls a tough drafting assignment that required
almost 11 hours. He and several other veterans skipped a
weekend soiree in order to complete it. When they delivered
their papers on time that Monday, the others who had gone to
the party and were delinquent with their papers booed.

The competition for high marks was intense, says Godley,
and anyone who got a Phi Beta Kappa prize at that time had to
be more than just a "greasy grind," he had to be very bright.

George and Barbara ran into the housing shortage that faced
everyone else. They found a large frame residence that had
been converted into apartments, in which were crammed 40
inhabitants. It was located off the main campus at 37 Hillhouse
Avenue. Just across the street lived Yale President Charles
Seymour.

Somehow, in the midst of all those housemates, Bush managed to meet his responsibilities efficiently. One must assume
that Barbara was a good partner, since with her he had the
mental and emotional equilibrium to accomplish all that he
did while in New Haven.

The environs of Yale were not that attractive. New Haven
then was a small industrial city of some 150,000 that had
started in the seventeenth century. It is located at the head of a
mini-estuary at the mouth of the Quinnipiac River, which
flows through the east side of town. Yale was founded in 1701
by several clergymen. It stands in the middle of the city, on the

west and north sides of the town green. This is a tree-lined, square park with churches abutting the other sides.

Winchester Arms, with which Prescott Bush had been affiliated, had its headquarters there. Yale itself was the principal cultural "activity," in addition to the Peabody Art Museum and the New Haven Symphony Orchestra. Its gothic buildings adorned the city. Its students enlivened it. Vehicular and trolley traffic choked its thoroughfares.

George Bush extended his education and reputation in the short time he spent there. His 1987 autobiography devotes some 90 percent of its passage on Yale to his athletic doings. Presumably he didn't want to present himself as an egghead during his presidential campaign. The fact was that he conquered what he described as the "dismal science": On graduation he garnered both a prize in economics and a Phi Beta Kappa key. He gave no indication that he noticed a development William F. Buckley, Jr. would attack two years later in "For God and Man at Yale." Buckley would assert that most of the teachers of economics at Yale were tending toward a liberalism that should shock good American conservatives. Buckley alerted his readers that individualism so dear to the private enterprise system was endangered. He cited the economists' increasing suggestions that America's social problems might best be solved by government intervention. This would not be the last instance in which Bush would be accused of insensitivity to conservative concerns.

In addition to his scholarly triumph, he could have been described as almost a carbon copy of Prescott Bush for his many-faceted prominence. As an athlete he made the varsity baseball team three seasons running. He played first base and was elected captain his senior year. The record shows this ball team was no ordinary college-caliber nine. By the spring of 1948, they almost went all the way to become national champions. They lost to the University of Southern California in the finals of the National Collegiate Athletic Association at Kalamazoo, Michigan.

Bush scored Yale's only run in the first game and knocked in two runs in the second game, which Yale won 8–3. He hit .167

for the series with 32 fielding chances handled perfectly. After 45 years, USC coach Rod Dedeaux told the *Omaha World Herald* that even 45 years later he would put Bush on his all-time all-opponent team.[1]

There was some talk at that time that major league scouts examined Bush's quality and almost made an offer. Bush threw left-handed and batted right and reportedly said that if he had batted left he might have done better since his left was the controlling eye. Bush also won a minor letter as a varsity soccer player. Teammate Jack Sloat recalls that he played the key center forward position and was noted for his goal scoring prowess.

Bush revealed again during the baseball experience his appeal to people at all levels and his immediate response to them. The head groundskeeper at the Yale athletic field, Morris Greenberg, wrote him a note of batting advice that if he would "put more power behind your swing, you would improve your batting average 100 percent."[2] Bush writes, "My first reaction . . . was to call Morris and thank him." Next, he took Greenberg's advice, deciding he had been swinging too defensively and should practice more on attacking the ball. This change brought up his average to .280 by his final game.

One of Bush's fellow students at Yale, Senator John H. Chafee, of Rhode Island, says that "wasn't just some Ivy League lackadaisical team he was on, that was a terrific outfit."[3] Indeed, after Yale five of Bush's teammates went on to be drafted by major league ball clubs. The standout was pitcher Frank Quinn, who went to the Boston Red Sox organization.

Bush admired Lou Gehrig, the great Yankee star, because Gehrig as a player at Columbia University "set a standard of excellence on and off the field. Nothing flashy, no hotdogging, the ideal sportsman." Yet a turn of the wheel put Bush next to another Yankee—the Sultan of Swat, Babe Ruth, not Gehrig, for an historic photograph. Not long before Ruth died of cancer, he presented the original manuscript of his autobiography to George Bush. As Yale captain, Bush received it for Yale's library in a public presentation.

Bush, like his father, also found time to participate in local

charities, in particular the United Negro College Fund, something he pursued after leaving Yale.

His leadership was felt in a general way by others at Yale.
Senator Chafee says "He was one of these fellows who was sort
of a golden boy: Everything he did he did well. We didn't see
much of him because he was married, but I guess my first
impression was that he was—and I don't mean this in a deroga-
tory fashion—in the inner set, the movers and shakers, the
establishment. I don't mean he put on airs or anything, but . . .
just everybody knew him."

Chafee is soft-spoken, especially about himself. Like Bush,
he entered World War II early and was among the first Marines
who landed on the beach at Guadalcanal. He modestly describes knowing Bush ever since Yale, even that they were in
the same fraternity, Delta Kappa Epsilon ("DEKE"). But "I
never remember seeing him there. He wasn't one to hang
around with the fellows." Chafee's roommate, Alexander Ellis,
married George's sister Nancy, so they both were ushers in the
wedding.

Bush was indeed in the establishment at Yale. One of his
supposedly secret honors was being tapped last—meaning he
was most highly regarded—for the Skull and Bones Club. This
took place as a sort of public spectacle that was later discon-
tinued, since it was humiliating to those who didn't get tapped
at all. Members of the junior class would mill around in the
beautiful greensward of the Branford College courtyard, waiting for the electrifying moment which might or might not
come.

The clubhouse for the Skull and Bones Club is windowless.
Perhaps this signifies that the focus of the group is inward, into
itself, away from the rest of the world. The practice is for
members, 15 at a time in their senior years, to get to know one
another deeply. There are sessions wherein, possibly a bit like
Alcoholics Anonymous, each man reveals his past and his
inner thoughts. The end product is a truly compact baker's
dozen of people who almost will be like a second family to one
another for the balance of their lives.

The Skull and Bones symbol stands for the thought that

everybody dies, and therefore it is important to make the most of one's brief stint on earth. Synchronous with the name of this club, its headquarters is called the "Tomb." Although the names of members are deemed confidential information, those of Bush's year were listed in the *Washington Post* in 1988.

Thomas William Ludlow Ashley
Lucius Horatio Biglow, Jr.
George Herbert Walker Bush
John Erwin Caulkins
William Judkins Clark
William James Connelly, Jr.
George Cook, III
David Charles Grimes
Richard Elwood Jenkins
Richard Gerstle Mack
Thomas Wilder Moseley
George Harold Pfau, Jr.
Samuel Sloane Walker, Jr.
Howard Sayre Weaver
Valleau Wilkie, Jr.

These 15 members of George's year in "Bones" have re-mained close friends—for the balance of their lives in some cases—since a few have died. When triumph occurs, they like to celebrate together; in times of disaster, they shore up one another.

It is said that both his father and his father's partner, Averell Harriman, had preceded George Bush as members. George had taken the secret club route before. At Andover he had been elected to one of the half-dozen or so such fraternities. Robert L. "Tim" Ireland, Bush's longtime supporter, who later served on the Andover board of trustees with him, said he believed he had been in AUV.[4]

"What's that? I asked.

"Can't tell you," laughed Ireland. "It's secret!" Both at Andover and Yale, such groups only bring in a small percentage of the total enrollment in any class. "That's a bit cruel to those who don't make AUB or 'Bones,'" conceded Ireland. As Jack Kennedy is credited with saying, life is not fair.

Prescott Bush continued as a strong presence in his son's (and other children's) life. At Yale, for example, former English professor George deF. Lord says, "You could not *not* meet Prescott Bush if you stayed at Yale at all. He often was coming to sing with the Whiffenpoofs. He was very enthusiastic about the college, dedicated and clearly influenced by the Yale milieu and Yale spirit, an old-fashioned Yale man—a gentleman."[5]

Despite his dignified ways on corporate boards and pro bono organizations, Prescott Bush had a colorful side. In 1988 the press revealed the complaint of an Apache leader about Bush. This was Ned Anderson of San Carlos, Oklahoma, who charged that as a young army officer Bush stole the skull of Indian Chief Geronimo and had it hung on the wall of Yale's Skull and Bones Club. After exposure of "true facts" by Anderson, and consideration by some representatives in Congress, the issue faded from public sight. Whether or not this alleged skulduggery actually occurred, the mere idea casts the senior Bush in an adventurous light.

Bush always strove for excellence, even at play. In golf he collected silver cups by the dozen, including the national senior golf championship in 1951, when he shot a 66 at age 56. He continued to be a strong swimmer and tennis player as well.

Someone as accomplished as Prescott Bush might well have wanted the spotlight all for himself. But according to his daughter, Nancy Ellis, he exulted when his children succeeded. Nancy tells of his skipping a CBS board meeting and its $600 fee in order to watch son George play on Yale's championship baseball team. He himself had been a baseball stalwart at Yale. Nancy avers it gave him great pleasure to see his sons do well, but there was no "pushing."

He sent his younger sons Jonathan and William T. ("Bucky") to Hotchkiss School in Lakeville, Connecticut, in part so he could easily drive up from Greenwich to see Jonathan play football. "Johnny" was a lean, high-stepping halfback star there.

His children doubtless felt considerable pressure to keep up with their paragon of a father. He clearly tried not to intimidate them. He had one endearing habit that Nancy Ellis describes. "When we came home [after all had gone away to school, college, jobs, marriage, and so forth], he would stand on the front porch waiting for us and then hug us all."[6]

Their mother, Dorothy Bush, also remained a strong current in their lives as they left the nest in Greenwich. Additionally, she became as popular in her own way as Prescott. She has admirers along the eastern seaboard from Florida to Maine. They tell of her good deeds, of her sharing her own rich endowments to help others.

Typically, she helped Bill Preston, a cousin by marriage, to recover from his war wounds. He incurred these at St. Lo, France, following D-Day in 1944. Hospitalized for months after German shrapnel hit him in the neck and immobilized his left side, Preston faced a dismal future.

Then Dorothy Bush took him in hand. She rented an indoor tennis court in Aiken, South Carolina. She was upbeat and inspired Preston to use tennis for therapy. She played with him, and thanks to her he overcame much of his paralysis. Gradually she worked with him until he could not only walk again, but also could hit balls across the net with some authority. Preston, who became a history professor, says that she made the critical difference in his recovery.

Then grandchildren began to appear to the extraordinary Prescott and Dorothy Bush. It was impressed on me how highly they were respected one stormy night in Manila at the end of World War II. I was aide to the Philippine Sea Frontier Commander Vice Admiral James L. Kauffman. We were expecting a typhoon. The admiral frowned as he entered our quarters at six P.M., stomping his feet dry. Rain already pelted the windows. I foresaw a hectic evening of meteorological bulletins—a disagreeable prospect.

Minutes later, the base messenger arrived with a radiogram marked "personal" for the admiral. The old sea dog read it. Abruptly the climate changed in his study where we were eyeballing maps of the Philippine archipelago. He broke into a grin that could have stopped a typhoon in its tracks. "Tell the

steward to bring drinks," he ordered. Minutes later he raised
an icy martini to "Prescott S. Bush, the third, my grandson!"

In 1947 the second grandson followed in New Haven:
George Walker Bush became the first of six more Bushes produced by George and Barbara.

By graduation in June 1948, George Bush already had made
his plan as a breadwinner. The prospects were numerous as he
mulled over which to pick. His father wanted to contribute
ideas and opportunities. As a member of the Pan American
Airways company board, he at least partially had been responsible for Pres Jr.'s going to work for them.

Brown Brothers, Harriman, where Prescott was still a partner, broke its tenet against nepotism to invite George to take a
position in the firm. Other possibilities loomed in the training
programs of big companies. With his sparkling record, George
would be a juicy catch for the body hunters—Yale's 1948
yearbook reveals 25 separate affiliations and achievements of
George Bush during his scant two-and-a-half years at New
Haven. Getting a job was no problem for him. Finding something that would engage his considerable energy and ambition
was a challenge.

It would have been all too easy with his connections to go
down to New York and be an instant winner on Wall Street, but
quite a few young men of his background began looking southwest and west. The economy was bursting, as consumer industries of many categories were at last driving hard to meet the
shortages left in the wake of war.

Suddenly one prospect focused his searching gaze. Prescott
long had been a senior director of Dresser Industries, an oil
enterprise with activities in the southwest United States. He
had been in at the beginning, in a sense. Brown Brothers,
Harriman underwrote the company when, after being a family
business for 48 years, it became a public corporation in 1928.
Neil Mallon, the president of Dresser, was put there at the
suggestion of Roland Harriman, Prescott's partner.[7] Now, in
1948, Mallon offered to take on George as the company's only
trainee that year.

Mallon, like George and his father, had been a star at Yale as an intercollegiate All-American basketball player and a member of the Skull and Bones Club. As George had been the navy's youngest pilot in World War II, Mallon, at 23, had been the army's youngest major in World War I.[8]

There were other possibilities, unrelated to George's family network, in New York and elsewhere. But his interest was piqued by the idea of physically, at least, cutting loose from his blood and school ties in the East.

This was a good way to penetrate the oil business from the bottom up. Despite his undoubted "in" with the president, George would have to begin as a laborer in a complicated and speculative field. It was a promising moment to get involved. The postwar boom needed oil to run its engines and build its products, especially those in the brand-new petrochemical industry. Texas was stirring in response to this beckoning future. Texas was the California of what would become a black gold rush. George was convinced. He agreed to start with Dresser immediately.

He gassed up his red 1947 Studebaker, arranged for his wife and son to follow, and headed for Odessa, Texas. He wouldn't be back for nearly twenty years.

CHAPTER 5

Businessman

A S GEORGE BUSH DROVE TOWARD TEXAS IN THE SUM-
mer of 1948, he was traveling the open road for the first
time. Until then he had moved from one structured environment to another: Family, where disciplinarian parents laid out
basic rules of life, with religious overtones; private school in
Greenwich, which taught him responsibility and socialization;
boarding school at Andover, where he was expected to be a
good boy, work hard and serve others (a pattern that determined his way of speaking and his moral code of friendship
and loyalty); the U.S. Navy, with its physical exigencies in
training and in combat; and a truncated stint in college where
he was marinated in the ethos of "For God, for Country and for
Yale." For 24 years George Bush had his agenda pretty well
laid out for him. Now, somewhat like a prisoner freed from
others' disciplines and expectations, he faced an uncharted
future.

This was, as Werner Erhard might put it, truly the first day of
the rest of his life.[1] From this moment on he never again would
have his days fully ordered for him. He was, at last, commander of his fate and master of his soul.

But when he arrived in Odessa, Texas, Bush found he wasn't quite yet on his own. Neil Mallon had arranged a trainee's spot in Ideco (International Derrick and Equipment Company), the oil drilling equipment division of Dresser Industries. Bush would take the position of equipment clerk. Mallon had explained there would be little money, but he would get a good grounding in the business.

His opening assignments were odd jobs, cleaning and painting the machinery and drilling parts. He did these chores and others so quickly and thoroughly, according to his boss, Bill Nelson, that Nelson was somewhat overwhelmed. He would go home at night and list the next day's duties for Bush, but when he arrived at work in the morning, he would find that Bush already had done them.

While still a trainee, Bush helped out as a salesman in the Ideco store. One day he was asked to deal with a visiting Yugoslav customer. Bill Nelson didn't like the idea of having to kowtow not only to a foreigner, but also a Communist to boot, so he passed the Yugoslav to Bush, his young trainee. It was Bush's baptism in diplomacy. He quickly won the foreigner's approval, and even entertained him in off-hours. The only sticky moment occurred when Bush took him to a local football game. The Yugoslav found it very different from European football (soccer). The noise of Texans cheering and jeering was so loud that the man put his hands over his ears.

Barbara and George Junior arrived after a few weeks. Their lodging was not too elegant, and certainly a change from New England. The little house stood on Seventh Street—a dirt road. In Texas such a structure was termed a shotgun house, because it looks like the box a shotgun comes in. In short, the Bushes lived in a frame building, bare boards nailed together without insulation. It was crudely partitioned in the middle. On the other side dwelt a mother-daughter hooker team, who shared the house's one bathroom with the Bushes. The hookers enjoyed a sizable, sometimes boisterous clientele, and during the nights no one got much sleep. During the days, however, the "ladies' " side of the house was quieter than a Trappist monastery. They seemed to lack the time or enthusiasm to socialize with the Bushes. The two families thus maintained a tacit standoff. This was a classic case of live-and-let-live.

The Bushes were determined to strike out on their own and were doing so on the cheap. Bush had only about $3,000 in his pocket when he went west, but he and Barbara were solidly upbeat on weathering any discomfort that might lie in their path. Their upbringing had given them the Judeo-Christian ethic for strenuous work and frugal habits. Now was their chance to put it into play.

George Bush continued to drive hard, whatever his varied responsibilities at Ideco. At the Christmas Eve company party that first year, he was drafted to bartend. Bill Nelson suggested that a good host drinks a glass or two with his customers. Once again, Bush met a tough challenge, but this time he ultimately lost. His normal intake has never been more than one or two drinks at any given time. At the party he pushed his limit.

Since then Bush has pointed out that he didn't know what his limit might be since he had never tested it before.[2] Alcohol is a depressant, of course, and so on this Christmas Eve, a great silence descended over the usually ebullient Bush. His family was waiting expectantly at home for him to trim the tree. Little did they know he had gone to sleep.

After the departure of Ideco's last guest, field salesman Leo Thomas kindly loaded Bush on the back of his pickup truck and delivered him to Barbara. Bush ruefully complains that this has been Barbara's version of the episode for the past 35 years, and he has had to listen to it without argument, since he can't remember what really happened.

Less than a year after he began with Ideco, Bush's apprenticeship with Dresser Industries took him to Pacific Pumps, another subsidiary in Huntington Park, California. There Bush joined the United Steelworkers labor union. He proudly declares that he paid dues and attended meetings while he learned the skills of an assemblyman.

Dresser next transferred Bush to Bakersfield, California, and let him practice his natural talent as a salesman. Barbara and George have lived in 28 houses in 17 cities, not counting the White House. They gave this record a jump start in California during the time George was peddling drill bits. In sequence they moved from Whittier to Ventura to Compton. He drove a thousand miles a week calling on oil well operators and discussing their drilling needs as he touted Ideco's wares.

Evidently Dresser liked his sales record. They shifted him to Midland, Texas, at a more advanced level. Midland and Odessa are basically twin cities separated by only 20 or so miles. The oil industry's blue collar workers tend to inhabit Odessa, where the wells and hardware are located. Midland's population is largely white collar clerks, salesmen, and management types. At that time the area's Permian oil reservoir was drawing entrepreneurs from all over. "Pretty soon Midland was the headquarters of the independent oil man in Texas."[3]

That's what Bush wanted to be. The way to make money, he figured, was not to limit oneself to a predictable salary. Despite the bright prospects in his present situation, outside opportunities beckoned Bush. After two-and-one-half years with Dresser, he decided to strike out on his own.

He felt a bit uneasy about how his benefactor, Neil Mallon, might react. He had been Mallon's protege and was slated for sure promotion. His father had long been a member of Dresser's board of directors. Leaving Dresser would be another cut of familial ties. He had known for some time he would do this when he went to Texas in the first place, but he didn't want to hurt or be ungrateful to his father and the man who had given him a start.

He needn't have worried. Mallon told him that if he were George's age he'd do the same thing. Whereupon he advised him how to go about creating an independent oil company. It's no wonder that Bush is devoted to this man; indeed he has named one of his boys after him: Neil Mallon Bush.

With Mallon still in his corner, Bush and his next-door neighbor, John Overbey, soon formed a small firm in Midland called Bush-Overbey Oil Development Co., Inc. Bush jumped from the security of a large corporation in which he was a minion marked for ascendancy to survival on his own.

Back in Compton his first daughter, Robin (Pauline Robinson), had been born. Now he had four mouths to fill. The challenge appealed to him. Perhaps an enterprising nature was his genetic imprint. Bush's great great grandfather, James Smith Bush, had left a comfortable storekeeper's existence in the East to try his luck in the California gold rush.

Midland was a more hospitable home base than Odessa. The oil fever had infected ambitious young people from different parts of the country and they were crowding in for a piece of the action. The Bushes found a house in what was dubbed Easter Egg Row. The housing contractor had thrown up dozens of rectangular dwellings with identical designs. To keep them from looking like the row houses they were, he faced them in different directions and painted each a separate, bright-hued color. The Bushes bought a light-blue Easter Egg at the standard price: $7,500 for 847 square feet. This bargain was due, no doubt, to the fact that the units were built with the help of a Federal Housing Administration loan.

The Bushes soon found themselves in the midst of lively and attractive prospectors hailing mostly from out of state: People like the Hugh and William Liedkes from Oklahoma, the John Ashmuns, the Toby Hilliards (with connections to the Mellons of Pittsburgh), Bailor Van Meters, Ferris and Fred Hamilton, and the John Overbeys.

Life was certainly gayer than in Odessa. Midland had collected a neighborhood of compatible yuppies who were aiming high. Many were fresh graduates from Yale and Princeton. They had come to make their pile in the American tradition, and to have fun while doing it. Fifty or more typical couples became companionable with one another. They dined together; played softball, tennis and golf; and shared information and tips about their common interest: oil.

John Ashmun met George Bush and Barbara in Midland. He remembers the day they moved over from Odessa. At first they had to stay in a motel called "George's Courts," about which Ashmun kidded Bush. Then there were Jim and Hopie Richie, Peter Douglas, George Potter, Dick Burke and Ferris and Mary Ann Hamilton—they only stayed about a year and then went back to Denver.

"In the evenings," says Ashmun, "we'd go over to George

and Bar's and she would rustle up some hamburgers. The door always was open for us.

"We'd all be downtown every day and bump into each other and then sort of congregate at each others' houses in the evenings. After supper the men would go off in a corner and talk oil again, infuriating the wives who would complain that we'd been doing that all day! We were all having kids every five minutes. None of us had any conception [pun intended] of family planning in those days.

"We were getting into the booming oil business any way we could, buying royalties and selling them to the big oil companies, acting as brokers."

They also would play the big oil companies on the stock market. Ashmun mentioned the time Texas Gulf Sulfur made a big oil find near Midland. Those on the spot realized the company was testing that site for a week before word got up to Wall Street, and the stock began to go up. Presumably those young men in Midland bought some before the rise. Now, of course, with the improvement in communications, the news would be in New York immediately.

Ashmun recalls, "Bush-Overbey got a little ahead of us because they were able to mount bigger financing, from Herbie Walker and his buddies in New York."

I asked for particulars as to how Ashmun saw Bush's New York family. He remembers Walker as tough, brusque, hard-charging, about average size. As for Senator Bush, he was "a very reserved man, patrician in bearing, interesting, wise, serious in demeanor, but you felt a sparkle. . . ."[4]

According to acquaintances of mine from that era, there was a certain amount of serious drinking and spouse-swapping under way, in the spirit of a modern boom town. Another reports that it was like a frontier settlement in the old West. Life was pretty raw. It was a time, in John Marquand's words, when "cocktails grew on bushes and we stayed out every night."

Speaking of the original frontiersmen pushing their way west, George expressed his own idealistic slant about them.

"You rode toward a new town and saw the silhouette against the sky. You would see just two buildings: a church and a schoolhouse. A place for the spirit and a place for our children to learn the great thoughts of man. We weren't saints but we lived by standards."[5]

My informants stress that the Bushes managed to be popular and amusing but always behaved themselves, avoiding the high jinks in which some became involved. They weren't prudes; they simply followed a different set of personal rules. They eschewed activities that would drain their health and vigor. George and Barbara Bush were more often engaged in the community, pushing for better hospitals, schools, music and museums for Midland.

Barbara joined the forerunner of the Junior League in Midland. George taught Sunday school at the First Presbyterian Church. People still recall that he was very effective in relating his war adventures to the precepts of the Bible. "He held everybody mesmerized. He was very nice looking, very intense and very energetic," says Henry Meadows, Jr., one of his students.[6]

Joan Baskin, former Chamber of Commerce president, says, "He was very deeply involved in Midland and in its growth and progress, whether it was the YMCA, the theater or the church."[7] Frank Trombley, a staff writer of the *Midland Reporter Telegram*, adds that "because of new ideas, a new culture, new education processes, and even a dress code that Bush and a group of about a half-dozen young men brought with them, their impact remains indelibly imprinted on Midland to this day."

Bush also devoted himself to the children of this growing town of 25,000. He coached Little League baseball and amazed the kids with his athletic skills and his fund of trivia about the game. Joseph O'Neill III, recalls a trick of Bush's. "He would take outfield practice with all of us and play catch with us. He had this ability to put his glove behind his back at belt level, drop his head [forward] and catch the ball behind his back." "And," said O'Neill, "I've often been at their house when he

has brought out shoe box after shoe box full of baseball cards
. . . and Barbara always was there with all those kids. She
always had a handful of kids around her at the Little League
park."[8]

· Bush picked up a cultural detail from Midland which he
embraced permanently. "A handshake was a man's bond. It was
a fundamental thing that I learned then and have reinforced
over and over." His probity was not lost on his neighbors of
those days, like Midland Oil operator Curtis Inman, who was
an avid badminton player with Bush. "He will be the most
honest person who has ever been in the White House. He is
capable, and he's smart. He's everything a person wants to be.
But he didn't show you. You had to search that out. He was for
the right things."[9]

Barbara was pregnant much of the time in Midland, yet she
had the energy and giving spirit that resulted in an open house
for other people's children. "I have heard neighbors of the
Bushes say that Barbara treated their children just like her
own. They were free to come and go and play in her home and
she was always there and had creative things for them to do,"
says Harriet Herd, a fellow member with Barbara of the Midland Service League (now Junior League).[10]

The Bushes entertained frequently in each of their three
rather small but successively larger houses as the years passed.
Barbara served simple food, like the hamburgers after church
on Sunday. She was noted as a good cook. Mrs. Earle Craig says
she still uses Barbara's recipe for Caesar salad. Mrs. Craig and
her husband, also a Yale graduate, were close friends with the
Bushes. The two wives also shared a New York and prep
school background.

Throughout his life Bush has shown evidence of reaching
out to touch those beyond his own privileged parameters. As a
child in Kennebunkport he made friends with "townies,"—the
yearround residents distinct from the summer colonists who
tended to keep to themselves. They still are friends. Barbara
remembers him bringing home a shoeshine boy for supper. He
kept in touch with the youth for many years. Midland was no

different in this respect. He personified Kipling's ideal of one who could "Dine with kings, nor lose the common touch."

The *Washington Post's* David Hoffman summed up the Bushes' style in Midland, "which is to say they had much more in common with the Lions Club than the country club."[11]

Bush's Midland contemporaries and others of that group went on to create great fortunes and/or great corporations. The Liedtkes made their name with the national firm Pennzoil. The Hamilton brothers were more individualistic. They started with one well and drilled it themselves. They became experts in the technology of extracting oil from both land and sea sites. Ferris Hamilton was an inventor who perfected numerous devices and techniques for more efficient operation. He and his brother, Fred, ultimately tried the fabulous North Slope reservoir of Alaska. Then with a semi-submersible platform, and in partnership with British Petroleum, they brought the first oil from the North Sea into Great Britain.

George Bush was destined to veer off this exciting pathway to oil riches and fame. When he and John Overbey began their joint venture in 1951, however, they talked only of their great future in oil.

Their scheme was similar to those of other independent operators: Search for land judged by geologists to be a likely site for oil deposits; buy drilling or royalty rights from the landowners; raise money to pay for these purchases. Beyond those steps they would search for investors to back drilling in the most promising spots. The search for backers would demand a lion's share of their time.

George's uncle, Herbert Walker, waxed enthusiastic about the new firm and invested nearly half a million in it. John Overbey exulted that this large financial dollop launched George's and his enterprise. But as Bush has said, in business or in politics, family and friends are an asset that can be stretched just so far. Still, they had connections, and connections have connections—networking was the buzzword. Moreover, Bush's reputation as a comer was spreading. Moneyed

Easterners were beginning to hear his name; presumably they wanted to see what Prescott Bush's son, who was also Herbert Walker's nephew, was up to and capable of.

Eugene Meyer, owner of the *Washington Post*, heard enough to invite George Bush and colleague C. Fred Chambers for breakfast at his house. Meyer's daughter, Katharine Graham, is the paper's current board chairman. Bush had called him to see if he would participate in a "sure-fire" deal in west Texas. Bush carried a certain advantage into this meeting. Meyer was an investing client of Brown Brothers, Harriman where Bush's father was a partner. Nevertheless, Meyer approached young Bush's proposition with caution, checking it out with his own specialist, who also counseled caution.

When the meal was over, Meyer hadn't committed himself, although the two young men had made their best pitch. They didn't press him. Conversation continued pleasantly, but he held them in suspense even as he took them to Union Station.

It was a briskly cold morning as they rode in his chauffeured limousine. They were impressed with the lap robe for their legs . . . very much in keeping with Meyer's VIP lifestyle. As it turned out, he was impressed too, for he signed up for $50,000 before bidding them goodbye. Then he added a bonus: "Since the tax ramifications are positive," he said with a smile, "put me down for [an undisclosed sum] for my son-in-law." This was Philip Graham, who later became a close and influential friend of John Kennedy.

While Kennedy was running for the Senate in 1952 with a healthy inheritance to back him, Bush was struggling to build his own bankroll. It was during the 1950s that Bush began to move into Republican politics. He wanted enough money so that he could pursue a political career without worry over supporting his family. He was in a hurry, perhaps, because in the back of his mind he realized that his father's sense of family duty had possibly kept him from running for office until it had become too late for him to go all the way to the presidency.

As George had been progressing through his own eventful and changing life, his father had been steadily adding plaudits to his own prominence.

During World War II he ran the national campaign for the U.S.O., the service group for soldiers and sailors away from home. He also chaired the National War Fund campaign, a consortium of about 600 war relief groups. The Republicans noted his talent for raising money and, after the war, chose him to chair the Connecticut state finance committee.

In 1950 Prescott Sr. took the inevitable plunge into elective politics by running for the U.S. Senate against William Benton, a nationally acclaimed advertising executive. An allegation made by Drew Pearson that Bush was promoting birth control helped to defeat him by a mere 1,000 votes. As Senator Bush said, "They handed out these notices at the church that said, 'Listen to the Pearson broadcast tonight about Senator Bush,' and he came out with this devastating attack. It certainly had a tremendous effect. Our telephone never stopped ringing. I can't prove it, but every political writer and every political leader in this state told me that that's what cost me the election." Bush denied the charge, but the election was only a couple of days off, and he couldn't shake it.[12]

Two years later when Senator Brian McMahon died in office, Bush beat Ambassador to Italy Clare Boothe Luce, among others, for the Republican nomination to fill the four years of his unfinished term. He went on to win the seat, defeating Abraham A. Ribicoff by 30,000 votes. He was sworn in with Jack Kennedy in 1953.

In 1956 Bush was re-elected over Representative Thomas J. Dodd (D., Conn.) by 138,000 votes.

In Washington Senator Bush performed as a flexible fiscal conservative, seeking moderate methods for containing the Tennessee Valley Authority and arguing against a public power development proposal for Niagara Falls. He sought ways to curb Senator Joseph McCarthy's excesses as an investigator. He also supported President Eisenhower's civil rights bills.

Additionally, the president liked him as a golf partner. He probably knew that Bush resisted press queries as to presidential prowess in that game. "People who play with the president don't reveal his score," Bush told journalists.

Prescott Bush retired from the Senate in 1962, citing poor

health. Bush was not the kind of man to concede sadness, so it is not clear whether the rather untimely end of his career as senator interfered with a larger ambition. He did say to some friends that he regretted leaving the Senate, that he found retirement a letdown.

His wife has said that he really wanted to be president and, had he started earlier, might have gone all the way. But, she is alleged to have said, he wanted to make enough money to raise his family first.

He certainly looked presidential: Six feet four and trim, he was fine-looking and courtly in manner. Claiborne Pell, who served with him in the Senate, remembers Bush as personally modest and diffident. This manner was appropriate to his background and did not detract from his effectiveness, according to Pell. By the time his son George was campaigning for president, that same Eastern establishment demeanor was attacked as "wimpish." Times had changed, it seemed. George's good manners were seen as too subservient. Or perhaps the strong personality of Prescott Bush impelled his son to be too diffident.

All this transpired as a *leitmotif* in the peripheral sight of George Bush. Aware of his father's accomplishments, George steadfastly made his own way. He strove hard to succeed with his partner John Overbey.

Despite George's fruitful fund-raising efforts, however, Bush-Overbey was destined only for mediocre profits. Bush would later comment dryly on this portion of his business life, saying that independent oil prospecting is risky and they were lucky to survive.

But at the time Bush went at the project with a full court press. The idea, as he explained it, was to buy drilling rights from farmers and then broker them to bigger companies. He traveled incessantly for two purposes: to find investors, and to locate potential oil plays.

He tells about one rumor he tracked down in North Dakota. He and another neighbor, Gary Laughlin, had heard of a major oil strike there called Amerada Iverson No. 1. So the two trekked north and persuaded some landowners to sell them options for the possibility of an oil find. The arrangement would yield royalties when and if the oil started flowing.

The deal sealed, the two headed south to Texas in Laughlin's Beechcraft plane. Former Marine Laughlin was a fine pilot, but when the weather turned sour he soon met conditions beyond his control. Clouds towered above; ice formed on the wings and they were unable either to get above the clouds or under them. Instrument flying had not yet spread to small private planes, and their visibility was zero. They had voluntarily committed themselves to financial risk, but now their lives were in peril to boot.

The two ex-military pilots claimed later they never had experienced anything worse during the war. For hours they meandered blindly over Montana, hoping their luck would change.

Finally it did. They spotted a small opening above Miles City and quickly slid through. Bush said the people on the field welcomed them, but twitted them for being aloft on such a day.

All in all this adventure had been exciting, but it netted them a loss after expenses. North Dakota still hasn't become a household word in oil circles.

With offices next door to Bush-Overbey in Midland, William and Hugh Liedtke started their own independent oil exploration company. Their business consisted of actually drilling for oil and gas. These two energetic Oklahoma brothers, trained as lawyers, proposed a merger with Bush-Overbey in 1953. Each side would raise $500,000, and together the amalgamated firm would buy shares in producing oil wells. Eschewing the old wives' tale against doing business with friends, Bush and his partner agreed to join the Liedtkes.

After an idea session, the four men decided to name their firm Zapata Petroleum. They hoped the name of the colorful Mexican revolutionary would catch the public eye, since Marlon Brando had just appeared in a film about him.

Hugh Liedtke was president and ran the company. His associates report he had a flushed face with heavy jowls, was about six-feet tall and looked like an ex-pro-footballer. They tell about the time he bought a Tip O'Neill face mask, went to a party and nobody recognized him.

George Bush was vice president. Before long Zapata began to turn a sizable profit. They had purchased 8,100 acres in what was known as the West Jamieson Field in Coke County, Texas. Within a year, by 1954, they were producing over a thousand barrels a day from 71 wells. Before the oil ran out, Zapata had drilled 127 wells without hitting one dry hole.

Bush minimizes the luck factor, saying that their geologists had studied the physical indicators and were convinced that it was a question not of whether but of how much oil was present.[13]

As business improved Bush had a new house built for him, and this time it included a swimming pool. He and C. Fred Chambers, another oil man in Midland, sat inside cooling themselves with ice tea one steamy Texas afternoon in the late 1950s. The children played and swam outside.

Apropos of nothing, Bush looked at Chambers and asked, "What are your long range plans for the future?" The two had met a year or two earlier and enjoyed a comfortable give-and-take on many of life's concerns.

Chambers replied that he was happy in the oil business and intended to stick with it. Bush then said, for the first time that Chambers can remember, that he was interested in public service and probably would enter politics to pursue this bent.

With capital assured by its pumped and still pumping wells, Zapata continued to prosper in numerous locales. Meanwhile, Bush began to look ahead for other possibilities in oil. He believed the common wisdom that the future was bright for offshore exploration. He and the Liedtkes formed a subsidiary of Zapata which they called Zapata Offshore. Bush served as president.

Soon Bush found a man who had created the necessary technology for Zapata's new division—an inventor named R. G. Le Tourneau. Hailing from Vicksburg, Mississippi, the site of one of General U. S. Grant's great victories, Le Tourneau was as unorthodox and strong-willed as Grant himself.

Le Tourneau had sold his earthmoving business in Peru, Illinois. Then he began to imagine a mobile offshore drilling machine. Shell Oil asked to see his design drawings. But he had none since he was not an engineer.

"He really was a 'mad inventor,'" says Hugh Liedtke, "and when George Bush and I went to see him in Mississippi, he showed us his plan to build a train that would transit the ice cap, in addition to a plan to build prefab houses simply by pouring cement into molds."[14]

Le Tourneau was a very religious man who gave most of his earnings to the church. He supported missionaries who would offer his inventions to help develop the countries to which they were assigned. He called this procedure the Point Four Program.

While Liedtke and Bush were talking to him at his office, they heard a whistle blow. "Is it lunch time?" asked Liedtke.

"No, that's no lunch, that's church," said Le Tourneau. "Twice a day we blow that whistle and that means that the workers can take ten minutes off to pray if they desire.

"I've had a profitable relationship with the Lord for about 30 years, but I never pray to him about price."[15]

Liedtke said George was just fascinated by the offshore drilling business and had developed confidence in Le Tourneau's idea. He and George negotiated a very favorable deal for Zapata: Le Tourneau would build "Scorpion," the first three-legged drilling barge, at his own expense. Zapata would advance him $400,000, to be refunded if Scorpion failed. If it ran properly, Zapata would pay him another $550,000 and 38,000 shares of Zapata Offshore common stock.

Le Tourneau completed the rig and towed it to Galveston to ready it for sea. It weighed nine million pounds and cost $3 million. The platform measured 180 by 150 feet. Under it extended three triangular steel legs. Each leg had 11 electric motors which could lift or lower it to the desired distance. At the lower end each leg had a metal base in the shape of a tin can.

When the legs, driven by the motors, reached the gulf bottom, these bases would be pushed beneath the sand until they formed a firm foundation. Then the motors on the legs, which had ratchets engaged with the pinions of the motors, would thrust the platform upwards some 50 to 60 feet above the water's surface. This height would enable the platform to be free of the waves even in a 100-mile-per-hour wind.

When solidly anchored this way, the platform crew would sink a drill to see if any oil was there. If a well were found, then the platform would be moved. This was done by reversing the 33 motors on the legs so that the platform would submerge into the water until its buoyancy would pull out the three metal base cans. Thus the whole contraption once again would be afloat and could be towed to a new exploration site.

Its place at the well would be taken by a permanent drill rig that would pump the oil. When the well was sucked dry, then the crew on the rig would "whipstock," or drill a curved hole to reach out for new contiguous reservoirs.

At present, Hugh Liedtke told me, there are a dozen idle mobile rigs like the Le Tourneau prototype. Liedtke says they are beginning to stir again as business improves.

Scorpion was commissioned in March of 1956 and represented the state of the art for offshore oil extraction. Early on, the rig developed mechanical failures during its shakedown days in the gulf. These hampered it seriously. Delays mounted and Zapata personnel became frustrated. Bush himself kept his cool. He swallowed hard and stuck with Le Tourneau as he perfected Scorpion. Le Tourneau then filled two more Zapata orders, for "Vinegarroon" and "Maverick," which cost $6 million.

Although the two divisions of Zapata operated amicably enough together, the Liedtkes and Bush realized more and more toward the end of the 1950s that they were in quite different businesses. The Liedtkes were exploring for oil and gas directly; Bush was renting rigs to companies who wanted to prospect in the gulf for themselves. After discussing the separate, perhaps incompatible, objectives of the two companies, Bush and the Liedtkes agreed to split.

The Liedtkes would stay in Midland with Zapata, and Bush would go to Houston, nearer the water, with Zapata Offshore. At this time Zapata owned 43 percent of Zapata Offshore. With the split Zapata sold these shares publicly, but they were taken over mostly by Liedtke's individual friends in Zapata.

In 1959 Bush, still president, set up headquarters in the Houston Club Building and gradually enlarged his company to an office force of 20 to 30 people with about 200 engineers and other drilling specialists who operated his rigs in varying places in the Gulf of Mexico. John Overbey and Bush also separated at about this time. Overbey stayed friendly with Bush, though he remained in Midland as well. He retired in 1969.

Hugh Liedtke, Bill Liedtke and Bush arranged the division of Zapata harmoniously over a private lunch. To demonstrate the mutual confidence and comradeship the three men enjoyed, the brothers decided to hold on to some of their personal shares in Zapata Offshore. The Liedtke-Bush friendship endures to this writing. The Liedtkes, among many other friends, unobtrusively labored to get their former partner elected president.

Nevertheless, it is possible to find an occasional critic nipping at Bush for his Midland days. One of his acquaintances from that era, a contemporary of Bush's from the East, conceded that Bush was well liked among his fellow Easterners. Still, he told me, some of the long-time residents from the area found his breezy, preppy manner grating. According to them Bush apparently was wont to show more enthusiasm for a topic than it warranted; and, they felt, he did so to get attention.

When asked if Bush was a star and leader among the Midland people, C. Fred Chambers says that no one there stood out particularly. "We were all out trying to find oil and customers and make a living," he explains. "There were no leaders as such. But," he continues, "George clearly was respected by the others as a potential chief, someone qualified to take charge."[16]

On leaving Midland for Houston, the Bushes carried with

them a scar that still sears. Their blond, pretty little three year old, Robin, had begun to feel listless and, at first, it seemed as if the Texas climate might be responsible.

One day, when George was in the county courthouse perusing deeds to possible oil acreage, he was called to the telephone. A family doctor had discovered that Robin had leukemia. The prognosis was hopeless. The medic estimated she had but two weeks left.

George refused to accept the doctor's chilling pronouncement. He insisted upon doing something. After conferring with his uncle, Dr. John Walker, and others, the couple took Robin to the New York Memorial Hospital, which specializes in cancer cases.

For six months, every step then known was taken. The child appeared to respond to treatment with periodic remissions. Robin fought with quiet courage and cheerfulness. Her parents were consoled during the ghastly process by friends from their various former dwellings. Fellow Skull and Bonesman Lud Ashley, then working in New York for Radio Free Europe, was particularly solicitous.

George commuted back and forth over weekends from Midland, doggedly keeping up with his business. He and Barbara forbade anyone to cry when they visited Robin. George lived up to this rule, but away from her he frequently and openly wept.

When the torture finally ended, the parents returned to Texas. Barbara found it harder to absorb the tragedy than George. His Christian beliefs allowed him to feel that it was God's will and that Robin was now at peace, and therefore her survivors must get on with their lives as soon as possible. The sympathetic messages and calls from their innumerable friends, as well as family, provided some relief. It has been said that Barbara's hair began to go white during this ordeal.

More children arrived to swell the Bush clan. Before leaving Midland they had five children: George Walker (1949), John Ellis ("Jeb," 1954), Neil Mallon (1955), Marvin Pierce (1956), and Dorothy ("Doro," 1959).

The Bushes settled in Houston in 1959, where they still legally are official residents to this day. One of George's young Houston employees, Charles R. Powell, still is awed by the energy and disciplined habits of George Bush. "He works too damn hard!" exclaims Powell. He cites the day they were planning a trip to Beaumont, Texas. It was a two-hour drive. They were to meet with Bush's Uncle Herbert Walker and others on a project. "What time shall we leave tomorrow?" Powell asked Bush. "About seven?" "No, no, we've got to get there by seven," insisted Bush. "He was outside my house at five with a cup of coffee ready to go," recollects Powell. His name is George H. W. Bush—that H. W. stands for 'hard work' as far as I have observed for the past 27 years!"[17]

Bush left no possibility for new business untended at home or abroad. Powell tells of trips he made with Bush to New York, London, The Hague, Mexico, and Trinidad. Combined with his war experience in the Pacific, Bush was laying sound foundations for a diplomatic career to come.

He also was exhibiting coolness during emergencies. His brother William (Bucky) Bush was on hand when the giant rig Maverick collapsed and disappeared in a Gulf of Mexico hurricane. Evidently it was a tornado within the larger storm that tore the rig apart. As a result of this bizarre meteorological phenomenon, which was little known at the time, efforts to find the wreckage were protracted. George himself helicoptered for many hours around the gulf during the search. Until the evidence was in hand, no insurance claim could be honored.

Back in the Houston headquarters, according to William Bush, people wrung their hands and tended toward hysteria. Not George, he affirms. At stake, after all, were his supporters' and his money. "Yet he remained as calm as a man sitting home smoking his pipe in front of the fireplace, and kind and thoughtful of the others. "Everything is going to be all right," he kept assuring his staff."[18]

Eventually it was, particularly in terms of cost. Charles Powell states that Lloyds of London paid the Zapata claim for the lost Maverick. It was the biggest such settlement in their history: about $8 million.

For George Bush another phase of his life was nearing its close. He would not relinquish Zapata Offshore for a few more years. But already he had been dipping his toes occasionally into a wide ocean that eventually would engulf him completely: national politics.

CHAPTER 6

Texas Politician: 1960–1964

G EORGE BUSH THE POLITICIAN EMERGED SLOWLY.
While in Midland he toiled at the grass-roots level for
General Eisenhower in his campaigns of 1952 and 1956. He
saw the seamy side of national politics when, in 1956, Texas
oil magnates and their lobbyists pushed Senate passage of a
bill to deregulate their industry. Senator Prescott Bush opposed the legislation. As an Easterner he believed it would
bring his region higher prices for oil and gas.

George tells of numerous attempts to scare him out of the oil
business if he didn't persuade his father to change his vote and
support the oil industry. Bush's response to this pressure was
that yes, he had expressed his and other Texans' views on the
bill to his father, and no, his father refused to budge.

One lobbyist called at two in the morning and threatened to
scuttle Bush's enterprise if Prescott voted against the bill. This
man represented Sid Richardson, a Texas oilman then thought
to be the richest man in the world. Richardson was leading the
charge for the bill. Bush recalls that the lobbyist was dead

drunk, and told him that if he couldn't turn his dad around "That's all she wrote for you, Bush, because we're gonna run your ass out of the offshore drilling business."[1]

George was concerned and angry. He met later that morning with Tom Fowler, a savvy practitioner in the oil business whom he had known and trusted since Midland days. Fowler, who was acquainted with Richardson, agreed to take action. Within hours the regretful, sobered lobbyist apologized to Bush.

More leverage was applied before the final vote. K. S. Adams, head of the giant Phillips Petroleum company, leaned on Neil Mallon, Bush's former mentor at Dresser Industries, saying "if Prescott Bush doesn't vote for this bill, you can forget selling any more Dresser equipment to Phillips, and you can tell George Bush to forget his offshore drilling business."[2]

Prescott Sr. commented on this episode in 1966.[3] He recalled that the bill in question, the Harris-Fulbright Act, indeed was favorable to the oil interests. He said that President Johnson and Oklahoma Senator Bob Kerr promoted it very hard. When the bill passed, after Bush had voted against it, the question was whether there were enough votes for an override. It was then, said Bush, that "The oil industry acted very badly. They tried to bribe Senator Case with $2,500. Senator Hickenlooper was offered some money . . . these things all came out in the debate."

The senator added that his son "was threatened that if his father voted against the bill, they'd drive him out of Texas. They'd put him out of business. He came up to see me . . . and said 'I think you ought to know about these things.' I said, 'Don't you believe them . . . They wouldn't dare. This will not affect you at all. I'm going to vote against the bill because on the whole I think that's in the best interest of my state, as well as the United States. But don't you worry . . . if there's any after-effects . . . just tell me . . . and we'll take care of that."

The senator went on to berate what Drew Pearson had said about the matter, to the effect that "Bush has got a son in the oil business. He'll do what he can for him." "It was perfectly ridiculous," Bush concluded. "What I did was the last thing my son wanted me to do."

The bill actually passed, but President Eisenhower vetoed it in irritation over the oil industry's excessive campaign to influence Congress. He expressed dismay at the industry's low moral standards.

This run-in with special interests didn't deter George Bush's growing desire to begin his career as a Texas politician. He did suffer two disadvantages in this ambition: He was neither a real Texan nor a natural politician. At least he didn't seem to be.

From his arrival in Odessa, Bush had thrown himself into becoming a Texan with fervor. But he was already 24 years old. At that age, one's personality and cultural background are formed and hardened. He was a New England prep-schooler and Ivy Leaguer like his father.

George Bush stepped into Texas and out of the groove so securely shaped by family, schooling and military service. Let's suppose he had not gone to Texas and run instead from Connecticut, New York, or even Massachusetts or Maine, all of which he rightfully could call home. It's a good bet that his entry into politics would have been smoother and his persona more familiar to his constituents. Had he stayed in the East, he would have had the same advantages as his father. His constituents would have known his kind. Politicians of his social stratum such as Franklin Delano Roosevelt and John F. Kennedy had earned their votes before.

But Bush is stubborn and persistent; he likes to cut his own furrows. He would be a Texan in his own mind if not in the minds of others. His gregariousness had exposed him to neighbors and colleagues in the twin cities of Odessa and Midland, and now in Houston. These people had grown accustomed to the migrating bird from the East, though he never would really shed his preppy-Yale plumage. The Texans would have to accept him for what he was, but it would be some time before they called him a Texan.

How about Bush as politician? His record teemed with credentials that suggest political strength. A wholesomely handsome, prize-winning college graduate, heroic warrior, successful businessman, generous participant in community service, devoted and happy family man—in short, Mr. Clean and Mr. Competence.

Yet in large measure he was, as his son George now says, a quiet man, someone who kept his own counsel and was modest to the point of shyness. At least his hands were large and beefy—great for shaking thousands of hands!

Doesn't all this rich bounty add up to instant politician? Of course it does—superficially. But there was another angle to consider. Until the moment he entered politics, George Bush never had to electioneer for anything. In grade school, high school, the navy, and college, he simply was himself and others looked up to him, gave him awards, and dubbed him their leader.

He was not immodest about this. Now that he had to try for people's votes he found himself in strange environs. He couldn't be his usual, relaxed self. He had lived too long as the automatic receiver of the royal mantle. He didn't seem to enjoy becoming an instant hustler. Indeed this was the onset of years of malaise at the mike.

Another factor evidently gave him pause, although he didn't speak of it. Indeed he denied it implicitly every time he insisted he was a real Texan. This was the training that had made him the person and personality he had become. Throughout his family, church and school years, he had been absorbing their creed: "The meek shall inherit the earth." "Gentlemen don't ask people to vote for them." "Real men don't boast." "It's more blessed to give than to receive." "Public service is the purpose for entering politics." These Eastern establishment shibboleths, scrupulously taught to and meticulously followed by George Bush, had formed his social persona. He had seen his father garner votes without really violating any of these creeds. But he had departed his cocoon. With wet wings he would have to learn to fly on his own, as an American politician without a natural constituency.

Politicians, environmentalists and public relations people

have something in common: Anybody can be one simply by declaring that he is. There is no formal schooling, degree or license necessary to enter these fields. As a result almost anyone interested in these subjects feels he can comment as an expert—and frequently does. More importantly, anyone who decides to practice as a professional will chart his own path based on his own talents and preferences. So George Bush began to chart his own political odyssey.

For politics it is useful to be a performer. Reagan showed the benefits of acting techniques. Jonathan Bush, George's brother, has been an actor as well as an activist in politics in New York City, though he never has run for office. Bush's sister, Nancy Ellis, affirms that George never has been an actor in any sense. He plays it straight, whatever it is. What you see is what you get.

Singing is another art form that can enhance acting and politics, for it depends on precise timing and the knack of projecting oneself to an audience. As an actor Frank Sinatra was a hit often because the timing of his lines was so perfect. Prescott Bush's political strengths certainly were enhanced by his gift as a singer. Unlike Reagan, who was a master of oratorical timing, George has found it difficult to wait for the punch line to sink in before going on with the next thought in a speech.

Pres Jr. claims that George always sang in church and could carry a tune. Yet he was the only member of the family that didn't join in their father's group singing, in the choir, or in any of the Yale Glee Club activities. For some unstated reason, he just said no when given the chance to develop musically. One or two of his cronies say they have heard him sing off-key. They insist that even though he claims to like country music, he can't even recognize the big names when he hears them because he has no ear. In any case, while the rest of his family was singing, George always would find something else to do. Perhaps this was an early step in distancing himself from his father. Still, this early choice is regrettable. Almost surely he deprived himself of a useful instrument for his political toolchest.

Curiously, Bush is a talented mimic. Yet to date he only has revealed this side of himself to close friends and family. When he returns from travels, he regales them with hilarious imitations of all kinds of people he has met, even the important ones. He does it perfectly, says his sister Nancy, down to their foreign accents.

Perhaps as chief of state he will go public with this engaging trait. Franklin Roosevelt employed it with sarcasm to put down his political targets. Americans from that era can still remember his sing-song sneering at "Martin, Barton and Fish," Republicans he ridiculed. Harry Truman enjoyed mimicking broadcaster H. V. Kaltenborn after he had misguessed the 1948 election results, saying that Thomas E. Dewey had won the presidency. Bush has long amused his cronies by poking fun at them and himself. Still, they concede that throughout his political career he has tended to guard against really being himself, either in front of a strange crowd or television cameras.

His friends and associates in Texas, however, encouraged him when he began showing an interest in public service during the late 1950s. Some were political heavyweights, like George Brown, who was close to Lyndon Johnson. As such, they were bound to be Democrats in those days. Ever since Reconstruction, when the northern Republicans came south to straighten out the "rebels" after the Civil War, the Democrats were the preferred party. They sweet-talked George, suggesting he might be a good candidate for the U.S. Senate.

They stipulated, however, that he would have to switch parties. Their rationale was that in Texas the two-party system consisted of liberal Democrats and conservative Democrats. As a Republican, they explained, he would fit in fine as a conservative Democrat if he decided to change.[4]

Bush waved off this idea. In his autobiography he asserts that he was philosophically a Republican and intended to stay that way. He also observed that the party was showing signs of new life under the leadership of state chairman Peter O'Donnell and Thad Hutcheson.

Bush's past was about to repeat itself. As in his earlier days, admirers came to him and bestowed their confidence in his abilities. Their first move was a modest offer. Early in 1962 the co-chairmen of Harris County's (Houston) Republican Candidates Selection Committee asked George to join them. As is true everywhere in the country, a certain number of eccentrics, some who probably belong in an institution, present themselves as candidates for state offices on behalf of both major parties. The committee's job was to screen candidates to avoid any embarrassment to the party and the political system. George clearly had the judgment for spotting troublesome types.

Later that spring, after George accepted this assignment, the Harris Company Republican party chief resigned. Then the Republicans approached George in earnest. The evidence was mounting that some Texans not only considered him a politician, but a man for whom they would be comfortable voting.

They urged him to announce for the post of Harris County Republican chairman. They explained that the John Birch Society was aiming to take over the organization. A strong gladiator was needed to carry the banner against this danger. Would he do it?

These forward-thinking Republicans included Roy Goodearle, Tom and Nancy Thawley, Jack Steel and others. Bush gave them lunch and his assent to be their instrument in the upcoming election. He says candidly in retrospect: "I didn't really need time to think it over. This was the challenge I'd been waiting for—an opening into politics at the ground level, where it all starts."[5]

As he jumped into this first contest, Bush was relaxed in attitude but vigorous in pursuit of the prize. He knew the people he was courting, if not individually, at least as Texans. He now had lived in Houston for three years, and had been in Texas since 1948, a total of over 14 years, less the two years or so when Dresser had posted him in California.

He still was managing Zapata Offshore, but took time off at nights and on weekends. Barbara went with him night after night as they met with every group, however small or large, throughout the county. He learned to capture audiences while she sat nearby and taught herself needlepoint. She said she needed something to distract her from hearing the same speech 150 times in a row. He won the county chairmanship.

For the next two years, he strove to broaden the party's strength in the midst of the Democratic majority. As a pleasant neighbor, promoter of charitable activities, churchgoer, and prominent businessman, Bush started his political forays with a good base of contacts. In all these areas people had come to know and appreciate Bush. They were potential converts, if not already Republicans, to Bush's missionary efforts.

The party grew larger and richer. This was an excellent first achievement for a man who would one day be chairman of the national party.

His reputation blossomed as he extended the Harris County party's membership and filled its coffers. His theme was unity. "We all shared basic conservative views, but to be effective we had to concentrate on tackling the Democrats, not each other."[6]

Ironically, considering his opponents' and some fainthearted supporters' criticisms of his 1988 presidential campaign, Bush wrote in 1987, "Jugular politics—going for the opposition's throat—wasn't my style." In business, he pointed out, "When competition gets cutthroat, everybody loses." He did concede that bare knuckles must sometimes be used as a last resort. But his personal approach to political jousts then as now was more consistently kind and gentle. His record shows him remarkably free of rancor and ad hominem attack, either by or against him. There have been exceptions, of course, as when Senator Dole called him a liar in the 1988 primary campaign; in that case he didn't respond directly. After the debate with Geraldine Ferraro in 1984, he made his crude statement to the steelworkers. He relishes competition, whatever the arena—politics, business or sports. He plays to win.

He pushes himself. In the 1960s his body rebelled a few times. One of his Zapata colleagues recalls that on long trips to Europe Bush would take "a big swig of Pepto Bismol" before going to bed. This tendency for heartburn twice progressed to bleeding ulcers, first in London (his trips there and elsewhere during those years were in pursuit of oil deals with foreigners), and later during his congressional race in 1966. Since then he has been more careful of his diet and has had no recurrence of that ailment. Indeed, his fondness for pork rinds ("fatback," as southerners call it), and hot TexMex chili dishes evidently settle his stomach. Most men his age would seek blander fare, especially those who have encountered abdominal problems. Bush's internal durability has improved continuously since the early 1960s. That is fortunate, for he was entering a life that would challenge the digestion of a garbage grinder.

Meanwhile, back in Houston in 1963 and 1964, the fledgling politician was busy building political popularity. A big payoff was looming. His youthful aura, sunny disposition and enthusiastic promotion of Republicanism in Harris County had evidently lit a fire among state party leaders. Like the Democrats before them, they saw in Bush the makings of a senatorial candidate.

Soon Peter O'Donnell, chairman of the state Republican party, contacted Bush and flattered him with remarks about his political powers. Without too much effort he talked Bush into challenging the liberal Ralph Yarborough for his seat in the Senate. The offer carried with it the burden of two primary elections before Bush could face Yarborough. There were several candidates in the regular primary that filtered Bush and Jack Cox into a runoff race. Bush beat him handily in what the *Corpus Christi Beacon Press* called a "landslide victory" on June 18, 1964. He got 67 percent of the vote.

This resounding nomination gave Bush the sendoff he needed for his siege against the comfortable incumbent. Was Bush really equipped to make this statewide goal a realistic one?

Yarborough's reputation was secure. He recently had attacked Lyndon Johnson as a "power-mad politician," however, and now he needed the president's support. Johnson, power-mad or not, put aside any irritation and spoke up for Yarborough. *Time* noted that Johnson's endorsement of Yarborough would make Bush the underdog. If not for the president, *Time* acknowledged, Bush might have been a viable contender.

But Bush was clearly a greenhorn in this race. His speeches were adequate. At forty years of age he had accomplished much in the military and business. He clearly was an educated, intelligent man. But his ability to command his listeners in large groups and on television was nascent at best. According to those who saw him on the campaign trail, he waved his arms and spoke in a high-pitched voice with sentences that sometimes ran together. He practiced eye contact in his tryout days as would-be county chairman. It was improving. But meanwhile he'd have to rely on his clean-cut, handsome and athletic appearance.

Texas presents a unique challenge to any statewide candidate who doesn't sport seven-league boots. Bush traveled tirelessly, but he started with the limited base of Houston, Midland and Odessa—beyond it, he was still Bush Who?

One particular frustration was his unsuccessful attempt to reach black voters. He appeared wherever they would receive him, and made it clear he opposed racial prejudice and bias of any sort. He had shown his desire to ally himself with their causes back at Yale where he led the United Negro College Fund drive in 1948. As GOP chairman in Harris County, he had deposited the party's money in a black-owned bank. He had established an office near Texas Southern, a major black college, to seek the support of its students. As a Republican politician, however, his message might be seen but not noticed.

It is difficult to get at the reasons for this problem. Blacks are reluctant to talk about it. Bush did win over individuals with his specially focussed attempts. Nevertheless, the reputation of the Republicans for being anti-minority, at least compared to the Democrats, was most likely the root cause.

This was but one hurdle in his ambitious quest for the Senate. By October Yarborough was so confident of victory that he showed up on Columbus Day in Columbus, Ohio. At a ceremony there I shared the podium with him. I was speaking as a member of the U.S. Mission to the United Nations. He was the featured orator and had a natural, down-home style that captivated the audience. "Don't you have an election to win in Texas these days?" I asked him, after his address. His answer was a big wink and a grin.

In 1988 he told me why he had not worried about Bush 24 years earlier. To win the 1964 primary, recalled Yarborough, Bush had to wrap himself tightly in the mantle of Senator Barry Goldwater. "When I started my campaign for re-election I was touting my record of six years in the Senate. But my speech advisors said, all you have to do is quote Bush, who had already called himself 100 percent for Goldwater and the Vietnam war. So that's what I did, and it worked very well."[7]

Yarborough didn't refer to the hardball that he and Bush played against each other, as reported in *Time*'s October 16 issue. Bush charged that his opponent was the exponent of left-wing radicalism, and reminded voters that he had accepted money from fraudulent financier Billie Sol Estes. Yarborough lashed back with sallies to the effect that Senator Prescott Bush couldn't send little Georgie down here to buy a senate seat!

As it became more and more apparent that Johnson would crush Barry Goldwater in Texas, Yarborough accurately teased Bush for mentioning Goldwater less and less. Yarborough, reported *Time*, attacked Bush's outdoor advertising: "You can find everything on those billboards except the word Republican . . . He's got it so small you have to . . . get out of your car and look for it with a magnifying glass."

Yarborough also assailed Bush for being the "darling of the John Birch Society" and a "carpetbagger." Lyndon Johnson echoed the last epithet, which evidently galled Bush. He complained that, since 1948, he had spent more time in Texas than Johnson.

Bush was determined to persuade others of his new identity, but his geographic background remained too apparent in his mannerisms and accent. Like the wolf impersonating Red Riding Hood's grandmother, he didn't wear his new costume comfortably. This fact badgered his political efforts for years to come. A simple answer might have been to give up trying to act like a Texas native, for the effort was unsettling to him. He is sensitive enough to realize that people didn't see him as a Texan. Why then didn't he drop the idea?

Although he could read the discouraging polls as well as anybody, Bush kept plugging away, and toward the end he caught up a bit. Indeed, his autobiography claims he was neck and neck with Yarborough in the home stretch. He fought from morning to night. His campaign manager reports that the days started at 6 A.M. with a cup of coffee. Did some aide get up and make it? No. George Bush got it for himself and his collaborators.

Freshman Senator John Tower, a new power on the Texas Republican scene, tried to help, boosting Bush in his own party speeches during that presidential election year. Tower, whom the party had put up as a sacrificial lamb, had entered the Senate through unusual circumstances. In the 1960 election Senator Lyndon Johnson had engineered a state law that allowed him to run for vice president and senator simultaneously. This was the act that permitted Lloyd Bentsen to do the same thing in 1988.

After Johnson vacated his Senate seat, Governor John Connally called a special election. There were 72 candidates: John Tower, who had been defeated in the 1960 contest, and 71 Democrats. There was a run-off among the Democrats that was won by William Arvis Blakely. Tower bested him, according to George Bush's political ally Nancy Thawley, because the liberals sat on their hands and vowed to challenge him in 1966. They would do this, but fail repeatedly until 1984.

By the end of the 1964 campaign, George Bush had tried everything: visits on his behalf by Barry Goldwater, Richard Nixon, and other Republican bigwigs, fancy rallies with country music and plenty of advertising. I remember seeing the huge Bush For Senate billboards still up on a 1965 visit to Texas, and marveling at the prominence of an ex-Easterner in this unlikely setting. Nevertheless, the prize eluded him on his maiden try.

By 11:30 on election night Bush had conceded. His statement was modest. *The Houston Post* quoted him as saying, "I have been trying to think whom we could blame for this and regretfully conclude that the only one I can blame is myself. I extend to Senator Ralph Yarborough, who I believe beat me fair and square, my best wishes."

But Bush could savor the satisfaction of garnering 1,134,337 votes, or 43 percent, which made him the top Republican vote-getter in Texas history.

CHAPTER 7

Texas Politician 1964– 1966

WHEN JOHN ASHMUN AND BUSH WERE FELLOW oilmen and neighbors, he noticed Bush's consuming competitiveness—not on any major issue like contact sports or business, but on the rug in his sitting room. "When I'd drop into the Bushes' house in Midland after work, George would pounce on me for a game of tiddlywinks," he recalls. "He'd sit me down on the carpet and pop those little things into an old-fashioned-size glass until he'd wump me; which he did soundly every time. Only then would I be allowed to get up and have supper."[1]

After Yarborough defeated him in 1964, Bush wasted little time nursing his wounds. The election had been a new experience for him. Until then his life had been an uninterrupted string of victories, whether in tiddlywinks, academics, war, athletics or business. He never before had lost a contest in which he was a serious combatant. He treated this as a painful but temporary setback in a longer contest.

Before continuing his new profession, however, the ever-cautious Bush took measure of the situation. Like a military commander, he needed to assess his assets and liabilities. First, as a nascent pol he really had done very well, conducting a creditable siege on the citadel of an incumbent senator. He had become an outstanding member of the growing Republican party in Texas.

In 1960 John Tower had paved the way to some degree as the first Republican to win a Senate seat since 1890. He was admired by the state Republican organization, but operated somewhat as a lone wolf. In contrast Bush was currying the party's favor and getting it, particularly in its Houston headquarters. Although he had no clear path to the next nomination and would doubtless need a primary to achieve it, as a candidate he would have widespread party encouragement.

Also, he had learned hands-on that running for office is no task for a dilettante. It demands every waking minute and inner resource of the vote-chaser. This reality would put stress on any serious candidate's competing duties as a business executive and family man. He would have to fish or cut bait before too much longer as to whether or not to maintain his leadership of Zapata Offshore. He further noted that he already possessed a precious gem for any political career: His own preternatural tendency to make and keep acquaintances and friends in all the walks of life. Along with this trait, he was honing his remarkable memory for names. He built a habit of writing prompt and affectionate notes to people with whom he was dealing. Any mnemonic expert would encourage this means for remembering because the physical act of writing adds a kinesthetic dimension to the eye and ear details, literally a memory in the muscles of the hand that writes the note.

The knack for names is a great advantage for people in public life. Some are better than others. George Herman Ruth made his living from the fans who went to see him swing a bat. In his era there was no television revenue, so a player's personal recognition derived more from his relationship with the crowds. Ruth could scarcely retain anyone's name, and this failing might have hurt a less resourceful fellow. He saved himself by the simple device of calling everybody "Babe." That's how he came to be known as "Babe."

James Farley, who did so much to advance Franklin D. Roosevelt's political fortunes, had a legendary capacity for name retention. It is said he knew scores of thousands. I met him when he was in his 80s and this great talent had dissipated somewhat, but his memory bank still seemed better than most.

When I accompanied Adlai E. Stevenson at the United Nations as his spokesman for a time, I saw that he had no special gift for recognizing individuals. Everywhere he went, of course, passersby would react to seeing him. Once as we emerged from his limousine, a big, burly stranger in a wrinkled suit strode up to him and said, "Hello, Governor Stevenson, I'll bet you don't remember me!" His tone was demanding and intrusive. Stevenson was known everywhere for his courtliness. This time the governor (he preferred this title though he was then our U.N. ambassador) looked the man coldly in the eye, said "That's right," and left him standing with his mouth open.

George Bush's inherent fondness for people helps him to avoid such needless confrontations. A determined politician, he taught himself early to slip free of most rude and hostile entrapments by strangers.

In 1965, Bush began to ready himself for the next moves toward political office. One of his first steps was to shuck off a bothersome trace from his 1964 campaign. He had espoused some conservative ideas that didn't jibe with his own moderate attitude. So he stated forthrightly to his Episcopalian minister in Houston, John Stevens, "You know, John, I took some of the far right positions to get elected. I hope I never do it again. I regret it."[2]

The minister took this affirmation in good faith, although he obviously felt that Bush had been regressive on civil rights. He said later, "I suspect that his goal on civil rights was the same as mine; it's just that he wanted to go through the existing authorities to attain it. In that way nothing would get done. Still, he represents about the best of noblesse oblige."[3]

Bush made a poll of the newly apportioned Seventh District, which was mostly the white, silk-stocking area of Houston, along with a small representation of blacks and Hispanics. There was no incumbent congressman since this was the first election for the Seventh. The poll indicated it was winnable by a Republican.

In February 1966 Bush filed from the Seventh District as Republican candidate for the United States House of Representatives. In mid-February he sold Zapata Offshore so he could put all his time into the campaign. This divestiture would properly distance him from the oil business, thus allowing him to avoid any possible conflict of interest in Washington. As mentioned in the last chapter, Drew Pearson already had aired assertions that Senator Bush was tilting his votes to aid his son in the oil business.

George was determined to avoid any such vulnerability. If and when he might be legislating on energy matters, he wanted to be able to think and act freely.

1966 was a poor year for selling. His colleagues from Texas repeatedly have asserted that Bush could have made "real" money if he hadn't bailed out just then. If he had stayed with his company just a few years more . . . up till the oil embargo of 1973, for example.

He sold his share of Zapata Offshore for $1.1 million. He was bid another $400,000, but the man who made that offer refused Bush's stipulation that he keep on the employees. With that guarantee Bush accepted the lower figure. This act of loyalty cost him almost a half-million dollars.

The stock Bush let go doubled within the next two years. Allegedly he said later to Barbara, "I could have made seven million dollars if I'd held on to that stock!"

By 1966 the country was just entering its long agony of Vietnam. Jack Kennedy was assassinated before he could come to grips with the war. Lyndon Johnson had embraced it vigorously and was busy selling his guns-and-butter package (read Great Society for butter). Students were beginning to bridle at the draft. Blacks were unsettled, their expectations for new freedoms were frustrated. Despite Johnson's legislative successes, he and many other Southerners were slow to shift basic prejudices formed in childhood.

If these issues seemed curiously irrelevant in Bush's try for Congress, it was because he and his opponent, conservative Democrat Frank Briscoe, looked at them from the same point of view. They both favored the Vietnam war and the right-to-work law, plus the need to cut Johnson's spending.

In his own account Bush modestly says that it figured to be a close race between him and former Harris County District Attorney Briscoe. He certainly played it that way. He persuaded Richard Nixon to fire the campaign's starting gun in Houston. The relationship between these two had become rather warm: two years earlier Bush's five-year-old daughter, Dorothy (Doro), personally had embraced Nixon when he alighted at the airport during Bush's Senate thrust. Both men are inclined toward homey touches; Nixon's famous 1952 "Checkers" speech lingers in memory.

Furthermore, Nixon almost had carried Texas over Kennedy, and captured the majority in Houston—"the largest metropolitan area in the country to go Republican in 1960."[4] He was a strong card to play. So was Jerry Ford, House Republican leader, who arrived later in Bush's 1966 campaign to help raise money for him.

Bush collected a formidable support group this time. Two friends—Jim Allison and Harry Treleaven—joined right away. Jim Allison from Midland became manager. Harry Treleaven took leave from a national public relations firm to create materials for the mass media. With them, Bush assembled a large team that laid siege to the voter via every avenue. Bush delivered 100 formal speeches himself; every advertising medium—radio, TV, newspapers, posters, and volunteer house-to-house calls from "bandwagons" circling the district—was used. Often he was accompanied by as many as ten attractive, young "Blue Bonnet Belles" distributing literature. He crafted a well-organized, well-financed team effort highlighting his experience and accomplishments.

His billboards and leaflets emphasized his particular appeal as a youthful candidate, with pictures of him always moving, in shirtsleeves, with a coat hooked over his shoulder.

Victory was in the air well before the election. Yet toward the end Bush lost some ground to Briscoe. The conservatives were unhappy at attacks Bush leveled at the party's "extremists." He evidently was keeping his pledge to Reverend Stevens not to veer right again.

One conservative, Tex Hale, sneered that the Democratic nominee was more conservative than Bush and predicted that "many Republicans will support Briscoe just to defeat Bush and, hopefully, prevent permanent party control by moderates and liberals."[5] Bush ducked discussion of his ideology, charging that "labels are for cans."

This was Bush's third run for political office. He was learning and growing professionally. Allison and Treleaven later wrote a history of the campaign. They cited Bush's talent for the people-to-people part. It served him well, they declared. Personal contact, away from the podium, was still his strongest suit. He already had perfected his natural knack of greeting people as if he had been looking foward to seeing them for the last two weeks. In the limited area of one congressional district, an individual can make himself known in the flesh to enormous numbers of the electorate. This task requires energy for working long hours and the discipline to schedule them effectively. I have seen candidates just as energetic and outgoing as Bush; but they run around in circles till they drop in fruitless exhaustion, unmourned and unelected!

Briscoe's campaign was low-key, without any memorable theme, and failed to bring much glow in the minds of voters. The registration in the district was six to one for the Democrats. But John Tower had won there in the special election for the Senate in 1961.

This year, Tower was running for re-election and both his and Bush's campaign committees agreed to conduct separate races unless some special reason for coordination should arise. Apparently it did not, for both men comfortably hewed to their respective lines.

What was Bush marketing this time around? He concentrated on the promise of more "action" in Washington. He wasn't offering much that was specific. What he was saying sounded very much like Jack Kennedy's simplistic theme of 1960: "Get America moving again." As in Kennedy's case it was probably his fresh, appealing youthfulness that made the difference at the polls. Briscoe, like Nixon in 1960, had average good looks, and was approximately the same age, but was less photogenic than his opponent.

The difference in Houston was sizeable. "George Bush Easily Defeats Briscoe" announced the *Houston Post* on November 9, 1966.[6] The tally was 55,619 for Bush and 40,367 for Briscoe, a 57.6 percent win. Bush's elation was given an extra fillip by the apparent response to his efforts among blacks and Hispanics. The total percentage of the ethnic vote for him rose from a mere 3 percent in 1964 to 35 percent this time.

When the voters' decision was clear, Briscoe conceded with a chuckle, "I have been elected to practice law!"

Barbara Bush might have said that night, quite truthfully, "I have been elected to be a congressman's wife!" As in the 1964 race for the Senate and the contest for Harris County chairman, she had traveled around to meetings and electioneered at his side with every spare minute. Now George Bush's score was improving: two wins and one loss.

This time she had added a personal, handwritten letter to the district's 73,000 women voters telling them about George. It read, in part,

"George has a marvelous sense of humor, a great sense of being openminded and fair. He is kind and a very hard worker, eager to learn more. All these qualities he uses to help bring up our five children.

"George leans heavily on his church and, in turn, serves his church. What I am trying to say is that George loves his God, his family, his friends and his fellow man.

"Please . . . vote with me for George!"

From the very start of their union, George and Barbara seemed to have a strong relationship. Both brought strong personalities into their marriage, yet somehow they found compromise when necessary without yielding individuality. She commanded the house and he didn't interfere in that any more than she interfered with his office downtown. She accepted his propensity for bringing friends home for meals, often with little or no notice. When any person entered their house, he would be enveloped in a warmth as easy as going home.

As their own parents had before them, the Bushes showered their progeny with love, attention and discipline. The children responded to this treatment and enjoyed their home. Doro, the youngest and now a mother with two of her own progeny, says she's a "homebody" because of her own happy childhood.

There were poignant moments, particularly on the subject of their little sister, Robin, claimed by leukemia just before her fourth birthday. The Bushes keep a picture of her on their dresser. When Doro was growing up, she says, "Dad would tuck me into bed at night, and he would tell me about Robin, and we'd both cry. I look at my four year old and think . . . you would never forget, never."[7]

Marvin recalls there being a sense of chaos and lots of different people around, at least 10 or 15. The house was a homing point for all the other neighborhood kids. The parents enjoyed the fact "that their place was a madhouse . . . but there were firm codes of conduct." Marvin spells out that the worst offense was to pick on others, poke fun at them, take advantage of their weaknesses, or hurt their feelings.[8]

Jeb states, "We were taught not to sit on the sidelines." The Bushes clearly saw the risk that their children might feel overshadowed by their busy and prominent father. So they were encouraged to step out on their own, as Jeb and his two younger brothers did when they published a weekly, neighborhood newspaper.[9] They presumably had seen copies of their grandmother Bush's weekly column in the *New Haven Register*—which was a topical commentary. Mrs. Franklin D. (Eleanor) Roosevelt had started this trend with her famous, sometimes ridiculed, little column "My Day," in the 1930s.

The Bush children saw almost limitless work by both parents in business, politics and helping others through the church, school and charity groups. Yet somehow all these activities were kept in smooth gear; their mother was a superb, orderly manager.

Now the whole gang had to pull up stakes and move to Washington. This meant leaving familiar surroundings and daily habits, friends and schools. Multiplied by seven—George and Barbara, plus young George (19), Jeb (11), Neil (10), Marvin (9), and Doro (6)—that was a lot of change. George was now at Yale and the others all would be moved to local schools near the capital.

Barbara would be in charge of finding a house. She did this by telephone. The father of then Senator Alan Simpson sold them his dwelling on residential Hillbrook Lane in the northwest section. Barbara settled her brood in swiftly and new routines soon replaced those of Texas. There were new tasks, new friends and a cooler climate.

The Bushes soon discovered pals in many quarters. There were old friends from Yale, or Andover, or business, and new ones in their expanding political coterie. As before, their closest associates would be next-door neighbors, or George's colleagues from his work on the Hill.

In the House of Representatives, 47 "freshmen" Republicans were sworn in during January 1967. Before long George Bush would distinguish himself among them.

CHAPTER 8

Congressman

SHORTLY AFTER GEORGE BUSH BECAME A MEMBER of the 90th Congress, he was embroiled in the leadership question concerning the 1966 class. After the election the Republicans had a net gain of 47 seats. One of the more than 50 new Republicans, Donald E. (Buzz) Lukens of Ohio, was buttonholing fellow freshmen to get their vote for president of the class. Lukens was a strong conservative, and his efforts were causing some irritation. George stepped into the fray, and soon he and Bill Steiger of Wisconsin prepared a slate that would appeal to the majority. Tom Railsback of Illinois would be treasurer, William O. Cowger of Kentucky, president. Bush did not pick a spot for himself.

Railsback grumbles with a grin now that one of the provisions they adopted was that anyone who skipped a meeting would have to pay a dollar to the treasurer. After the first assemblage was over, one congressman, Bill Scott of Virginia, refused to pay his dollar and complained to Railsback about it for years. If only the Congress cared so much about the national debt!

Curiously, Congressman Lukens ended up as president of

his class—but it was another class, some years later, after he had held an interim position outside of Congress and then been re-elected.

Without much delay Bush assembled a staff to run his offices both in Washington and Austin. From Texas he brought his veteran campaign people: Pete Roussel, Jim Allison and Aleene Smith. For manager of his office, "Administrative Assistant (AA)" in Washington parlance, he found Mrs. Rosemary Zamaria. She had been a staffer with former Houston Congressman Albert Thomas. She was savvy in the ways of the Hill as well as Bush's district.

Mrs. Zamaria still has vivid recollections of Bush's two terms. Even now, over 20 years later, it is clear that she was a top-flight AA. Her accurate command of detail, her commitment to Bush and her sense of the strategic requirements of her congressman's career all are apparent as she talks.

"We put in long hours to keep up with all the activity he generated," she says, "but we were happy and enjoyed our days with him. He was always so upbeat and jovial when he arrived in the morning. He would speak to everyone without fail, usually making light jokes. He was so grateful and would thank us for every task we completed. His attendance was almost perfect," she recalls, "although he traveled nearly every weekend to see his Texas constituents."[1]

With his office organized and functioning, he turned quickly to the question of committee assignment. A mix of alertness, luck, timing and (some say) a telephone call from his father, won Bush a coveted seat on the Ways and Means Committee. This committee, the nation's ultimate authority on taxation, was a convenient proving ground for the man who would one day utter the memorable phrase, "Read my lips: no new taxes."

It was also a way station on the path of a man who would always know how to get on with the boss, to give him unswerving loyalty in good times and bad. Chairman Wilbur Mills was at the peak of his reputation when Bush joined his committee. No one in government, it was said, had a more extensive grasp of the nation's fiscal affairs than Democrat Wilbur Mills, who was responsible for tax legislation. Bush thought he was a model of what a congressional leader should be.

Mills also won the young congressman's fealty by forcing a star witness, Chief of the United Automobile Workers Walter Reuther, to stay long enough to be interrogated by Bush.

Junior committee members had to wait their turn. On this occasion the hearing on a bill that concerned the automobile union had lasted after 5 P.M. Reuther was getting restless. He had a plane to catch. Thanks to the chairman's insistence, however, he held still until Bush had a crack at him. News that the fledgling legislator had quizzed the famous labor leader reached Houston's radio and TV screens and newspapers. Good for Congressman George Bush. Thanks to Wilbur Mills.

Years later Mills' career crashed amid public alcoholic escapades with dancer "Fanny" Foxe. Bush maintained his professional respect for him. Today he salutes Mills for his courage in regaining his health and usefulness to society; Mills, in control of his alcohol addiction, has been a tax counsel in the reputable law firm of Shea and Gould since 1977.

Meanwhile, the Vietnam war and the draft were disrupting the lives of more and more young men. Bush was sympathetic with their views. Vietnam was controversial; in earlier days, diplomat George Kennan's Containment (of Communism) Policy had been accepted. It had succeeded in Greece, the Philippines, Malaysia, and Korea. In Vietnam it was backfiring: The North Vietnamese Communists were winning; the South Vietnamese "good guys" were floundering. But more to the point, what did all this have to do with the United States?

Bush believed the war was a valid action, and thought it vital for young citizens to understand what it was they were being asked to do and why. He left orders with his staff to interrupt him, even in meetings of the Ways and Means Committee, whenever youths from Texas or anywhere else in the country asked for an audience.

Rose Zamaria remembers many of them emerging from one-on-one sessions with Bush after he had listened to their worries and queries. The boys always were grateful. They would say, "Mr. Bush didn't agree with everything we said, but he would explain why he was for the war."[2] They felt that although they didn't turn policy around, the system was working. A political leader had heard their story and taken the trouble to clarify the government's position for them personally.

Bush's concern for the young didn't stop outside his own front door. His instructions at the office, according to Mrs. Zamaria, were to put through his own children's telephone calls no matter what was going on. Those remain his orders today.

In 36 years of observing Washington careers, I have witnesed innumerable domestic strains and breaks caused by the habits of workaholic husbands. Bush made certain that his family transferred the relaxed atmosphere of Houston to the pressure box of Washington. For example, they continued their custom of Sunday barbeques. Friends and neighbors like the Potter Stewarts (he was Supreme Court Justice), the Bill Steigers (he was in Bush's Congressional class), and their children would congregate just like informal Texans. Eventually the Bushes sold the Simpson house, at a loss, and bought a better one on Palisades Lane where there was a rural environment with more lawns and trees. It still was only 15 minutes from Capitol Hill.

Marvin Bush, now a strapping six foot two, recalls being a little boy in those days and what his father was like. "He always was impulsive in day-to-day things," says Marvin. "I remember there was always a chaotic environment in our house. Happy, but chaotic in the sense that Sunday morning my dad might bump into somebody at the grocery store and have them come on home for lunch. And he'd just show up, with three or four people, then two others would hear about it. The next thing you know, they've got a cookout with 22 people eating lunch there."[3]

When the Bushes went on trips together, the moment for departure would arrive and Barbara would have the bags packed, the kids' hair slicked down and her foot tapping well in advance. But where was George? He would show up with about 23 minutes left before flight time and say "Let's go!" The children suggest that perhaps that's how Mom's hair got white.

The most exciting getaway occurred one day when they were leaving Nashville for Christmas in Houston. George drove the family up to the door of the terminal with three minutes left before scheduled takeoff. They traipsed into the airport in unison. George put the car keys into the hands of a startled baggage attendant.

"I don't know you from Adam," he declared, "but I trust you. Please do me a favor and park my car for me. I'll take care of everything when we get back. I'm George Bush."

Who the heck's that?

"I'm the congressman from Houston."

Well, the guy took care of it, as Marvin says. The keys were waiting at the ticket counter on the Bushes' return, and the car was in the parking lot.

Despite his spur-of-the-moment surprises, the children knew how well organized their father was. They saw that he had very little spare time and had to be as spontaneous as possible to cram as much as he could into his brief freedoms.

"Other things he did at home," as Marvin put it recently, "besides sports, was reading some. He wasn't much of a TV watcher. Every once in a while you'd see him reading himself to sleep in the late afternoons. He spent a lot of time with us, trying to figure out what the heck we were up to."[4] With five kids. . . .

Or he'd be in his office. He always set up an office wherever he lived so that he could be at home as much as possible. His door never was shut against the children. They could burst in on him without notice and not be thrown out on their ears.

Additionally, Bush eschewed, as had his father before him, getting caught up in Washington's ceaseless social swirl. Even when key constituents came to town looking for things to do, Bush usually brought them home for dinner. It wasn't very elegant. The kids were ever-present, making noises when the constituents were trying to talk and tripping over their feet in the living room. It was very down-home-on-the-farm. But when the kids grew up, Bush's well-earned boast was, "They all still come home."

Meanwhile, down at the shop, so to speak, Bush put in the same all-out effort as all the other ambitious young legislators—and not without effect. Only months had passed when the *Christian Science Monitor* wrote a series on the emerging leaders in Congress. Republican freshmen formed a "power elite," said the *Monitor*, and listed Bush first among them: "Rep. George Bush of Texas, the first new congressman from either party to serve on the Ways and Means Committee since 1900."[5]

Other leaders featured in the article included William A. Steiger of Wisconsin, who had become a close comrade of Bush; William O. Cowger of Kentucky, whom Bush had earlier helped to steer into the class presidency; Thomas F. Railsback of Illinois and Donald W. Riegle Jr. of Michigan. Riegle later switched parties and became a senator. Many Republicans, including Bush, Railsback and myself, tried to dissuade Riegle from leaving the party. In time he settled comfortably among the Democrats just as former Congressman and Republican Mayor of New York John V. Lindsay had done.

Railsback was a fellow "jock" who frequently played paddle ball with Bush in the Rayburn House Office Building gym. In his early forties, Bush still was fiercely competitive in sports. In the spring, he played first base for the House Republicans on a team with pitcher Bob Michel (later minority leader), and they beat their Democrat peers a dozen times.

Bush's closest pals on the Hill were Republicans William Steiger of Wisconsin, Tom Kleppe of North Dakota, John Paul Hammerschmidt of Arkansas and Jim Leach of Iowa. These young Republicans took their lead from Minority Leader Jerry Ford and Minority Whip Mel Laird as they learned the ropes in Congress. Ford and Laird proved to be distinguished role models—a future president and an eight-year secretary of defense, respectively.

From them Bush declares he picked up four rules for excelling in Congress:

Never get personal.
Do your homework.
Persuade, don't intimidate.
Be considerate of your colleagues, above or below your rank.[6]

Now that Bush had become a national lawmaker, what laws did he introduce, or floor manage to passage during his tour in Congress? The answer is rather skimpy, if one is listing bills of his own initiative. It is important to understand how the system works. Legislation is scheduled for consideration by the chairman of the appropriate committee. The chairman always is a member of the majority party at any given time. The Democrats were in the majority when Bush arrived in Washington. Even if a minority member introduces a bill, it often is co-opted by the majority as their own.

Therefore, there were two reasons why Bush would be blocked from guiding his own bills through Congress: First, he was a Republican (minority) member; second, when he arrived, the old rule that a freshman should be seen and not heard still was in force.

Despite these institutional barriers, Bush did make his mark in the House. For example, he introduced an ethics bill that would require every member of Congress to make a full disclosure of assets and income, as he had done voluntarily. He also laid on the floor numerous bills dealing with pollution and other environmental matters.

He expressed his views on most big issues, in general on the conservative side. He supported curbs on wasteful government spending, wanted control of education to stay local, urged returning a portion of federal taxes to the states, favored voluntary prayer in schools, opposed busing to achieve racial balance and fought federal registration and licensing of guns.

On matters such as the environment, he was more moderate to liberal. He chaired the Republican Task Force on Earth Resources and Population. After early hawkishness on Vietnam he came around to favoring an all-volunteer army and withdrawal from Vietnam.

He was designated a member of the U.S. delegation to the Ninth Mexico-U.S. Interparliamentary Conference.

One bill did catch his complete attention: the Fair Housing Act of 1968. This bill prohibited the sale, renting, or financing of housing on the basis of race, color, religion, sex or national origin. Bush voted for this proposal. Aleene Smith, his secretary of many years, hasn't forgotten the heat he took back in Houston for his liberal position while representing a conservative constituency. After the vote angry mail began to pour in. It finally became so heavy and venomous that Bush went home to face the music in person.

He drove to a large rally in the Memorial-West section of the district. A previous speaker had warmed up the crowd by suggesting that the new law would "lead to government control of private property, the Communists' number one goal."[7] The people were angry and ready to vent their displeasure when Bush appeared.

He stood up and talked quietly at first, citing famous British statesman and orator Edmund Burke. He used the perfect quote for a congressman who strays from the majority views of his constituency: "Your representative owes you not only his industry, but his judgment, and he betrays instead of serves you if he sacrifices it to your opinion."[8]

Bush then argued against the inequities of denying any American the right to live where he wishes because of his race or color. Bush brought his logic to a crescendo with the reminder that even as he spoke, blacks and Hispanics were risking and giving their lives in Vietnam to protect the freedom of all Americans. He closed by saying:

"Somehow it seems fundamental that a man should not have a door slammed in his face because he is a Negro or speaks with a Latin American accent. Open housing offers a ray of hope for blacks and other minorities locked out by habit and discrimination."[9]

When Bush finished, there was no reaction, not a sound. He gathered his notes, silent and convinced his plea had foundered. He turned to nod at the moderator. Then it happened. The audience stirred. Scattered handclaps began like the first drops of a summer rain. They waxed rapidly into a cloudburst of applause and cheers until those Texans rose to their feet to salute the man they had come to jeer.

Bush had spoken from his personally held values. He clearly had found the decent core of those who had heard him. Complaints against his vote on this issue slowed to a trickle. This matter was another marker on his trail toward the acceptance of black Americans.

Not long after this night, in the wake of the murder of Martin Luther King, Jr., blacks from all over American marched to Washington. This was the summer of 1968. They came to dramatize inequities in America's democracy. In front of the Lincoln Memorial thousands of them erected what they called "Resurrection City" with hundreds of tents. Rains turned it into a quagmire, but youths of all colors and creeds came to show their approval. My college-age nephew and a black fellow student joined the tide of sympathizers. They stayed in my house but spent many hours talking under the stoney gaze of Abraham Lincoln. The boys would return late at night, still dripping with mud from "The City." George Bush also visited the encampment and met at length with the Reverend Ralph Abernathy, who was the leader of this poor people's campaign. Bush's outreach to minorities didn't seem to disturb the white majority in his district. It likely eased their conscience to some degree.

Meanwhile, he and his staff did excellent "case work"— responding to the routine questions, requests and criticisms from constituents that require much attention from every legislator. Publicity on his performance as congressman was favorable.

Still it came as a happy fact when no Democrat challenged Bush for his seat. He returned for another term without opposition.

From Bush's first day in the House of Representatives, his good-naturedness seemed to beam across the partisan ravine. Ohio Congressman and fellow "Bonesman" from Yale Thomas Ludlow Ashley and Gillespie V. (Sonny) Montgomery of Mississippi were two Democrats who grew close to Bush.

Another less-likely comradeship had developed with Lyndon Johnson and rose to a poignant peak of sorts when the
president departed Washington as Richard Nixon was being
sworn in on January 20, 1969. Bush decided to skip the ceremony as a gesture to Johnson, and he went out to Andrews Air
Force Base to see him off.

Saddened and battered by the waning period as president,
Johnson appreciated Bush's generous act. Although members
of his cabinet and a smattering of senators and congressmen
were there, Bush was the only Republican. "Thanks for coming," Johnson said, before boarding Air Force One for the last
time.

Bush noted that his old opponent Ralph Yarborough had not
found it necessary to show up. Yarborough had ridden the
president's coattails (at Bush's expense) back into the Senate in
1964. Would this selfish omission make him an easier target
for Bush in 1970?

Johnson later reciprocated Bush's kindness by inviting
George and Barbara to his ranch. There he gave them the
standard treatment: an 80-mph race around the dirt roads near
the Pedernales River in his open Lincoln Continental. One
might wonder whether Bush ever thought of returning the
compliment with a wild ride in his speedboat "Fidelity" off
Kennebunkport. There are similarities between the two men;
perhaps it's just the Texas air.

It is alleged that to accomplish anything significant in Washington one should never take the credit. From his school days
Bush had been loathe to boast. His mother had been adamant
on this trait. It was in character for Bush to claim that saying
goodbye to Johnson was his assistant Rose Zamaria's idea. If so,
Bush also might have thanked Rose for the advice Johnson
later gave him as Bush pondered another run for the Senate.

In the first place, Bush was hearing indirectly that the Nixon
White House was beginning to think Bush ought to challenge
Yarborough again. Speculation was spreading in Texas about
this possibility. Reporters were bugging Bush to comment.
Temptation was tickling his fancy.

Although safe in his Seventh District seat, Bush realized that real power in the House comes with seniority. By 1970 he would only have two terms under his belt. That meant many years before committee chairmanship, and probably longer before he could hope for party leadership.

Yarborough was losing popularity in Texas; he was considered too liberal. Bush had made a strong showing in 1964, despite being a neophyte. Now, with Johnson out of the picture, Yarborough seemed vulnerable. Why not ask LBJ, the master politician and Bush's trusted fellow Texan?

Bush promptly called on Johnson at the ranch. He flew there with longtime adherent and friend Jack Steel of Houston, who one day would run Bush's vice presidential office in that city. Johnson wasted little time before telling Bush what he wanted to hear. But first he reminded Bush that he would have to forbear encouraging a Republican to threaten any Democratic incumbent. Having cleared his conscience Johnson then went into one of his colorful monologues. He conceded that serving in the House of Representatives was an honor. He had done that himself. But he also had been a senator. From his own experience he had discovered there was a difference between the two. "It's the difference," he slapped his thigh, "between chickenshit and chicken salad."[10]

Bush's fever was rising. The top Democrat in the land privately had spurred him on. The leading Republicans were nudging him. He was close to decision. Another senior friend, his father, still was an important factor in his life.

When George moved to Washington in 1966, he had in some measure returned to the turf of his father. In his ten years as senator (1952–1962), Prescott Bush had left a large imprint on Washington. At first, as a candidate for the Senate, Prescott seemed more like the zealous Yalie that he was than someone who would fit in the dignified legislative body for which he was aiming. A Yale freshman at the time, who is now a political historian, remembers his appearance on the campus with General Dwight D. Eisenhower. The general was making his first run for the presidency. It was a cold, blustery day. The very tall Bush wore a raccoon coat, acting as a sort of cheerleader for the general. He was trying to be the "jolly populist," says this informant. He was waving his arms and getting in front of the general so much that the students called out more than once "Down Bush!"

But this was all in the spirit of good fun; the old Eli had become a politician and he wasn't stepping out of character to behave this way. He knew how to endure such treatment from his peers, after all, from the ordeal of initiation to his college fraternity. The seniors had forced him to sit naked for several hours on a large cake of ice. Even his grandchildren learned of this assault on his dignity, though they didn't dare talk of it in his presence.

Once in the Senate, Prescott Bush became a strong and popular member of that most exclusive "club." He successively became a member of the Banking and then the Armed Services committees. He spoke out on the key issues forcefully. He voted against Joseph McCarthy. He was a friend of John F. Kennedy, and even went to the University of Virginia at Kennedy's request when his young brother Teddy was being named to a prestigious position.

One of his fellow members, Senator Margaret Chase Smith of Maine, ended up being his friend, though the two of them fell into a dispute over a dinner he organized. The affair was a kind of salute by Republican senators in honor of President Eisenhower. Unfortunately it was slated to be held at a men's club which refused to bend its rules so that Senator Chase could be included. After she gave vent to her disgust the decision to permit her to attend was reversed, but at that point she had become nearly intractable. It took a great surge of persuasion by Bush to get her to finally accept.

Stuart L. Pittman, whose parents were friends of the senator, has a warm memory of his exposure during the Armed Services Committee hearing on his appointment as assistant secretary of defense for Civil Defense. "He was extremely forceful and knowledgeable about the Department of Defense, and clearly held in respect by his colleagues," says Pittman.

When he declined to seek another term in 1962, the elder Bush indicated several times that he missed his job in Washington. Perhaps this regret in his own case influenced Bush's assessment of his son's aspirations for the Senate.

He advised George against leaving his secure base in the House. George thanked him for his opinion, but he determined to run nevertheless.

One critical writer says this was the first time Bush ever stood up to his father.[11] Perhaps so, although the record is moot on this point. Through his membership on the board of Dresser Industries, Prescott Bush had been instrumental in George's striking out on his own. For those who argue that he never really shook loose from parental influence, this event surely suggests the opposite. His brother Jonathan explains that George left the House of Representatives because he saw the Senate as a better route to the White House.[12]

White House!? Is this what George Bush had in mind all along? This remark was the first to hit print to that effect; and the print date was 1988. But a detective might have collected some clues as far back as 1970.

Imagine the United States as a page from a child's coloring book. Already Bush had crayoned in a number of states he could call home: Massachusetts, where he had been born and went to prep school; Connecticut, where he had been raised and gone to college; Maine, where from infancy he had spent summers; Virginia, where he was stationed while in the navy; Texas, which he had obsessively adopted since 1948; California, where he had toiled for Dresser Industries; and the District of Columbia, not yet a state but big enough to color in fully. They didn't add up to enough electoral votes yet, but Bush never went anywhere without creating bonds. Aleene Smith says that George Bush already had about 4,000 best friends when she worked for him in the 1960s and 1970s.

In 1970 Bush couldn't yet be judged guilty of presidential ambition, but already he could be rounded up among the usual, or at least possible, suspects. Maybe that's why his father was waving him off the senate quest: He wanted to protect him from the most incurable political disease of all.

But George was off and running for the Senate. He had been correct about Yarborough's weakness. He was ripe for the plucking. Indeed, Lloyd Bentsen plucked Yarborough off in the Democratic primary before George had a chance at him. Now it looked as if ex-Senator Prescott Bush knew something about which George hadn't thought. His opponent would be no pushover.

Bentsen could be seen as almost a clone of George Bush. Both were close in age—Bush was 46 and Bentsen 48; both were tall, comely and aristocratic in demeanor; both were fighter pilots with bemedaled combat war records; both had headed their own profitable business firms, both were congressmen; Bush with two and Bentsen with three terms; and both were judged to be at the conservative end of the Texas spectrum. The comparison dipped in Bentsen's favor, however, because he was a Democrat in a Democratic state and possibly because he appeared to be more wealthy.

But George set his jaw and ploughed ahead. He had faced tough opposition before and he was accustomed to taking risks. Besides, he was entering this battle far better equipped than in his somewhat quixotic thrust of 1964, when he had been untested and unknown. Nixon was even more supportive this time. He contributed $100,000 from a White House fund for favored candidates. He and Vice President Agnew both barnstormed Texas for Bush in numerous public events, along with five cabinet officers. Bentsen later said he thought the administration's intervention was overkill and might have backfired against Bush.

In any case Nixon reportedly promised Bush a safety net in case Bentsen won by offering a high appointive office in Washington. He also had said earlier that there was a need for more congressmen like George Bush.

From the Republican Senate Campaign Committee, Chairman John Tower (the Texas senator) earmarked nearly twice as much in party funds for Bush as for any other candidate: $72,879. He also said, "I believe Congressman George Bush would make an outstanding senator."

Bush announced his candidacy on January 13, 1970, and formed a strong, tightly knit organization mostly of volunteers. Again he employed every advertising and marketing medium, worked hard, traveled incessantly and met as many voters as he could find.

Recently I was able to review his electioneering style on a videotape recorded for a local Texas TV station. It caught him in midsummer. One could feel the unbearable sun of Texas in June. Bush's cheeks were flushed, his coat lying beside him, his collar open and necktie pulled down, his brown hair wet from perspiration and slightly mussed. Still, he seemed at ease with the reporter, serious and attentive to his questions. Although words flowed from Bush, his sentences were ragged, ran into each other, and tended to leave thoughts hanging and ideas incomplete. I was reminded of a younger version of General Eisenhower whom I had observed in a 1952 meeting with his campaigners at the Commodore Hotel in New York.

Despite the four-to-one advantage that Democrats enjoyed in party membership, Bush approached the finish line competitively. Johnson, out of office but still formidable in the eyes of Texans, had endorsed Bentsen but did not stump for him. Bush tried to stay nonpartisan and stressed the positive. The October 27 *Washington Post* reported his performance at Southern Methodist University, where he "lectured with great feeling on the problems of pollution and population control. The speech seemed nonpolitical, without a single jab at his Democratic opponent." The *Post* waxed lyrical on Bush's charms "though he is 46 years old and the father of five, [he] managed to convey the youthful modesty of a high school quarterback who had just been kissed by the prettiest cheerleader."[13]

A disagreeable rumor that may have hurt Bush bobbed up just before the election. Allegedly tipped off by a White House intimate, David Broder wrote in the *Washington Post* that the Republicans might dump Spiro Agnew from the 1972 ticket and replace him with George Bush. The catch was that this would happen only if Bush became a Texas senator. Everybody officially issued denials, but some Republicans in Texas may have felt they were being manipulated, and may have turned against Bush in pique.[14]

A more proximate cause for Bush's defeat was, according to the *New York Times*, two proposed constitutional amendments in Texas, one to allow saloons, and one to allow all undeveloped land to be taxed as farmland. These possibilities frightened great numbers of farmers, who normally wouldn't have bothered to vote. Rural conservatives voted in great numbers to defeat the first and carry the second. The nearly 300,000 extra voters lost on both counts, but they evidently brought victory to Bentsen.

He won with a total of 1,153,000 to Bush's 1,005,000.[15]

Added to Bush's general disappointment was an especially painful coda: Evidently, Barbara Jordan had brought in black votes for Bentsen with her endorsement. Jordan, from Bush's home town of Houston, had been the first black ever elected to the Texas State Senate.[16]

Bush returned to Washington to complete his duties in Congress and plan for his now somewhat-beclouded future.

CHAPTER 9

At the United Nations

IN LATE NOVEMBER 1970 GEORGE BUSH AND
Charles W. Yost, U.S. Ambassador to the United Nations,
both faced an uncertain future. Bush was a lame duck congressman, having lost a tight race for the Senate. Yost, a career
ambassador and Democrat, was a lame duck permanent representative to the United Nations, having lost the patronage of
his mentor in the White House. For the moment both men were
pawns in the hands of President Richard M. Nixon.

To induce Bush to drop his safe seat in the Congress and
make the Senate run, Nixon had dangled the possibility of
political sugar plums.

In appointing Democrat Yost to the U.N., Nixon had advertised his willingness to conduct a bipartisan foreign policy as
well as to install a professional instead of a political hack. He
made this decision just after achieving his lifelong goal of the
presidency in 1968. He was happily acting the "New Nixon,"
who could reach out and be president of all American people
and factions.

Actually, he already had tendered the opening to Hubert
Humphrey and Sargent Shriver, much more prominent Demo-

crats. Both said no. Yost knew this but accepted the job—despite the fact that Nixon was someone he had "always disliked, both for his personality and his policies."[1]

Yost, whom I served under both at the U.N. in 1964 and 1965 and when he was ambassador to Laos in 1955 and 1956, was counting on Nixon to end the Vietnam war. Although mild in manner, Charles Yost possessed a sharp mind and steel will. He remained a cautious optimist and idealist throughout his career.

When he saw that Nixon wasn't yet ready to leave Vietnam, however, Yost grew dispirited. Nixon eventually became dissatisfied with him, presumably over the policy differences he sensed. But in person he congratulated Yost effusively on his handling of the post as late as September 1970. As was his habit, the president avoided personal confrontation.

Yost thought it now time to retire and quietly made plans to do so. But the president beat him to it. First, a rumor leaked that Daniel Patrick Moynihan would replace him. This gave way to an official announcement that George Bush would be nominated. Nixon had said nothing to Yost about this shift either before or after making it.

While breaking his covenant with Yost, Nixon kept it with Bush. John Haldeman, his chief of staff, summoned Bush after the election and spelled out the president's wishes. Bush heartily agreed to this new twist on his career course. He would be a cabinet member, an ambassador, and would have to develop instant expertise in foreign relations. He also stipulated that he be free to weigh in with policy suggestions to the president and secretary of state. Haldeman consented on behalf of the president.

The news went to press on December 11, 1970. Debunkers in the media and in Democratic circles had a field day with Bush's appointment. The *Washington Star* and the *New York Times* summed up the widespread reaction to the new ambassador: There seemed to be "nothing in his record that qualifies him for this highly important position."[2] Senator Adlai Stevenson III waited three months before dropping his rather personal bouquet, to the effect that Bush's appointment was "an insult" to the U.S.[3] As spokeman to the senator's father when he was U.N. permanent representative, I felt that he would have been too civil to make such a comment.

Bush expected some static and rode out the storm with confidence. He believed he was qualified for this post. After all, he had been an exponent of policy both as a political candidate and congressman. He had spent four years in the Congress negotiating with some of the country's top bargainers. And ever since his business days he had been a salesman. Now he could be dubbed "the American salesman in the world marketplace for ideas." Nixon viewed the U.N. in the same light and was comfortable with Bush's capability.

The new ambassador landed in New York prepared for action. He buckled down and studied his domain, learning and analyzing the issues and people with which he would be dealing. Other delegations and the U.S. Mission to the U.N. were alike in their concern about this tenderfoot loose in the big leagues.

Ambassador Jacov Malik, the Soviet permanent representative ("perm rep" is the jargon), was quick to give him the new-boy-on-the-block treatment. He called a big power powwow with Britain, France and the United States shortly after Bush was sworn in. He wanted to raise the matter of Israel's withdrawal from the Gaza Strip (which Israel had occupied during the 1967 Six-Day War). He began the discussion with the accusation that Washington was taking orders from Israel. Bush retorted without hesitation that the charge was too ridiculous to justify a full reply, and that if this was the Soviets' way of seeking peace they couldn't be serious about it.[4]

Malik was the tough old cold warrior who had one favorable deed to his credit. It was he who as the Soviet delegate boycotted the Security Council meeting on the North Korean invasion of South Korea in 1950. He did so because of Moscow's position that the wrong China was seated in the Security Council, since Mao was by then ruling all of mainland China. This act made it possible for the United Nations Korean operation to take place without a veto.

Ambassador Christopher Phillips, whom Bush had asked to

stay on as his deputy (he had been deputy to Yost), said that after their first brush, Malik and Bush "developed quite a good personal relationship. They would kid each other a bit, joke with each other. All of this happened rather quickly."[5]

Bush's staff were gratified to discover their neophyte chief could think fast and clearly under the parry and thrust of Soviet misbehavior. Within a month they saw that he could back up his native hutzpah with solid knowledge. He still followed the dictum to do his homework that he picked up in Congress.

The heavy hitters in the U.N. were the British, French and Belgian ambassadors. Many of the Western Europeans were top-skilled diplomats, according to Phillips. "In no time at all," said Phillips, "he won their confidence. And you talk to almost anybody in the secretariat [the permanent personnel in the U.N. bureaucracy] and they will tell you that he turned out to be an outstandingly effective American representative."[6]

Barbara Bush soon let it be known that she was part of the team. She and her children had joined Bush in the capacious living quarters for the U.S. permanent representative on the forty-second floor of the Waldorf Astoria Hotel on Park Avenue. This posh space comprises three separate apartments connected into one.

On her own initiative Barbara asked for the diplomatic Blue Book, which lists all the permanent representatives, their first names, the first names of their wives, and the names of the key members of their delegation. Additionally, Rudolph (Foxy) Carter, Bush's personal assistant, attests that Barbara requested specifics about individuals. "We, of course, did this," Carter says, "and we would see someone at a reception and tell Barbara, 'See the lady over there with the big headdress who just arrived? You might wish to talk to her, because she's interesting, and was educated at Harvard, and we're having a problem with her husband, or we're trying to get him to join us in some political action at the U.N.' And Barbara would say, 'Fine, please introduce me to her.' Barbara would then take her to meet George." It was gracious, professional teamwork.

The U.S. ambassador to the U.N. has three communication

terminals in Washington. For day-to-day instructions, his mission reports to the assistant secretary of state for International Organizations (IO); for more weighty matters, the secretary of state may talk directly to the ambassador (others on his staff can take orders from IO). Finally, because he is in the cabinet and is the personal representative of the president of the United States, the president may tell him directly to handle issues which may have domestic as well as international ramifications. Such interchanges may be outside the State channels. In fact, State may be kept in the dark.

So before he even begins conducting relations with the nearly 150 foreign missions in New York and dealing with the bureaucracy of the U.N. secretariat, the U.S. permanent representative has plenty of opportunity to get it wrong. He must have a clear head, steady emotions, a nearly flawless memory, and—preferably—long familiarity with foreign affairs.

For years the U.S. mission had faced a test in the General Assembly: The annual credentials vote to decide whether Taiwan or mainland China would hold the Chinese seat, both in the General Assembly and as a permanent member of the Security Council. This strange situation had devolved from a continuing loyalty to the China that Chiang Kai-shek had headed at the inception of the United Nations. When he was driven out to Formosa by the Communists, the United States still clung to the fiction that he was in charge of mainland China. The illusion was kept alive by the so-called China Lobby, but now it had run its course. Each time the vote had grown closer, with the People's Republic of China approaching the majority needed for entry.

In 1971 the United States at last pulled its head out of the sand. It could no longer ignore the right of the world's most populous country to join the United Nations. But it wanted to have its cake and eat it too. Accordingly, Washington devised the two-China policy called "dual representation," membership in the General Assembly for both the P.R.C. (People's Republic of China) and Taiwan, the original Republic of China. Under this scheme the P.R.C. also would occupy a permanent seat in the Security Council, displacing Taiwan there.

Unfortunately, the U.S. position was not finalized until the summer of 1971. By then many friendly delegates who had been inquiring anxiously since January felt obliged to make their own policies without regard to the U.S.

George Bush marshalled his troops at the mission to lobby foreign delegates to vote for dual representation. He divided his area specialists into tactical groups. His two deputies, Christopher Phillips and W. Tapley Bennett, and more junior officers plied their "territories" throughout the U.N. for months. At strategy sessions back at the U.S. Mission, Bush and his strike force found the nose count discouraging. But if every promised vote held, there was a chance.

Unfortunately for Bush that was the year that Kissinger and Nixon secretly had decided to renew diplomatic ties with the People's Republic. Actually, they didn't maintain enough secrecy, for in the midst of Bush's campaign for dual representation, news surfaced that Henry Kissinger was in Beijing. But with his penchant for security regardless of its impact on his operatives, the president chose to leave Bush uninformed.

Meanwhile Bush steadfastly strove for his hopeless goal. Not only did he not give up, but also when the vote came he expected to win on the strength of pledges that had been made to him. He didn't win because some delegates who had said they were on the U.S. side either abstained or cast against the U.S. The tally was 59–55, with 15 abstentions. In Bush's lexicon a broken word is the cruelest wound. He says he still remembers which countries reneged on October 25, 1971, when the General Assembly voted to expel Taiwan—an ally of the U.S. Bush called it the most serious setback since the U.N. opened its doors.[7]

Third World critics were delighted to see America take its lumps after so many years of unchallenged domination. Delegates of the Third World took that occasion to razz the United States crudely and noisily in the huge, elegant hall of the General Assembly. Brian Urquhart, the storied undersecretary general of the U.N., was no defender of America's obsolete position on the seating of China. Still, he writes favorably on George Bush, who "as representative of the U.S. fought valiantly to the end, suffering the indignity of the famous 'dancing in the aisles' incident when the vote went against the United States. His position was made even odder by the fact that Henry Kissinger had already been on a secret mission to Beijing to work on the 'opening to China.' "[8]

After the episode was over, Bush escorted the Taiwan delegate from the General Assembly to his limousine outside. Observers recall tears on Bush's cheeks.

Still, he remained commander of his forces. Once the PRC was admitted, he bent over backwards not to be bitter with the incoming delegation. He told his mission people to be courteous and helpful as representatives of the host country. Without pandering to the P.R.C., he insisted that his colleagues put the loss firmly behind them.

During his short tenure Bush had his share of alarms and excursions. His tour was no tea party. Foxy Carter says he had to awaken Bush in the small hours of the morning on numerous occasions. Classified telegrams had to be delivered from around the world, slugged "immediate" by people who perhaps didn't understand time zones. Bush would receive Carter in his pajamas, unperturbed.

One night, while Bush was at dinner with the Belgians, a refrigerator in an apartment at the Soviet mission was "creased" by a bullet fired from the street through the window. The record doesn't tell whether chlorofluorocarbons were released to threaten the ozone layer, but the Soviets certainly felt threatened.

Bush appeared promptly on the scene and assured the Soviets that he would turn the city upside down to prevent a recurrence. The Soviets were abusive and dubious, but Bush contacted Mayor of New York John V. Lindsay, the police department, his own security functionaries, and asked that the U.S. Secret Service assign people as necessary.

The Jewish Defense League at that time was involved in various violent protestations against persecution of Jews in the Soviet Union. The New York Police arrested a member of the JDL for possession of the rifle that had been fired into the Soviet mission. Although that suspect was released by the courts, the JDL incidents were interfering with Bush's diplomacy at the U.N. and U.S. Ambassador Jacob Beam's task of maintaining sensible relations in Moscow.

One day Bush bared his teeth, a rare act for him, to the JDL's Rabbi Meir Kahane. Kahane showed up unannounced at the U.S. mission and tried to block Bush from walking through the front door. He was obviously seeking a confrontation. "Why won't you talk to me? All I want is a dialogue," demanded Kahane.[9]

Bush strode past him, saying, "Because I've seen your idea of a dialogue—those shots fired into the Soviet Embassy, and I don't condone your group's violence any more than violence directed at Jews by Arab terrorists."[10]

Ambassador Beam reports that he wrote to President Nixon about the JDL's harassment of Soviet officials, especially in New York. When the president didn't answer, Beam "turned to [his] colleague George Bush . . . who was also being embarrassed by the JDL attacks. Bush went directly to the president and was responsible for the creation of the special Executive Protective Service which now guards foreign officials in the U.S."[11]

During that period of Jewish unrest Bush was lunching with ten or twelve foreigners one day at the Palm Restaurant, near the United Nations on the corner of 45th Street and Second Avenue. Walter J. Ganzi, Jr., now president of the Palm Restaurant Corporation, tells the terrifying event of that day.

The Jews were unhappy, he says, because the United States had announced that fewer arms were going to Israel than previously. Members of the Jewish Defense League along with others were demonstrating outside the U.S. Mission to the U.N. Then someone told them where the U.S. ambassador was dining. Several thousand people marched to the Palm, filling Second Avenue wall to wall with demonstrators as far as you could see, says Mr. Ganzi. They were hostile, screaming and yelling. They were demanding to see Ambassador Bush.

Mr. Ganzi recounts the rest of the story. "Mr. Bush got up and went outside and talked to them. With no mike, he stood on a step next to the restaurant so they could see him. There were only a dozen or so policemen plus a couple of Secret Service guards with Mr. Bush. There was no way they could have saved him if the crowd had attacked, and they seemed in a mood to do so. The Palm's waiters were so impressed they followed him and called to him, 'We're behind you all the way, Mr. Ambassador.'

"When he began to speak, he calmed that crowd right down. It was amazing to see his leadership take effect like that. He explained what the U.S. position was on Israel and the arms issue. Then he answered their questions. There was no more noise. After about ten minutes of listening to Mr. Bush, they seemed to understand and accept his remarks and see that he was responsive to their concerns. Then they quietly dispersed. Thousands of them just walked away. Bush returned to his table in the Palm and finished his lunch."[12]

Ganzi says that incident convinced him Bush was an outstanding leader with a strong future. He and Bush struck up an 18-year friendship during which he has received more than 40 letters and notes, as well as telephone calls every year or so, from Bush.

Bush invested much time and thought into creating rapport with the foreign delegates. He was so enthusiastic and thorough in his official entertaining that the mission protocol officer called him "the Perle Mesta of the U.N." He didn't stop with the big ceremonial parties. He took a dozen or so members of the U.N. Economic and Social Council with him one night to sit in his Uncle Herbert Walker's box at Shea Stadium to watch the Mets play baseball. He took others for Sunday meals at his parents' house in Greenwich, Connecticut. Sometimes he brought key delegates to the exclusive Lynx Club in New York. He often lunched at the nearby Palm Restaurant with one or another of his "clients" from the U.N. He maintained this caring attitude in his daily business with the other missions. Unlike his successors Patrick Moynihan and Jeanne Kirkpatrick, Bush avoided harsh rhetoric and polemics to make points that might appeal to American constituents.

Brian Urquhart, a Britisher who had been with the U.N. since Gladwyn Jebb recruited him in 1945, had risen to be assistant secretary general by the time Bush came to New York. Urquhart later observed "Yost, Bush and Scranton (former Governor of Pennsylvania William Scranton) were more traditional ambassadors who commanded respect by their restraint and patrician style. In the long run the aristocratic embrace is more powerful than a slap in the face."[13]

While ambassador to the U.N., Bush occasionally traveled abroad. On one trip he visited African countries, including Kenya. In Nairobi he and Barbara stayed with U.S. Ambassador Robinson McIlvaine, a career foreign service officer and Republican. McIlvaine describes Bush as warm, friendly, fun and funny as a guest in the official residence.

His schedule was full and went smoothly—except for the press conference. One journalist unsettled Bush with his question about the U.S. policy on buying chromium from Rhodesia. The Africans were angry that this practice was enabling controversial white leader Ian Smith to stay in office. In short, profits from the U.S. purchases provided him with the support he needed. Neither Bush nor the U.S. as a whole could give Africans the answer they sought on this complaint.

McIlvaine tells an ancedote about Bush the human being. It concerns the game called "Thumper." After returning late in the evening from the formal dinners Bush had to attend in Nairobi, he would have the energy to sit down on the floor with McIlvaine's niece and her Peace Corps pals to play Thumper. This was a game like Slap Jack in which the players had to bang their fists on the carpet when a certain card was turned face up. If one thumped late, that person lost the hand. Bush reveled in this pastime and on his Christmas messages in succeeding years, he would ask who had been the best Thumper lately. One year he enclosed a picture of Khrushchev pounding his shoe on the Soviet desk in the General Assembly. His note said, "You see, we play Thumper at the United Nations too!"

As his deputy Tap Bennett visualizes them now, Bush's speeches at the General Assembly and Security Council were well and convincingly delivered. Urquhart concurs that Bush was a "good presenter" of the U.S. messages. Of course, as statements of policy that affected U.S. dealings with the whole planet, it was essential that every word be cleared with Washington.

Bush wasn't getting much practice polishing his oratory, except for the extemporaneous toasts and periodic informal talks for domestic audiences. Bennett and his other colleagues at the U.N. agreed that he had a strong presence.

With familiarity and personal contacts, he became increasingly effective. Out of courtesy he sat through lengthy sessions at which allies of the U.S. spoke, often for hours at a time. Foxy Carter would furnish him with supplies of small note cards at those occasions. Bush would write continuously, thanking fellow delegates for their help or hospitality, suggesting future activity, or simply relaying personal messages. If the delegate was present, a staffer would deliver these missives on the spot. Carter records that this habit of Bush added to his growing popularity, not to mention his incoming mail.

Christopher Phillips stresses that the wide acceptance Bush won at the U.N. was due not only to his geniality, but also, more importantly, to the impression of personal integrity that he conveyed.

After less than two years Bush was called to Washington to head the Republican National Committee. This happened early in 1973, on the eve of the Watergate travails.

Bush's departure from New York stirred considerable displeasure and frustration among the other delegates. What was the point of the effort to build up a relationship if the U.S. was going to pull its representative out so soon? It was clearly shortsighted to yank a man who was doing so well. Delegates wondered whether the U.S. really took the U.N. seriously. Some countries left their envoys there for 15 years or more.

Bush's feelings seemed somewhat mixed. He valued the world body but understood its limitations. For a man attuned to getting things done, he doubtless felt manacled by requisite diplomatic mating dances. He would have been happier, most likely, had he served there in Dag Hammarskjöld's day, when the U.N. was more action-oriented.

Bush underwent a wrenching personal sadness during his

U.N. tour. His father developed lung cancer and fought his
illness in a nearby hospital, while his mother stayed at George
and Barbara's apartment. Prescott Bush died on October 8,
1972. Perhaps the greatest giant George Bush had ever known
exited Bush's life. He said simply, "We had lost a best
friend."[14]

In its "Man in the News" farewell story, the *New York Times*
indicated that Bush's U.N. duty had taken its toll: "The light
blue eyes seemed more tired and the lines around the mouth
deeper than when he showed up . . . looking, as a Swedish
diplomat remarked, 'absurdly young for 47.'" Still, he took his
leave cheerfully, hoping to tell Congress about the "worth-
while activities of the organization that deserved support."
Kathleen Teltsch, who interviewed him, noted he still was
"breezily casual—an impression reinforced as he stood talking, wearing a wrinkled suit, hands stuffed into his pockets."[15]

Ambassador Seymour M. Finger, a veteran foreign service
officer on Bush's staff, summarizes his recollection: "He was
personable, very hard-working, most conscientious, and well
liked by foreign delegates."[16]

Ambassador John Stevenson, who then was chief of the U.S.
delegation to the U.N. Law of the Sea Convention and now is a
partner at Sullivan and Cromwell in New York, declares that
Bush "did a very good job at the U.N., much to everyone at the
U.S. mission's surprise. The old hands said, "Frankly, we
didn't think he would work out there, given his total lack of
experience. In fact, we thought he would likely fall on his face.
He did so well everyone was delighted."[17]

Bush had surmounted the perceived obstacles, but, once
again, he was facing a mountainous new challenge. The chairmanship of the Republican National Committee was a difficult
mission—perhaps impossible.

CHAPTER 10

Salvager of the Republican Party

PERHAPS IT WAS BECAUSE CONGRESSMAN GEORGE
Bush had been considered one of Texas's most charismatic
public officials, or perhaps it was because of his well-known
energy and loyalty, that President Nixon thought of him and
called him down to Camp David after his formidable re-election in 1972. Another possibility might have been that Nixon
was worrying that the Watergate burglary issue still bubbled
under the surface. If so, did he see Bush as a brave and
dependable trooper to fight the public indignation that might
lie ahead? Certainly the president didn't mention any such
concern to Bush.

Nixon was contemplating a new cabinet configuration, one
that would feature five super-secretaries. George Shultz, slated
to be "super-secretary" of the Treasury, intercepted Bush in
Washington en route to Camp David and invited him to be his
deputy secretary. Bush demurred and asked for time to see
what the president wanted.

At the camp Bush found Nixon relatively relaxed and in an

expansive mood. He came to the point directly: "George, this is an important time for the Republican party. We have a chance to build a new coalition in the next four years, and you're the one to do it. I want you to run the Republican National Committee."[1]

Bush realized what this would entail. He would replace Senator Robert Dole, who had been called an "irreverent and independent" chairman.[2] He also was aware that Nixon was busy assembling a more tightly knit team around himself. He had begun to do this almost before the votes were tallied. His first move had been to ask all White House appointees from his first term to submit their resignations. This was an intelligent move, though the insensitivity of its timing didn't please every Republican in his administration. In fact it diminished the joy of quite a few over Nixon's overwhelming mandate.

Bush doubtless drew some comfort from seeing that the president thought so highly of him. It was flattering to be invited to the inner circle of the second term. Nixon informed Bush that he knew Shultz already had propositioned him for the Treasury job and that that was acceptable if Bush had his heart set on it. But he made it clear that he would prefer Bush to help him restitch the party into stouter fabric. With the Franklin Roosevelt coalition of labor and liberals weakening at last, Nixon saw his chance to lead Republicans back to their majority days.

As he spoke rosily to Bush of victories ahead, did Nixon realize that his administration was terminally ill with Watergate? The break-in had occurred in June of 1972. I well remember that June was when John Erlichman made an abrupt exit from the U.N.'s global environment meeting in Stockholm. Erlichman had made it a point to be there as a member of the United States 65-person delegation to demonstrate the president's belief in the issue. While there, he and I discussed a possible bilateral environmental agreement with the People's Republic of China, and he asked me to call him in Washington. He didn't explain his sudden departure, but his manner suggested he was overwrought about something unrelated to the conference. I did telephone him the following day, but he

George Bush and his only sister Nancy.

Left: George Herbert Walker Bush at two years.

Teenagers Barbara Pierce and George Bush, with his brother Bucky.

Facing page, top: On U.S.S. San Jacinto, *fall of 1944,* George Bush flanked by crewmen Joe Rechert, *left, and Leo Nadeau.*

Facing page, bottom: George Bush, Navy pilot, 1944, in cockpit of TBM (torpedo bomber).

Above: George Bush, captain of championship baseball team and graduate of Yale in two and one-half years after war service. Phi Beta Kappa in Economics.

Left: Ensign George Bush plots his course.

Below: September 1944, rescued fliers including George Bush, front row second from left, and crew of submarine U.S.S. Finback.

George Bush and Barbara Pierce
married in Rye, New York,
January 6, 1945.

Businessman George Bush and
growing family in Midland,
Texas, 1959.

George and Barbara Bush at home with brood in Houston, Texas, 1964.

Elected to Congress, 1966.

Above: *Father and son, Prescott and George Bush, 1971.*

Left: *U.S. Congressman George Bush in Washington, 1970.*

Below: *Envoy to China and Barbara Bush in Beijing, 1975.*

Inaugural stroll: 41st president and Mrs. Bush on Pennsylvania Avenue, January 20, 1989.

Taking the oath as leaders of Congress watch.

Already at work, President and Mrs. Bush in Oval Office, January 27, 1989.

First family in full, at White House, January 21, 1989.

didn't respond then or later. The cover-up presumably started soon after his return to Washington.

Still, ensuing events indicated that the president and his men thought they could control the Watergate disease, and that he genuinely wanted Bush to extend the Republican renaissance. At first Bush tried to persuade the president to give him, instead, the number-two job at the State Department, as deputy to Secretary Henry Kissinger. Foreign affairs was his top priority, he said. Nixon was cool to this idea, and Bush capitulated. At least that was the purport of Nicholas Lehman's piece in the *Washington Post* in 1988.

But before agreeing to take the chairmanship of the Republican National Committee (RNC), Bush sought counsel from Lud Ashley, his friend of congressional days, and from others. Most of them, and apparently his family, took a dim view. They pointed out he would be stepping down from a VIP cabinet level post into the political rough and tumble, with a less important title.

In fact, Bush had brought this invitation on himself. Through his own initiative he had caught Nixon's eye during the campaign. While at the U.N. he had accepted speaking engagements on Nixon's behalf around the nation. The speech schedulers in presidential races often have more opportunities for the candidate than he himself can fill. Surrogate speakers, whose names or speaking ability will be influential in building support for the candidate, are sought. Bush's skill on the political stump in this role was so good that observers commented favorably to Nixon. Bush proved to be at his best as a tub-thumper without a text with a topic he believed in—in this case the president. The RNC assignment was a logical follow-through by the president. Bush had demonstrated himself to be a professional and loyal politician. It is easy to comprehend Bush's decision to accept the RNC chairmanship and keep up the good work.

But he did act on his friends' advice to require a free hand in running the committee and continued access as a cabinet intimate. With assurance on these points, Bush entered the RNC headquarters early in 1973. The president also had granted him a small office in the Executive Office Building adjacent to the White House; it was located close to Nixon's own private room away from the Oval Office.

Once again, Bush was presented with a challenge. His goal was a bigger, stronger Republican party. But this was alien territory. He never before had held a national political post.

The RNC's membership consists of the chairperson of each of the 50 states, the Virgin Islands, Puerto Rico, Guam and District of Columbia committees, plus the national committee man and woman from each. These people literally elect the chairman of the RNC, but when the sitting president is a Republican they function like the Electoral College. They vote for whomever he chooses. The term of office is two years.

The RNC home office is housed in a four-story building at 310 1st Street, S. E., Washington, DC. Its present staff comprises some 250 paid hands. Volunteers join for particular projects such as fund-raising, research, registration drives and information distribution.

When Bush was elected to the committee in January 1973, staff had to be cut to stay within the RNC's budget. Republican donors didn't realize that their money had been syphoned off to support CREEP, the Committee to Reelect the President. The RNC had become the party's impoverished stepchild.

Firing people was one of the many bitter tasks Bush faced as he came on the job. The reduction in force brought the number to a third of its former size—about 85. Bush then grasped the nettle again: Some staffers had been a little lax about alcohol during working hours. Bush firmly laid down the law and the practice stopped.

Because he handled these thorny responsibilities in a kind way, Bush is remembered by the veterans of those days as a decent man. Nancy Thawley, for example, spells out how when terminating staffers, "he called them in and told them himself. He was very upfront and honest about it and talked to them, and told them why it had to be done."[3]

Mrs. Thawley had been a neighbor and political colleague from the era in Houston when Bush was running for Harris County chairman. Recently she reminisced about these days when she and he first collaborated in 1962. He still was running Zapata Offshore and was a bit dubious about whether he could spare the time. She recalls he wagged his head and said: "I'll do it, Nancy, if you will be the vice chairman, because I can't run a business and do this, too, full time." Nancy now says that "We ran, I think, a most effective organization."

Recalling her stint with Bush at the RNC, Nancy says "Under Bush's management we had a good organization there, too."

As chairman he set standards—no deals, no corruption. I asked Mrs. Thawley how he got this word out through the committee staff. In the first place, she said, his behavior was above reproach. He flew coach, never first class. He drove a small American Motors car, whereas Bob Strauss, a fellow Texan and his counterpart at the Democratic National Committee, had a limousine and a driver.

"It was kind of fun. But we had no expense accounts as such; if someone spent over the budget which we had pared to the bone, he had to call people in and get a little tough and say I'm not accepting this. He and Barbara were very generous in entertaining at their home and never submitted a bill to the committee."[4]

Mary Louise Smith of Iowa joined George Bush as RNC co-chairperson in March 1974. They co-existed happily together from the start. She says now that "George let me have the freedom as a co-chairman that enabled me to branch out on my own and start an innovative, grass-roots program." To this day she stresses that Bush "notwithstanding his present position on the Equal Rights Amendment [he opposes it], has the best understanding of anybody of full partnership for women—in business, politics and professions." Mrs. Smith said that while the two of them co-chaired the RNC he was in favor of ERA. He changed his stance only after he became the vice-presidential nominee in 1980, when ERA was removed from the platform statement. He never was threatened by women with strength, Mrs. Smith states, he welcomed them. He always involved me in the RNC decision making, Mrs. Smith emphasized.[5]

As Mrs. Smith talked, I was reminded of an anecdote about

Prescott Bush, who was so popular with both men and women
in his days as a senator. It was told to me by a woman who was
a prominent figure in both political and literary circles of
Washington in the 1950s and still is today. I'll never forget the
first time I met Senator Bush, she laughs. "To make conversation I asked him if he had seen John Hersey's story in the
New Yorker about Hiroshima. "No," he declared, insulted, "of
course not. I never read women's magazines."[6]

George Bush had the RNC humming in short order. I had
several interchanges with his office. I wanted to know more
about the committee because I was active in Rhode Island
Republican matters at the time. I also sought his guidance on
whether to run again for the Congress, having been the party's
endorsed candidate in 1970. I was impressed by his prompt
and thorough replies by mail. I found his counsel wise.

He seemed pleased with his new responsibility, writing in a
letter to me: "I'm going to miss the U.N., but this new challenge is fantastic." He was determined to build the "New
Majority." As a postscript to his rather formal letter, he scrib-
bled some more about his RNC plans:

"There are two main functions:

A. Party building—wow, there's lots to do there.

B. Plus the establishment of a centralized campaign organization to hone in on target districts—plus a large sum for
White House support. We pay the political costs of the presidency, etc. etc. etc."

George Bush was careful not to push any ideological buttons.
He concentrated on bringing the conservative and the more
moderate, or liberal, wings together.

That was not easy, judging from my own experience that
year. A friend of mine, E. Taylor Chewning, Jr., who had just
sold his business was looking for new worlds to conquer in
1973. He had been such a successful chief executive of his
company for so long that he realized a huge profit from the
sale. Physically and mentally he was in *la force de la vie* as the
French say, in his prime, at about 54.

I suggested that he might put his assets at the disposal of the

Republicans. He could bring a great deal, I judged, to a party trying to grow. He asked me to find out whether the RNC would like his participation in its fund-raising division.

I quickly called a senior RNC financial official to tell him the good news and arrange a meeeting with Chewning. I explained that this man was the kind of person who, once he committed his time and abilities to a cause, also would commit sizable portions of his own capital.

The official thanked me for the idea and promised to call me back. Dead silence followed. This neglect seemed strange, particularly in the face of such a generous offer. Three weeks later, a polite letter arrived from him saying:

"We appreciate Mr. Chewning's willingness to donate his skills, etc., to the party. Unfortunately, however, I must report that we checked the record and discovered that in 1962 he voted in a Democratic primary in Virginia. This naturally means that we cannot ask him to join us. . . ."

Since the majority of American voters register Democratic, I wondered how this attitude would lead to fulfilling the president's hopes of winning the majority back for the Republicans. George Bush had to contend with such backward thinking. Furthermore, he had to contend with Watergate and what that unfortunate scandal was doing to his stewardship of the Republican party.

He fought back although the odds against him in this battle were the worst he had ever faced—short of the live ammunition fired against him over Chichi Jima. He spoke frequently throughout the country, urging Republicans to meet the crisis positively. It was not the party's fault, he reminded his listeners. For the party to stay viable, he pled with them, its stalwarts should keep putting up and electing good Republicans at the local, state and national levels.

This is not the place to recreate the whole pageant of Watergate obloquies, except in terms of its impact on George Bush and the RNC.

Fifteen years later, in 1988, he portrayed the effect the tug of war had on him: "I had two stacks of mail, one of letters asking 'how come you're not doing more for the president?' and the other saying 'how come you're keeping the party so close to the president?' Therein lay a very serious dilemma."[7]

For 12 months of the controversy, until the Supreme Court ruled 9-0 against the president's right to executive privilege on release of the tapes, Bush defended Richard Nixon. He covered the country like a Republican brush salesman for a total of 124,000 miles, giving 118 speeches and 84 press conferences.[8] Wherever he went he passionately inisted that no White House hand had been in the Watergate jam pot.

At a dinner for him in August of 1973, party regulars from all over Rhode Island gathered at John Slocum's Bellevue Avenue estate in Newport. Bush spoke to several hundred worried Republicans seated under a giant tent. He used no notes, looked out at his audience, and pounded home his point that "now is truly the time for all good Republicans to come to the aid of their party." His words excited the crowd; they jumped to their feet and cheered him at the climax. It was a bravura performance to which we Rhode Islanders were not often treated.

There as everywhere that year Bush emphasized that the party, not any specific president, was the important issue; that even if the president ultimately should be found to have committed an illegal act, the party should not be held accountable. It was vital that the presidency and the two-party system should survive.

The White House staff became disenchanted with Bush early in his RNC role. Haldeman, Erlichman and Chuck Colson had assumed he would be their "point man in a counterattack against investigators leading the Watergate charge."[9] Bush's speeches quickly disabused them of this dream.

As the flames of Watergate spread during the following spring and summer, White House personalities repeatedly pressured Bush to join their last ditch schemes to rescue the president. General Haig leaned on him the hardest; he was trying not only to sustain the president, but as chief of staff, he also had to keep the administration alive. At the very end,

Father John McLaughlin,* one of the last sailors on the sinking hulk, pleaded with the RNC for aid. McLaughlin, who earlier had served as a speechwriter for Nixon, now was pitching in wherever he could contribute. He requested RNC lists of Republican stalwarts around the country from Bush so that he could solicit them for letters and statements in favor of Nixon. Bush said no.

Against all such demands, Bush held to his position: The party and the president are two separate entities and the RNC can't be responsible for his behavior. Still, Bush resisted any personal criticism of Nixon, even after it was evident he had lied to the country. Bush never abandoned his civility toward him.

RNC Co-Chairman Mrs. Louise Smith still praises him for his self-restraint. She conjectures that Bush found it difficult to forget that Nixon and Senator Prescott Bush held high mutual regard for each other during the 1950s, or that Nixon often had helped his own rise in government. Also, Mrs. Smith stresses that Bush's loyalty is a hallmark of his character. In any case, he never turned vindictive; although Nixon's follies wrecked his tour at the RNC. Given the damages, the Republican party failed to garner the new coalition Bush had worked for on his watch at the RNC.

Yet Bush salvaged a great measure of respect for the Republicans and himself. Party chieftains in all corners of the nation still remember that he kept the flag flying during the dark ordeal. They know that at the key moment it was Bush who spoke up and told the president the time had come to resign.

Characteristically, as when he fired his underlings, Bush calmly and respectfully told his boss of his duty. On the next day, August 7, 1974, he sent the letter that became history.

It read, in part, "Dear Mr. President, It is my considered judgment that you should now resign. . . . I believe this view is held by most Republican leaders across the country. This letter

*Mr. McLaughlin is the current, feisty national TV talk show host.

is much more difficult because of the gratitude I will always feel toward you. . . ."[10]

During the aftermath of Nixon's abdication, Washington teemed with those wishing to maneuver themselves into the vice presidency under Gerald Ford. Bush let Ford know of his own interest in the office.

A complete picture of the log-rolling and turf struggles hasn't yet been drawn. According to then-Secretary of Defense Mel Laird, a majority of Republican state chairmen weighed in for Robert Dole.* On August 10, just after taking office as president, Ford announced that he would poll Republicans in and out of government and throughout the rest of the country. The *Washington Post* lists the survey findings as 255 for Bush and 181 for Rockefeller as vice president. No one else was close.[11]

Then, according to the *Post*, RNC official Tom Evans threw in allegations against Bush to the effect that National Republican Committee members named him because they had to route their preferences through his office. Furthermore, said the *Post*, Evans claimed that key RNC personnel found Bush inept on substantive matters. Others raised the fact that Bush had received $100,000 from Nixon's White House fund called "Townhouse" to finance his 1970 Senate race. That was true, but these same infighters were hinting that part of it, some $40,000, had been reported improperly to the IRS.

Laird declares that Ford liked Bush and knew him well from their days together in Congress. Eventually he chose Rockefeller over both Dole and Bush, Laird says. It would appear that Ford reasoned that Rockefeller's was the better-known name and would be more acceptable to U.S. opinion, regardless of party.

This choice infuriated the conservatives; they never had accepted the liberal Rockefeller. It is said that Rockefeller later admitted that picking him was a mistake and helped Carter defeat the ticket in 1976. With the clarity of hindsight, some Bush champions argue that Ford's denial of Bush may have

---

*January 5, 1989, interview with the author.

been a bigger blunder than his denial on TV that Poland was Communist.

Bush received the sad news at Kennebunkport. Ford telephoned him just moments before announcing his decision for Rockefeller on national television. Bush kept his cool, saying, "Yes . . . Well, Mr. President, you've made a fine choice, and I appreciate your taking the time to call. You really didn't have to. . . ."[12] When the press interviewed Bush a few minutes later, they asked how he could be so cheerful. He replied that they didn't know how it felt inside. What he didn't reveal was that Ford had encouraged him to expect an important assignment soon.

Another roller-coaster ride was over for Bush. His most influential patron had slid from power after an astonishing political comeback. Once more his own future seemed in doubt.

Any professional political analyst could have assured a continuing upward spiral for this talented, industrious Republican artisan. But in what direction? Should he campaign for office again? Where and for what? He had given up a solid seat in the House of Representatives. He had come close to beating Bentsen for the Senate, but Bentsen and Tower now were firmly ensconced—no opening there. Appointive office? Possibly, but having just missed the gold ring for the vice presidency, anything might feel flat. Well, he'd wait and see what prize Ford had in mind for him.

It was a good moment to take a spin in his Cigarette boat "Fidelity" in the sparkling, healing waters off Kennebunkport. Several spins. Which is exactly what he did.

CHAPTER 11

Ambassador in China

G ERALD FORD SWEPT INTO THE PRESIDENCY ON A wave of public relief. The contrast of his arrival with Nixon's exit was so dramatic that he began his truncated term in an instant honeymoon. His cheerful and positive statements met with universal approval. Here was a man of unblemished reputation, a Midwesterner with an honest face and long government experience. He was a president one could trust.

He promptly honored his pledge to George Bush. He told Bush that he happily would accord him his pick of two top ambassadorships: London or Paris.

George thought quickly. The president of the United States was proffering the two most-sought-after diplomatic plums in the foreign service. The situation reminded him of the choices before him upon graduation from Yale. Then, too, he was offered a full grab bag of opportunities—openings in rich, respected business firms in Wall Street, or elsewhere in the elite Eastern establishment. He had earned the right to enter these prestigious companies. As vice president manqué and distinguished performer at cabinet level, Bush was no ordinary political office seeker. He would be a credit to the president wherever he went.

Bush opted for untried territory, where he hoped he could learn more about the world and make headway for the United States. Bush replied to Ford by asking about China.

China? The president scratched his head. Why do you want to go there? Like George Bush the president understood the uncertainties and possibilities that nation posed. After a generation, the People's Republic of China was blossoming again as a potentially amicable member of the world community. But brutal internal upheavals had left the people and their present government shaky and timid in their dealings with foreigners.

Nixon and Kissinger's rapprochement between the U.S. and the P.R.C. in 1972 had led to an exchange of liaison offices in Beijing and Washington. Veteran diplomat David Bruce, the first head of the U.S. Liaison Office (USLO), was languishing in China. Although personally esteemed, Bruce had been unable to break through the wall of unfamiliarity and shyness.

What's the point of a vigorous young fellow like you going into career escrow for a couple of years? Ford didn't exactly say this, but as a practical man trying to reward Bush for his loyalty and achievements, he was baffled by Bush's request. So was Dean Burch, Bush's close friend in the White House at that moment. Burch admits now that he thought it was a strange move for Bush. Yet even he has come to see what Bush then saw in a P.R.C. posting. "I was shocked then," says Burch, "but it proved to be a valuable experience, broadening his feel for foreign affairs—the P.R.C. in particular—and enhancing his image as a potential world leader."[1]

When he was persuaded that Bush really wanted to represent the U.S. in China, Ford started the wheels turning. Since Bush would not, as chief of the U.S.L.O., need confirmation by the Senate, he could start preparing for China immediately. And since, under the same administration, he had the rank of ambassador at the United Nations, he could carry that title to Beijing. The Chinese and others could speak to him as "ambassador" even if he could not sign his mail that way.

Jack Kennedy sometimes is credited with saying that "You

should never get so angry with an opponent that you cannot some day be his friend, nor should you get so close to anyone that you will be unable to fight him when the need comes." George Bush had followed this tenet at the United Nations. He had tried to interdict the P.R.C.'s entry in place of Taiwan. Yet when he lost that battle, and the Chinese sent their first permanent representative, Ambassador Huang Hua, Bush had tended carefully to their needs in his role as the perm rep of the U.N.'s host country.

He also had met China's deputy foreign minister, Quiao Guanha, when Quiao made his country's maiden speech as a member of the U.N. Quiao had excoriated both the United States and the Soviet Union in that speech.

When Quiao rose to be foreign minister, it was he who received Bush's first formal call as chief of the U.S.L.O. Soon thereafter he invited George and Barbara to a private dinner at his own house.

Already this meant that Bush was violating Secretary of State Henry Kissinger's instructions for his China tour. Kissinger had explained that Bush was to be little more than listening scout for the U.S. He was not there to implement policy. Initiatives would be handled by Washington, meaning Kissinger himself. Bush thought he could do some good for the relationship by getting to know more Chinese; Kissinger indicated that the effort wouldn't be necessary.

In fact, Kissinger was so solicitous of the U.S.-P.R.C. budding friendship that he took extreme precautions to prevent leaks that could injure it. Bush discovered this as he was prepped at the State Department for his post. Tight security was the watchword as classified briefing papers were pulled from the files just long enough for Bush to read them.

As he sat studying in the quiet corner that the State Department had provided, Bush began to reflect on his own future. The time he would spend in China would serve as a kind of sabbatical, a time to absorb the lessons of his busy years in several walks of life. He could mull over the disappointments: his failed tries for the Senate, an expanded Republican party, and the vice presidency; and he could recover from them.

More importantly, he could use the new setting to ponder the vast geopolitical tides that had swept the planet during the brief span of his own life. Some were movements made great by tyrants with schemes for dominating mankind. It had been proven that megalomaniacal dreams could exceed mere chimera—they could even approach success. Hitler's Berlin-Rome-Tokyo axis had very nearly vanquished the democracies.

Incredibly, the U.S.S.R. bounced back in the late 1940s to impose its own hegemony. After suffering 20 million killed and nationwide ravages from Hitler's Panzer and Luftwaffe machines, the Soviets somehow had retained the strength to swallow half of Europe at one gulp.

Lenin's cry "Workers of the world, unite; you have nothing to lose but your chains" for the first time seemed all too possible. When the Communists of Chou En-lai defeated the armies of Chiang Kai-shek, the political map of Europe and Asia took on a distinctly reddish hue. The Communist monolith was spreading in every direction.

America had made countermoves against Communist internationalism. As undisputed Free World champion, the United States had drawn a line around the bulging Communist perimeter. This containment policy suggested by the State Department's George Kennan was implemented first by creating alliances like NATO, CENTO and SEATO; next by dousing the flames of Communist-fomented wars of liberation in Greece, Malaysia, the Philippine Republic, Korea, Vietnam, Cuba, Nicaragua, Angola and even the new Republic of Congo.

The news media exposed Communist weaknesses: The U.S.S.R. and Red China had murdered scores of millions to maintain control at home even as they strove to control the whole earth. The Communist juggernaut had, happily, hit some reefs and shoals. Cracks appeared in the heretofore seamless Red empire, first in Yugoslavia, then Poland, and then China.

From one giant, swelling cell, communism had split into polycentric pieces, no longer amalgamated. Indeed, George

Bush had seen firsthand the U.S.S.R./P.R.C. enmity at the United Nations. He was present when Huang Kwa, the P.R.C.'s first ambassador, shunned the handshake of Ambassador Yakov Malik on the day the People's Republic joined the U.N.

Now Bush could witness as a semipermanent guest the changes China had undergone during this titanic process. To him as to most Americans, the Red Guards, Cultural Revolution and Let a Hundred Flowers Bloom had registered as little more than names in the newspapers. Then at the U.S. Mission to the U.N., they began to assume additional dimension in the classified documents and think pieces to which he was privy.

By 1974, when Bush came to Beijing, China had barely emerged from the recovery room after the terrible surgery it had endured for nearly a generation.

In 1948 the legendary Mao Tse-tung came back from "The Long March" away from Chiang Kai-shek. In 1949 it was Mao who chased the generalissimo and his followers out of the country to Taiwan, whereupon Mao proceded in earnest to communize China. He ruled with a merciless grip on the citizenry. His regime systematically annihilated millions. Then it brought to a virtual standstill all intellectual, cultural and commercial activity, killing many leaders in these fields during the malevolent Cultural Revolution. When these individuals were liquidated or banished, the People's Army largely filled the empty places. Trade at home and abroad ceased, except as a function of the central government.

Now that Mao had established his ruthless reign, he began to look beyond his borders. He realized China couldn't live in total isolation from the rest of the world. His diplomatic outreach commenced gently about 1970. With confidence in his control at home, he was able to ease up on tyrannical measures initiated by the Cultural Revolution.

By the time Bush arrived in 1974, China was returning slowly to internal peace. Now it was gradually convalescing. Shorn of its top layer of educated experts like college professors, engineers and doctors, China was trying to compete in the technocratic twentieth century.

Bush comprehended that the P.R.C.'s accession to Nixon's courtship did not stem only from its fear of the U.S.S.R. Mao Tse-tung would seek intellectual, scientific and ultimately commercial exchanges with the U.S. in order to speed development. But Bush also knew that it was too soon to participate much in this process. It still was sticky even to schedule routine courtesy calls on foreign ministry officialdom.

Kissinger had warned Bush he would be bored out of his mind from the inactivity. To some extent this was true. Like the first chief of the U.S.L.O., David Bruce, and his wife, Evangeline, before them, the Bushes soon found themselves filling long evenings with books and writing letters or, now and then, the Chinese Opera. Or they could sightsee on journeys to the Great Wall or the Ming tombs, witness the unearthing of terra cotta soldiers from centuries of burial, appreciate the embroidery at Souzhou, or visit the huge bridge over the Yangtze River that is studded with obsolete rivets and decorated with cracking concrete likenesses of Communist worker heroes.

One political critic back in the U.S. sneered that the only Chinese Bush met were the boys sent over by the foreign ministry to play tennis with him. But Bush never stopped trying to widen his acquaintance among the citizenry despite their reticence to mix with foreigners.

Two initiatives helped. First, he and Barbara went about town on bicycles, both to avoid the dangers of motoring on roads thronged with thousands of Chinese cyclists and also to satisfy their endless quest for physical exercise. Second, they attended the national day celebrations of other diplomatic missions in Beijing. Since some countries boasted better relations with the P.R.C., the Chinese also would attend the affairs, and the Bushes would have the opportunity to meet them.

At the liaison office the Americans numbered approximately 30. Nevertheless, except for immediate staff like Jim Lilley, Harry Thayer, his deputy from Philadelphia, special assistant Jennifer Fitzgerald, and a few others, the Bushes quite frequently were alone.

Alone, that is, until the visitors came from the United States.

There is no count available, but the family dog, C. Fred Bush, *
seems to claim that while in China there were wall-to-wall
house guests. They ranged from family and friends to official
junketeers of various types. Friends like Charles Whitehouse,
then ambassador to Thailand, said, "George asked me casually
one day to come see him." Whitehouse airily obliged but then
discovered it entailed almost two weeks of travel time to stay
one week with Bush in China because he had to go via Tokyo.

Senator Charles Percy of Illinois, also a friend, headed a
delegation to China at about the same time. It was the first
group of representatives from the U.S. Congress to make such a
voyage. Mr. Xu Han, the P.R.C. Liaison Office chief in Washington, worked out the details with Senator Percy. It was
agreed that Jacob Javits and Claiborne Pell and others would
go.

Whereupon Xu Han, who later became ambassador, told
Percy that he must chair the delegation. Percy said that he
couldn't because Senators Javits and Pell were senior to him,
but that he'd be glad to handle the appointments in Beijing
through George Bush.

The Chinese Diplomat said, "No, this is a Chinese mission;
we want you to be in charge, we will take care of the schedule
in Beijing. You have asked permission to come to China for
longer than any other member of Congress and more than
many other embassy delegations. You have seniority by our
rules." So Percy went as chairman; Javits and Pell were furnished equally big limousines when they got to China, however.

Percy asserted (to me) that Bush was in useful contact with
all the ministers the group wanted to call on and that the
Chinese thought well of him. "Bush is a curious man, and he
was trying to learn everything he could," says Percy. "He was

*From *T. Fred's Story*, slightly edited by Barbara Bush. This book, written in
a light vein, is authored by C. Fred Bush, the cocker spaniel given Barbara by
her son Marvin and named for the Bush's close friend C. Fred Chambers of
Houston. The book's rather considerable profits went to literacy organizations selected by Barbara.

doing an extraordinarily good job early in the relationship and he helped break a lot of ice. He had a sophisticated understanding, I felt, of foreign policy."[2]

The Bushes took China in stride, down to the security watchman that motorbiked around at a respectful distance wherever they went. And there was the glue story. Barbara and George were in a guest house during one Kissinger visit, and she noted that their quarters were beautifully supplied with every personal need they might have. The only thing missing, she pointed out to George, was that there was no glue on the stamps. Nobody was present to hear her comment except the Bushes and John Holdridge, George's deputy. Yet in the morning, after breakfast, Barbara discovered a pot of glue sitting on the blotter of her desk next to the stamps.

The visits of Secretary of State Henry Kissinger were always high drama. On one arrival George recalls, with a touch of irony, so many security guards (he lost count after six) accompanied Kissinger that he suspected for a moment the president would materialize instead of Henry. After warm hellos from the welcoming Chinese VIPs, Kissinger was whisked off along with his wife, Nancy, and his two children, David and Elizabeth.[3]

George was left standing in the dust of the departing dignataries—not the usual treatment of the U.S. top diplomat when the Washington nabob comes to negotiate with the host government. But it was symbolic of the way Kissinger liked to operate, often excluding everyone but him and the president from substantive discussions. He liked to keep a personal hand in all the dealings with big countries, which, as Charlie Whitehouse says, is fair enough. He was brilliant at this game, according to Bush, and the Chinese had the highest regard for him.

Bush comments gently on this particular stay, when he caught up with the secretary at the formal meeting with the Chinese. "Henry was in an expansive mood, trading pleasantries with his Chinese hosts. I'd seen him like this on other occasions. Whenever he was center stage, the secretary seemed to come alive, like a political candidate working a crowd back home."⁴

Bush knew how to work a crowd too, in fact it was one of his specialties at home or abroad. The two men did it differently, though each knew how to exploit self-deprecating humor: Bush would appeal to individuals, making himself one of them, remembering their names, showing his warm appreciation of them. His approach is not unlike actor James Stewart, with his modest intonations of *Mr. Smith Goes to Washington*.

Kissinger did it with histrionics and sardonic one-liners, dazzling them with his verbal skills—not always easy through translators.

Both were wise enough to keep each other comfortable despite their differences of style. They obviously were an effective team in China. After two more visits by Kissinger and one by President Ford, everyone concerned in both governments seemed satisfied with the ongoing bilateral progress.

As for Bush, he had had his sabbatical, his rest, his familiarization with the other side of the globe, and as they say in the navy at the end of a watch, he was "ready to be relieved."

Back in Washington Gerald Ford was ready to move him once more. There were openings at the Department of Commerce and the Central Intelligence Agency, and Ford had two candidates to fill them: Elliot Richardson and George Bush. Some wags have said that when he selected Bush for the CIA and Richardson for Commerce he somehow got his cue cards mixed up.

With a business background that went all the way back to winning an economics prize at Yale, Bush was a natural for Commerce. A familiarity with the CIA while he was undersecretary of state and the lack of business experience rendered Richardson better fit for the CIA.

Yet the Kissinger telegram of November 1, 1975, calling for a new director of the CIA went to George Bush, and the Commerce assignment went to Richardson.

The telegram from Henry A. Kissinger to Ambassador Bush read in part: "The president asks that you consent to his nominating you as the new Director of the Central Intelligence Agency. . . . The President feels your appointment to be greatly in the national interest and very much hopes that you will accept. Your dedication to national service has been unremitting, and I join the President in hoping that you accept this new challenge in the service of your country. . . ."[5]

Bush was shocked by this spin of the Washington roulette wheel. The message said the president wanted to make the announcement on November 3, so instant acknowledgement was required. But first, another complex analysis by Bush. What was behind this startling, hurry-up request for Bush's services in a totally new arena? He had followed the press accounts of the beleaguered agency. Senator Frank Church's Select Committee on Intelligence had forced the present director, William Colby, to subject the "family jewels" to public scrutiny and revealed secrets that most CIA professionals thought never should be released.

Among them were activities like "Chaos Operation against the antiwar movement, the surveillance and bugging of American journalists to locate sources of leaks of sensitive materials, and all the connections with the Watergate conspirators." Additionally, such subjects as the mail intercept program and "bizarre and tragic cases wherein the Agency experimented with mind-control drugs, including the one of a CIA officer who, without his knowledge, was given LSD, which caused a deep depression and eventually his death."[6]

These comments from CIA Director William Colby were extended to discuss the questions of assassination of Lumumba, Castro and Trujillo; and the embarrassing time when a dart gun for shooting shellfish toxin and/or cobra venom was exhibited on television. As he appeared on the same program, Colby's briefing paper had him describe the gun as a "Nondiscernible Microbioinoculator."[7]

Many observers thought that Church's presidential aspirations were behind his investigation. Its effects on the public perception of the CIA were compounded by a simultaneous study of the agency by the House Select Intelligence Committee under Congressman Otis Pike.

The *New York Times* and CBS/TV's Daniel Schorr took the lead in media revelations of the agency's real and supposed nefarious doings.

Some friends of Bush worried that White House Chief of Staff Donald Rumsfeld had engineered Bush's selection to replace Colby as CIA chief. They wondered if he might be trying to demolish Bush's future as a presidential hopeful. Surely, to be shunted into the agency at this unfortunate point in its history would do little for Bush's political appeal.

The Democrats, on the other hand, were suspicious that the CIA post might add allure to Bush and actually be a jumping off place for him to enter the 1976 campaign, even as Ford's running mate. Bush shucked off all the static and focused the picture for his own decision. The president of the United States wanted him to do this job. That was enough. He signalled his acceptance.

In reality, the fate of the administration or the country was not hanging in the balance, depending on which man went to which department. Each was a proven utility infielder who could acquit himself well in any position. William D. Ruckelshaus, Elliot Richardson and George Bush were the three Ivy League "Mr. Cleans" that Nixon had used repeatedly to escape from the jams in which he kept getting himself.

For instance, in a situation similar to the present CIA anguish, Nixon had plugged Ruckelshaus temporarily into the FBI as director. Remarkably, all three men possessed presidential qualities, and although Nixon gave them responsibilities, he was careful not to give them too much power.

Once again Ford needed a reputable executive seasoned by past tests. Bush was familiar with the shallows and narrows of Washington politics and bureaucracy. He could navigate the CIA out to the open sea and leave it free to ply its own quiet course again.

In retrospect, what course should Bush have chosen? If he was interested only in public service, either Commerce or the CIA would do; although the Agency was involved more vitally in national security.

If he sought a straighter shot for the presidency, then the CIA posed definite risks. There were two in particular: First, despite its critical value to America's protection from a dangerous world, the CIA at present had lost much credibility. Even in the best of times, the mere idea of a department of dirty tricks and spies long had been—like an agency of propaganda—unpopular among Americans.

The inquiries of Senator Church and Congressman Pike had heightened the agency's malodor. For Bush to be associated with CIA would certainly besmirch him in the minds of many voters.

The second risk of joining the CIA was paradoxical. The Democrats were afraid that Bush might exploit his prominence as CIA director to catapult himself into the vice presidency. To disabuse them and win Senate approval, the president would have to bind and shackle Bush so tightly that he couldn't possibly be a candidate.

This moment was dismal for George Bush. He and Barbara called Maureen O'Ryan, British wife of an Argentine diplomat in Beijing, to come over and cheer him up. Mrs. O'Ryan says he was just sunk over his next job. The two of them, according to her, were lamenting that they wouldn't be able to go back to their house in Houston. He was sure that this new career trail would lead him away from the presidency forever.

Maureen asked why he would allow himself to be manipulated this way. He answered that he considered it his duty. She was impressed with his attitude—so much so that even as a foreigner, she later served in Washington as a volunteer on his presidential campaign committee in 1987 and 1988.

As the three sat together in the Bushes' residence, they recalled happier times in China. Maureen and Barbara frequently had spent days together at the Ming tombs just a few miles from Peking. Maureen would do rubbings of the statuary which later would make beautiful replicas suitable for framing. Barbara would take her ever-present needlepoint. She finally finished a large, carpet-size piece representing her time in China which now appears wherever the Bushes live. Over sandwiches they would keep an eye on C. Fred, the spaniel, who tended to bother the Chinese with his sniffing and yapping.

The Bushes remembered their first tries at entertaining the Chinese. Cross-cultural differences would pop up; for example, at their July 4th celebration when they buried presents in a tub full of sawdust. The Chinese were asked to reach in and pick out something as a surprise. This was, in effect, a grab bag.

During that period the Chinese believed they shouldn't accept favors from foreigners. So, according to a British reporter, European guests "eventually found themselves carrying away the "gifts" as the Chinese dared not be seen leaving with the books, toys, and sweets they had collected during the party."[8]

The family had been split over Christmas in 1974, when Barbara went to the States to be with the children, who were in school. George's mother was on hand for the holiday. She was amused when the Chinese took him on Christmas day to examine their mammoth tunnel system under Beijing. They had burrowed a vast air raid shelter in fear of a surprise Soviet atomic bombing. Mrs. Bush called attention to the irony of celebrating the birth of the Prince of Peace by inspecting works of war.

Four of the Bushes' five children had been able to share the Chinese cultural experience. They came in the summer of 1975—all except Jeb (22) and his new wife, Columba, from Mexico. He had to stay with his job in the Texas Commerce Bank. George, now 29, had graduated from Harvard Business School. He was planning to follow his dad into the oil business. Neil, 20, who had overcome his dyslexia, was a student at Tulane and on his way to two college degrees.

When Neil's dyslexia had been diagnosed some years earlier, Barbara dedicated herself to beating it. Barbara tirelessly had taken him to eye specialists; attended reading classes with him over weekends; found large-print books; gone over practice tapes; and encouraged him, "learning as much as she could about dyslexia and other reading impairments."[9]

Marvin, now 19, had been accepted by the University of

Virginia and was keen to see China. He came along with Doro, who had her sixteenth birthday and christening in Beijing.

One aspect of the Bushes' sojourn in China—the environment—very nearly was intolerable. George, Barbara and C. Fred Bush suffered through Beijing's air pollution—the most severe pollution in Asia. Bush joked about C. Fred's blond coat turning gray every day or so. He mentioned that the pollution had exacerbated a cold. Yet this front-line exposure to filthy air never translated into much of a domestic political issue for Bush, at least not until the campaign of 1988.

In the time since their stay, the Bushes have referred to China as their home away from home and developed warmly reciprocated friendships with many of the official Chinese they knew at the U.N. and in Beijing.

As Bush wound up his affairs in China, what did his record there say about the man? What about his wish to go there in the first place? He had made himself a favorite of the Republican party. As skipper of the RNC, he had steered its fortunes through the worst imaginable storms. He had shown such courage and skill that the party faithful of all stripes and levels admired him.

With Nixon gone the tempest had passed. A calm new president already had begun to restore public confidence in the government, even in the Republican party. What if Bush simply had remained with the RNC for the duration of Ford's term? He would have been beautifully placed to run for president or vice president in 1976. Rockefeller was fated to have worn out his welcome by then, and instead of the somewhat irascible Dole, Ford could at last have picked Bush to run with him. With Bush at his side, Ford might well have been re-elected.

On a more modest plane, the ambassadorship to London or Paris would have provided continuing visibility at home. Those posts still seem prestigious to the average American. Was it shrewd to refuse?

Kissinger had warned him he would be bored on this tour. Given the secretary's fascination with China and his predilection for doing everything himself, Bush had ample evidence that his presence in Beijing would be insignificant. He was playing in Kissinger's sandbox. Bush did the backslapping and tailwagging as a mere public relations man while Kissinger came and went on his high-level, substantive dealings with the Chinese power wielders.

The China episode, after all, might be judged as little more than an exotic interlude for George Bush in terms of advancing his serious ambitions.

CHAPTER 12

Director of the Central Intelligence Agency

G EORGE BUSH COMPLETED HIS FINAL DAYS IN CHINA at the accelerated pace of an old Keystone Cops movie. President Ford's rush visit to Beijing would end on December 5, 1975; two days later George and Barbara were bound for Washington, where Bush was slated for immediate Senate confirmation hearings.

In his meeting with Chairman Mao, President Ford received ample evidence that Bush was leaving in a modest blaze of glory. Chairman Mao smiled at Bush and exclaimed "You've been promoted!" Then he turned to Ford and declared, "We hate to see him go." At a ceremonial lunch, Vice Premier Deng Hsiao-ping assured Bush that he always would be welcome back in Beijing, even as head of the CIA.

This comforted Bush, who felt some trepidation about being transformed publicly from a diplomatic into an intelligence and covert action role. A fellow diplomat also soothed him with the reminder that ex-CIA chief Richard Helms once had been named ambassador to Iran. The Soviet ambassador, formerly a KGB minion, asked a high Iranian official what he thought about having the CIA head in his country as ambassador. The Iranian laughed that it was better to have been sent America's number-one spy than what the Soviets had sent: their number-ten spy.[1]

Promptly at 10:05 A.M. on December 15, 1975, the Senate Armed Services Committee commenced its examination of George Bush for the office of director of the Central Intelligence Agency. As Bush's home state senator, John Tower led off with a customary bouquet of compliments. Bush grinned appreciatively when Tower remarked on his "eminent good judgment to move to Texas, where he has spent all of his adult life."[2] At last he was being recognized as a Texan.

Bush delivered a strong, cogent rationale for being approved, affirming his belief in a vigorous CIA. He asserted he would have the proper access to the president, that he would seek to eliminate duplication in the intelligence community under his command, and that he would eschew personal political moves.

In fact, he said, "If some individual or group comes forward promoting me for vice president when I am director of the CIA, I will instruct them to cease such activity."[3]

Still, he stipulated that he wouldn't go as far as a Shermanesque disavowal. Civil War General John Sherman had responded to pressure on him to run for the presidency with the still-famous words: "If nominated, I will not run; if elected, I will not serve."

Bush then raised a unique point: What would he say if, without lifting a finger to encourage anyone, and indeed actively discouraging others from advocating him for the office, the nomination were offered him?

Bush declared "I cannot in all honesty tell you that I would not accept . . . and to my knowledge, no one in the history of the Republic has been asked to renounce his political birthright as the price of confirmation for any office."[4]

Finally, Bush was candid about his own reaction to being named for the post, in view of the controversy swirling around the agency and its obvious barriers to a political future. "My answer," he stated, "is simple. First, the work is desperately important to the survival of this country and to the survival of freedom around the world. And second, old fashioned as it may seem to some, it is my duty to serve my country. And I did not seek this job but I want to do it and I will do my very best."

He also declared his concern over the public beating the agency had undergone: "Frankly, many of our friends around the world and some who are not friendly are wondering what we are doing to ourselves as a nation as they see attacks on the CIA. Some must wonder if they can depend on us to protect them if they cooperate with us on important intelligence projects."[5]

The hearing filled two days, and Bush faced some thorny inquiry. The burden of it was that his was a political background and a political nomination, and that by training and experience he was not equipped for the job. Jet lag after the long trip from China and insufficient time to prepare rendered him more vulnerable to criticism.

The committee was at an impasse until President Ford issued a statement: "If Ambassador Bush is confirmed by the Senate as director of Central Intelligence, I will not consider him as my vice-presidential running mate in 1976."[6]

After the president succumbed to the Senate with this mollifying gesture, Bush was passed by the committee with a 12-4 vote, and then by the full Senate 64-27 in January. Friend and neighbor Supreme Court Justice Potter Stewart swore him in at CIA headquarters in Langley, Virginia.

The Bushes moved back into their former house on Palisades Lane and renewed their old Washington acquaintances from six years before. Bush's typical 12-hour workday was not so different from his earlier career, but he found that his home life had changed. For the first time in his marriage, he couldn't discuss what his day at the office was like when he and Barbara sat down to supper together.

The directorship entailed not only running the agency, but also managing the rest of the intelligence community at Defense, State and the National Security Agency as well. Bush saw that he would need to do some heavy studying before he could do more than take advice from the professionals.

His first priority was to counter the bad press stemming from testimony and leaks about malfeasances of the agency. Surprisingly, the CIA has a public information office, which then was under the direction of former newsman Angus Thurman. Bush huddled with Thurman to devise an outreach program to tell Americans about the agency's accomplishments. Actually, there were quite a few accomplishments in the agency's short history—the pictures that revealed the Soviet missile implants in Cuba were a prime example.

With some positive stories generated to improve the public perception of the CIA, Bush addressed the more sensitive issue of internal morale. By opting for Langley as his main office, he sent the first signal to his people that he was one of them. Second, he obtained approval from the president to select his own deputy. He chose Henry Knoche from the professional ranks of the CIA. He then installed Admiral Daniel J. Murphy of the U.S. Navy as his deputy for administration. Next, he managed to get acquainted with many of the personnel.

The basic divisions of the agency are called directorates. In addition to Administration, Science and Technology, and Intelligence, there is the directorate of Operations which deals with foreign intelligence, counterintelligence, and covert activity. Bush was impressed to find that the specialists in these divisions amounted to over 1,400 people, whose advanced degrees spanned a dozen or more disciplines.

Not long after taking office, he also circulated among some foreign posts. Cord Meyer, the agency's chief of station in London, recounts that Bush came to see him. At Bush's suggestion he arranged a meeting with all the United Kingdom's top intelligence officials from the Ministry of Defence, MI5 and MI6 at his residence. Meyer, a former World War II hero and founder of the World Federalists, recalls that the Britishers liked Bush and were flattered by this courtesy from such an important fellow.

Then, whether he liked it or not, Bush had to traipse to

Capitol Hill to brief the numerous committees with CIA oversight responsibility. He appeared 51 times on the Hill in less than a year.[7]

Once a week Bush would conduct briefings at the White House for President Ford. Additionally, he would make reports as called for by the National Security Council (NSC). The council comprises the president, the secretaries of State and Defense, the NSC advisor, and the director of the CIA. Others in those briefings recall Bush standing before the maps and spieling out names and figures. Nevertheless, he always kept an experienced expert at his elbow in the event of questions being thrown at him that he could not answer.

There was one emergency meeting of the NSC which President Ford called to determine how to offer American citizens a safe exit from beleaguered Beirut. This took place in 1976 just after U.S. Ambassador Francis E. Meloy, Jr., was assassinated. Bush mentions it in his autobiography. Besides the president, the small room held Secretary of State Kissinger, Deputy Defense Secretary William Clements, and Deputy National Security Adviser Brent Scowcroft (Kissinger was both NSC adviser and head of State at that time). Also present was Ambassador L. Dean Brown, a former foreign service officer, then a civilian. Kissinger had asked him informally to attend the meeting since he recently had been in Lebanon.

Brown remembers that Bush gave the intelligence briefing, which included details on potential escape routes for Americans. One of these routes was an overland passage with heavy air and ground support by U.S. armed forces. The president's decision was to determine how to get those Americans to safety. Apparently the military personnel present heavily favored the overland option. Although Bush had shown the maps and given the specifics of available military cover for the operation, he didn't enter the discussion. He saw his part in this as giving the intelligence, not in trying to make policy.

The president then asked Brown what he thought. Brown took Bush's maps and suggested that the Americans simply walk or ride down to the beach where they could be rescued by landing craft of the U.S. Navy. The president made his decision. I like that idea, he said, we've had enough macho actions already.[8] Thereafter, the Americans who chose to leave were moved expeditiously and without incident away from the dangers of Beirut.

Bush's recollection of the action taken was slightly different. He said that hundreds of American and foreign civilians boarded the ships, but that "others left Beirut in three convoys headed toward Damascus, Syria."[9]

During his tenure at the CIA, Bush pushed through a budget item of $500 million for high-tech improvements, including two satellite systems that could perform photoreconnaissance through clouds. Also added were four ground stations to intercept other countries' communications plus satellite and navy projects for the same purpose. "All this hardware has served the agency well, according to past and present CIA officials."[10] Bush hadn't lost his interest in the cutting edge of new technology—which years earlier in Texas had led him to bet millions on R. G. Le Tourneau's mobile offshore oil exploration rig.

Bush did find himself in one very controversial matter of substance at the CIA. The president's Foreign Intelligence Advisory Board, whose membership comprised several conservatives, was not happy with the CIA's estimates of the Soviet military threat. In 1975 the PFIAB urged Bush's predecessor, William Colby, to allow an outside group to provide their estimates based on the same data the CIA was employing. The PFIAB was composed of two senior retired military officers, Clare Booth Luce, and four chief executives of major corporations. Colby said no. The same suggestion was made to Bush in 1976. Against the advice of his CIA colleagues, Bush accepted the offer. Some complained that he was scratching the backs of the conservatives.[11]

"B"-Team then was formed, with conservative Harvard Professor Richard Pipes as chairman. B-Team read the CIA files, and to no one's surprise, delivered an opinion that was far more pessimistic about Soviet intentions that those of the careerists at CIA.

When the *Washington Post* covered the story of Bush inviting sharp disagreement both inside and outside of the agency, the headline ran in part "At CIA, a Rebuilder 'Goes with the Flow' Avoiding Intellectual Debate. . . ." In the story, however, the *Post* did provide a recognition of Bush's action: "Bush did it to clear the air," former deputy Murphy said, describing the A-Team, B-Team episode as "wheel-spinning." It was "an example of Bush biting the bullet, and it neutralized the outside bitching," Murphy said.[12]

The *Post* also concluded that Bush had "tiptoed successfully through this mine field, leaving everyone involved feeling unbruised. Both the career analysts on the A-Team and Pipes and his B-Team felt they had prevailed."[13]

Other confrontational issues claimed Bush's attention at the CIA. There were personnel weaknesses in the upper ranks of the agency, and he set about reducing them. When he found replacements, he personally informed those who were being weeded out. There were no pink slips, and no lack of appreciation for professional achievements of old hands. He faced them with kindness, as he had when firing people at the Republican National Committee.

Furthermore, he dug into the ranks of careerists to fill the empty chairs. He started with Henry Knoche, his top deputy. After leaving the agency, Cord Meyer wrote that Bush "quickly proved by his performance that he was prepared to put politics aside and devote all his considerable ability and enthusiasm to restoring the morale of an institution that had been battered enough. Instead of reaching outside for defeated Republican candidates to fill key jobs, he chose from within the organization among men who had demonstrated their competence through long careers in intelligence."[14] Meyer went on to tout Bush's determination to protect the agency's objectivity and avoid slanting its estimates to fit in with the president's preconceptions.

Meyer also stressed that because of the president's obvious confidence in him, Bush had access to the White House and the wider Washington bureaucracy. This new acceptability that Bush furnished for the agency did much to raise morale.

Some felt, however, that he had a proclivity for picking

assistants more on the basis of compatibility than ability. There were those who put Knoche in this category. He was a tall, athletic and very personable man much in the mold of Bush himself. Critics thought that he lacked the broad experience his position required, particularly in the field of covert operations.

About six months into his stewardship, Bush appointed William Wells to be deputy director for Operations, which upset the professionals. They saw Wells as a jolly, attractive man, but short on the qualities needed for that severely taxing assignment. He was relieved of that position shortly after Bush left the CIA. According to officials present in those days, Bush made this selection without consulting anyone.

For observers watching the agency from outside Langley, it is difficult to assess such judgments. There is always the possibility that they stem from long-lasting turf battles kept alive by gossip.

Although it nearly is impossible to track Bush's daily schedule and performance at the CIA given the secrecy there, vignettes do circulate. Admiral Daniel Murphy, a staunch Bush adherent, allows the real man to emerge through all the tributes. For example, I asked him whether Bush ever loses his temper. "He's not a screamer," reports the admiral, "and he will not bang his fist unless he's very mad, and I only remember him doing it once." It was a meeting of three, the admiral, Bush, and a man from the Defense Department. The latter, a senior official, addressed the admiral abusively, disrespectfully and at some length. Bush remained silent at first. Then he rose and practically climbed over the top of the table toward the man from Defense. Almost nose to nose, he said, "Don't you talk to the admiral that way. You want to complain about what we're doing, you can talk to me about it. But don't you ever talk to him that way."

The other guy was two inches taller than Bush. "He backed down," the admiral chortles, finishing the reminiscence with relish.

Admiral James Holloway, who was chief of naval operations

when Bush was at the CIA, tells of an NSC meeting he witnessed. For his briefing Bush was accompanied by his usual maps-and-papers aide plus a second man. Before the briefing Bush explained to the president that he had brought the extra man, a senior officer of the CIA, who disagreed with the points that he, Bush, was about to make to the NSC. He thought that in all fairness the man should be allowed to speak for himself because he would be making important contrasts with Bush's position.

Admiral Holloway cited that act as the finest example of inspired leadership and fairness that he ever had seen in his long career in the navy.

Holloway also cites the time Bush made a remarkable gesture to the Joint Chiefs of Staff of the army, navy, air force and Marine Corps: He invited them all to lunch at the Alibi Club, the small, prestigious restaurant on 1 Street in Washington. "He came alone, with no aides or colleagues." No CIA director had ever had the imagination or thoughtfulness to reach out to the military like that, the admiral remarked recently. "We had a wonderful time with him, and will always remember him."[15]

A gossipy anecdote from one national TV news commentator has it that when George Bush was running the CIA, his favorite pastime was to read all the intercepts. He was said to have had a little boy's excitement about them, because they are so secret. Intercepts are whatever is picked up from foreign cable traffic, radio signals, and so forth. They enable us to learn what other countries—especially our enemies—are saying, particularly when they don't know that we are listening.

Then there's the Dan Schorr story. The TV news pundit, who worked for CBS at the time, was driving in a blizzard one evening when his car slid into a snowdrift and stuck there. While he and his companions puzzled over their predicament, a limousine pulled up behind them. Out stepped CIA Director George Bush.

"Let's get you out of this," he announced, and within minutes he helped push the car free.

After they had proceeded, one of Schorr's friends exclaimed,

"Isn't this a wonderful country where the head of an important agency like the CIA personally rescues you from a pile of snow?!"

"I guess so," said Schorr, "but I wonder why the hell he was following us in the first place!"

Bush's time with the CIA was short—barely a year—because President Carter refused to leave him there in 1977. Bush let it be known that he enjoyed his duty and felt that if Carter didn't appoint a new man it would show that he didn't consider the CIA a political operation.

But Carter had used the agency as a whipping boy in his campaign, and, regardless of what his personal feelings might have been, it probably would have looked inconsistent for him to have kept Bush.

Bush has spoken often and fondly of the CIA; it is clear that he cared for the people and the work there as much as any in his varied experience.

Leaders as diverse as William Colby, whom he replaced during the agency's troubled period, and Richard Helms, the veteran director of many years, combine in their praise of Bush's contributions. Colby stresses how successfully he restored morale within the agency and its reputation on the Hill.[16]

Helms gave his comments at a dinner in 1983, when he won the William J. Donovan Award. "Soon after taking over the agency, Bill Casey commented that 'out there at Langley they think that guy—meaning you, Mr. Vice President—walks on water!' Maybe you do, maybe you don't; there is no doubt of the respect and affection in which you are held by intelligence officers everywhere."[17]

CHAPTER 13

Barnstormer for the Presidency

W HEN OUTSIDER JIMMY CARTER CAME TO WASH-
ington in 1977 and turned the insiders out, George and
Barbara Bush agreed to leave. They left for Houston to start
plotting their way back in.

They bought a house on Indian Lane, a dead-end street.
There they found a place to decompress and find old friends
after their momentous involvements of the previous six years.

Life was changing yet again. At least for now there was no
formal commitment to either the government or the Republican party. George was jobless for the first time since
leaving college in 1948! Here they were in Houston again, but
that was different too, for there were no children to be mus-
tered and enjoyed around the house. No longer was Barbara
the mother that their son Jeb would describe as "supermom,
serving as Cub Scout mother, carpool driver and Sunday
school teacher. Dad was the chief executive officer, but mother
was the chief operating officer. We all reported to her. She did a
good job of keeping the family intact."[1]

Now only Marvin and Doro, 20 and 17 respectively, were basing their lives out of Indian Lane, and they were in school most of the year. All five children still came home, as George liked to boast, and Kennebunkport still was a magnet in the summer time. In fact, before long George would buy outright the big house on Walker's Point from the rest of his family. But most days would find George and Barbara back where they started: as two people sharing a house.

George didn't stay unemployed very long. Like Winston Churchill, when a man of George Bush's drive and ambition is left to his own devices, he is soon busier than anyone around.

George began with business initiatives. These would serve not only to build up his coffers, but also would lead to travel around the country and abroad. With his eye on a political future, it was essential to keep and build on his broad network of contacts. Commercial connections could contribute to that process.

Within weeks he joined the executive committee of the First International Bank in Houston. With an office there as his headquarters, he then joined several corporations as a board director and consultant. He also was brought into the Dallas International Bancshares Corporation, the largest Texas bank holding company, in a similar capacity. There he was paid $75,000 annually as a consultant.

The *Washington Post* failed to ascertain precisely what Bush did for this fee. Neither the company nor Bush would divulge the details during the presidential campaign of 1988. From his income tax returns and voluntary disclosures, however, the *Post* listed his total income from these four corporations for two-and-one-half years, ending in May 1979, as $275,000.[2]

Additionally, Bush was an active investor during that period. With his friend and occasional tennis partner Robert Mosbacher, he put $50,000 in a partnership to buy small barges to transport oil products.

This deal became profitable both in increased share values and in what appears to be a $20,000 annual income for Bush for the foreseeable future.

He combined these commercial ventures with community-oriented deeds; as a director of Baylor Medical College; adjunct professor of Rice University; a trustee of Phillips Academy (his alma mater in Andover, Massachusetts), a trustee of Trinity University in San Antonio, and chairman of the American Heart Fund.

These pro bono relationships projected the concept of a thoughtful and generous citizen. The roles were valuable to the community and to the political Bush. For a man thinking of a greater role for himself in public service, as Bush was, these associations were essential.

Ideally Bush could have benefitted from a public program like the Rockefeller Brothers Fund's "Special Studies Project." This was organized in 1956 on the premise that the country had a need for long-range thinking. By 1960 the fund had produced six major reports: The Mid-Century Challenge to U.S. Foreign Policy; International Security: The Military Aspect; Foreign Economic Policy for the Twentieth Century; The Challenge to America: Its Economic and Social Aspects; The Pursuit of Excellence: Education and the Future of America; and The Power of the Democratic Idea.

Henry Kissinger participated in the project until 1958 when he and Nelson Rockefeller, who had been chairman, resigned. A book on this project entitled *Prospects for America*, was published.[3]

The net value to the country and Nelson Rockefeller was positive. The reports and his book provided him a stage from which to share his newly acquired wisdom. The voters, to the extent they bothered with such matters, could see this politician (he had become governor of New York in 1958) as knowledgeable and caring about the welfare of the United States.

Although Bush lacked the resources of the Rockefeller Brothers, he needed to extend his reach in some similar fashion. Through extensive travel as a speaker and businessman, he was physically widening his skein of friends and acquaintances among leaders both at home and abroad who could further his ambitions. But he could have used an impersonal vehicle that would recommend him to the public and the poohbahs of the Republican party.

He also needed to craft for himself the shape of the country and its government for which he was striving. He should be articulating just what he had in mind and why it was vital for America to follow him as a leader. This would have been an appropriate moment for him to have written some sort of treatise or book in which he could outline where he stood.

In the years to come he would be criticized by supporters and attackers alike for not offering clear goals for government—even oversimplified ones like Kennedy's "Let's get this country moving again!" Bush would call the criticisms his "Vision Thing," in reality meaning "the lack of a plan."

As for his own goal, it was no longer a question of what George Bush would do next—it was only when, how and with whom. He kept alert for political polls around the nation. He spoke frequently and wherever his presence would keep his potential future alive.

Stories proliferate as to who was present when Bush decided to run for president. According to the *Washington Post* and several Chinese friends, he considered the ultimate political peak while he was chief of the U.S. Liaison Office in Beijing. Allegedly he told a visiting Bonesman, "I am going to run for president." The guest asked, "For which company?" Bush laughed and said, "The United States."

Jing Xianfa, correspondent for *The People's Daily,* reported to me that Bush was considering it again on his return to China in the late 1970s as his steamer sailed through the spectacular, perpendicular Three Gorges of the Yangtze River.[4]

George and Barbara often traveled together during his interregnum from formal, full-time, titled positions. From China they managed to enter Tibet, where Barbara was said to be only the third American woman ever to put foot on the soil of that exotic nation.[5] The couple took advantage of his freedom to go for both profit and to imbibe international culture and political insights. Stops included Hong Kong, Australia, Singapore, Iran, Jordan, Egypt, Israel, Greece and Denmark.

Throughout this period he allowed the idea of a George Bush presidency to germinate quietly in his own mind as well as in the minds of others around the United States. The idea wasn't exactly taking fire. In 1978 he appeared as the lunch speaker at the Republican Men's Club of Dallas. Jim Oberwetter, a long-time loyalist and his former press aide in Congress introduced him. This was a big, elaborate event at the now defunct Baker Hotel. Oberwetter said, "I am proud to present to you a man who is a prospective Republican nominee for president." Oberwetter remembers that his pronouncement met with silence because no one believed him. After all, he says, they saw Bush as a man who had twice lost in his bids for the Senate and then quit the House of Representatives. How could he be serious? It didn't make sense.[6]

Bush nevertheless remained determined. On May 1, 1979, his candidacy was sure: He announced it formally at the National Press Club in Washington, D.C. with his family at his side.

His speech was straightforward and spoke of leadership with "new candor." He began it negatively, saying he would not promise simple solutions but offer hard choices; would not buy our way out of problems; would not protect our freedoms on the cheap; would not substitute something less for credible military strength.

He proceeded more positively and insisted that he would bring the virtues of personal commitment and self-discipline; government policies for a balanced budget and a stronger dollar; greater opportunities for women; inspiration for young people to build not simply a greater, but also a better society; and restoration of pride in the American ideal.

He then quoted President Eisenhower in calling for "a middle way between the untrammeled freedom of the individual and the demands for the welfare of the whole nation. This way must avoid government-by-bureaucracy as carefully as it avoids neglect of the helpless."

He wound up promising, again in Eisenhower's words, "a leadership confident of our strength, compassionate of heart, and clear in mind, as we turn to the great tasks before us."

In short, he spoke honorably but blandly and without any magic thoughts or originality. He needed a good speech writer for this vital step. He should have galvanized his listeners,

instead he merely soothed them. He was being his unpreten-
tious self: a fine person, a courageous, principled citizen offering himself for the ultimate public service. He possessed
charm, energy, dependability and experience. He lacked fire.

Perhaps he believed what Jack Kennedy reportedly said: "If
you're strong, your strength speaks for itself. If you're weak,
words make no difference."

Bush was strong in determination, physical vigor and intelligence. His family had no doubts. He inspired them and they
stepped out to many corners of the country to campaign for
him. All of his children campaigned, although young George
only spent half his time at first—he worked at a half-time job to
support himself.

The candidate left the podium at the Press Club to com-
mence a four-day swing through ten cities in Connecticut,
Massachusetts, New Hampshire, Vermont, Maine, Florida and
Alabama.

He had collected a good team to work for him, mostly as
volunteers. James A. Baker, III, old friend, political aide and
recent undersecretary of Commerce under President Ford,
managed the operation from campaign headquarters in Alexandria, Virginia. David Keene, a young conservative Republican, was the political advisor. A vital cog in the new
organization was its national finance operation, started and led
by Bush's long-time friend Robert Mosbacher. He was aided by
Fred Bush (no relation) in Houston and Jack Sloat in Washington. Money didn't come easy; George Bush was still
"George Who?" in those days. This team would have to accomplish near-miracles to keep the candidacy rolling.

Elsewhere around the nation, Bush committees began to
sprout. Jim Oberwetter started putting a program together in
the North Texas area, in effect for Dallas County—the third
district and one of the largest Republican districts in the country, with about 700,000 people in 1979.

Texas presented immediate problems: First, Ronald Reagan
had done very well in the primaries of 1976 and already was
strong for the coming 1980 race. Next, the popular ex-governor
and ex-Democrat John Connally entered the contest and

promptly made a whirlwind tour of about 35 cities and towns that the Bush strategists had been counting as theirs.

After Bush's launching both he and Barbara rented a house for the summer by the sea in Kennebunkport. There he gathered a diverse group, in sections, to pick their brains on defense, agriculture, environment, international affairs and other issues. He drew experts from universities, business, and government.

They met three days a week for six weeks in seminars from 9 to 5. Neighbors of the Bushes housed them. By the end of the sessions, 45 men and women had come and gone.

Being George Bush, he left his advisors feeling as if they had been to a jolly jamboree. After long discussions in a public building of the tiny village, George would invite his collaborators back to his house for lunch. In the evenings he and Barbara would picnic and barbecue for them on the rocks of Walker's Point.

Andrew Falkiewicz, former spokesman at the CIA and White House, was there as a foreign policy specialist. He says that despite the hard work, the participants came away refreshed by the upbeat atmosphere.

Falkiewicz had met Bush when he was ambassador to the U.N. Bush had heard that he was an expert on Eastern Europe and sent for Falkiewicz to come to New York and brief him. Later, at the CIA, Bush had brought him from the press office of the White House to be his assistant for external affairs. The two men had become friends and in the ensuing years had sailed together on Falkiewicz's 30-foot sloop.

Falkiewicz laughs that after an hour in Chesapeake Bay, Bush said "Well, that's about as long as I need to watch you handle the sails."[7]

By summer's end Bush had the nucleus of a campaign strategy and a growing coterie of campaigners for the long slog through the primaries of 1980. At Newport, Rhode Island, he informed the press that in his drive for the Republican nomination he would concentrate on the early primaries and caucuses in Iowa, New Hampshire, Vermont and Massachusetts.

At that time, like Bush, I was between government assignments and spending part of the summer in Newport. I had offered my services as a surrogate speaker to the Alexandria headquarters. I had seen the fresh faces of young volunteers— including Bush's own children—appearing in fund-raisers and party meetings in Rhode Island and elsewhere. In Newport, I was busy with Jonathan T. and Elizabeth Isham, William and Eleanor Wood-Prince of Chicago—summer residents in Rhode Island—and others on Bush's finance committee.

In September we offered a $100-per-plate dinner at my seaside house. Bush addressed 200-or-so Rhode Islanders from all over the state, and told them that he would try to mount a major effort in their state; but not until he built momentum for himself elsewhere.

George's talk was low-key, a kind of get-acquainted pitch highlighting his busy bureaucratic background. He didn't say much about his own platform, but pledged it would carry no phony promises. Thus he still was repeating his opening thoughts from the May announcement, always a sound practice.

He was asked who his opponent would be, if he were to garner the nomination. He believed, as fewer and fewer did at that time, that Jimmy Carter would be chosen by the Democrats in 1980.

As he stood and spoke on the lawn beneath a tent, Bush was informal in manner and dress. He had changed into a fresh white shirt before dinner, but his dark grey, pinstripe trousers were baggy from travel. Except for his New England accent, he came across as an educated, weather-ruddy Midwesterner—a hardworking, sincere, politician whose charisma was most apparent face to face.

To become familiar with his audience, one would have required a political road map, said Charles Bakst of the *Providence Journal*.[8] The group typified the mix of individuals that Bush would attract in months to come: People who had known him from his numerous walks of life—as a student, in government, the military, politics and business.

Rhode Island's Republican Senator John H. Chafee, an old

schoolmate from Yale, showed up even though he was leading the presidential charge for Senator Howard Baker.

Claudine Schneider, a 1978 congressional candidate who would be elected in 1982, joined others who wouldn't commit to Bush but were willing to pay to hear him speak.

Mrs. Eileen Slocum, who was supporting former Governor Connally, had colorful words: "Any Republican is a good Republican. . . ." Then she added, "George is so attractive and has such intellectual depth, but has he the common touch and strength to handle Teddy Kennedy?"[9]

That fall had produced a large harvest of White House hopefuls in both parties. President Jimmy Carter proclaimed a malaise in the country, a condition which more and more voters were blaming on him. Bush now was trotting in a full pack that had been assembling for well over a year. Some already had dropped out or decided against entering at all.

In 1974, for example, William D. Ruckelshaus's name had gained some currency. As deputy attorney general, he had followed Attorney General Elliot Richardson's resignation with his own after the Saturday Night Massacre. This was the occasion when the two refused President Nixon's order to fire Watergate Special Prosecutor Archibald Cox.

Ruckelshaus's luster from that incident, plus his good performance as the first head of the Environmental Protection Agency and his considerable oratorical abilities, had produced an afterglow in the minds of three candidates in the 1976 campaign. Ronald Reagan, Gerald Ford and Eugene McCarthy each had pointed to Ruckelshaus directly or indirectly as their preferred vice-presidential running mate. As we know, George Bush was not available that year, Ford having sworn in writing that the CIA chief would not be a candidate.

Those confidential boomlets for Ruckelshaus fizzled before decisions were finalized in 1976, but some interest lingered in 1978. He rejected a privately tendered bid that he enter the presidential sweepstakes. Soon afterward he threw his weight behind Bush as a surrogate speaker and silent advisor.

Bush could have used a legion of speakers in 1979 and 1980.

There were ample opportunities that arose out of his stalwart performance as head of the Republican National Committee. District chairmen and other delegates remembered how available he had been in the hardship days of Watergate. Many now showed their gratitude with invitations to make appearances. His Alexandria staff was able to schedule him almost solidly during the weeks before the primaries. David Bates and Jane Kenny were usually the only helpers that ventured forth to accompany Bush on his travels.

Bush was unfailingly well received at small meetings, where his natural charm was in play. In the early months, however, his platform spark was missing. The oratorical skills so vital before large groups, or on TV, were thin to absent.

He hadn't yet found a central, passionate theme to dramatize his candidacy. His amiable but bloodless address at the Newport dinner in September seemed to have come from a different man than the one who delivered the superb fighting speeches of 1973 there and elsewhere. Then, he had been the champion of the embattled Republican party, fierce to save it from sinking in the slough of Watergate calumny. He believed in the party deeply and his performance resonated what he truly felt. His own candidacy somehow failed to excite him in the same fashion.

During the early briefings his supporters had set up in Washington, two of his friends tried to prep him for doing better on TV. One day at the International Club they ushered him into a room with a videotape machine, where they peppered him with questions. One of the first was "Why do you want to be president?" His reply: "Aaaaaah. . . ."

Teddy Kennedy had answered the same question posed by Roger Mudd in precisely the same way, except that it was on live TV. The exposure did much to kill Kennedy's chances that year, and perhaps forever. In his autobiography Bush candidly writes, "Kennedy was faulted for not coming back with a quick, articulate reply; but any presidential candidate honest with himself had to wonder: What would I have said if Roger Mudd surprised me with that question?"[10]

Despite imperfections of style Bush plugged away toward

the critical Iowa caucuses of January 1980. Reagan already was judged front-runner in the polls. But Bush was starting to roll. Although the pundits had him behind in Maine, he came in first against Howard Baker, John Connally and all other hopefuls when a straw vote was held in November.

The locale was a Republican convention in Portland. This victory rang sweeter than the mere vote count, for many of the Republican delegates leapt up in reaction to his speech. They especially liked a line he had been belting out with conviction: "I am sick and tired of hearing people apologize for America!" This point, of course, was aimed at Carter's unfortunate remark about American malaise. One sobering note on the Maine result was the absence of Reagan on the slate.

Meanwhile, Bush's staff in Washington was growing. The state committees for Bush were proliferating; his campaign seemed to be creating some momentum, as he had promised. In January, pollster Gallup gave a national reading among registered Republicans. Bad news again: It pegged Reagan at 45 percent and Bush with 6 percent.[11]

Over the years Bush often had done his best when facing long odds. Nicholas Brady, the head of Purolator (on whose board Bush served), was also a tennis companion. He claims that Bush fights hardest when the score gets lopsided against him.[12] On hearing Gallup's numbers Bush shifted into overdrive. He blasted his points with more vigor in his speeches and spurred his Iowa support troops.

Yet only days before the caucuses, the *Des Moines Register and Tribune* clocked Reagan with 50 percent and Bush with 14 percent.[13]

Then on January 21 Bush scored a political knockdown in Iowa. He defeated all the candidates: Bob Dole; Phil Crane; John Connally; Howard Baker; the maverick John Anderson; and Reagan, the California heavyweight, whom he edged by 2,000 votes.

Suddenly the Bush effort took on the heady ambience of a bandwagon. He had developed some momentum. He dubbed it the "Big Mo" to the embarrassment of associates when the phrase was jeered at by critics as too preppy and juvenile. It

was encouraging for him to land on the cover of *Newsweek* and
have a whole planeload of newsmen and women follow the
Bush caravan to New Hampshire.

Furthermore, it was now a two-man race, something for
which the Bush camp had hoped. He had risen above the pack.
There were only two front-runners, and he was one of them.

David Keene, his senior aide of that time says, however, that
Bush was already 17 points behind Reagan when he got to
New Hampshire. Moreover, the Republican party potentates as
well as the rank and file favored Reagan, as the polls demonstrated, although they had doubts as to whether his age had
weakened him.[14]

The televised debate in Manchester, New Hampshire, at
which all the candidates spoke, proved to dubious Republicans that Reagan was strong enough for the presidency,
according to Keene. When the notorious debate at Nashua
loomed, all the party regulars wanted to be sure of was
whether Reagan was adequate.[15]

For Bush, his immediate future was an accident about to
happen. The evening he and Reagan met in Nashua, he had
had no relaxation for three weeks and his mood was somewhat
frenzied. A rested Bush might well have sized up the situation
and avoided being upstaged by professional actor Ronald Reagan.

The debate was sponsored by the Nashua-Telegraph and
scheduled for the stage of the city's high school, on Saturday
night, February 23. Ronald Reagan had underwritten the event,
a fact not known by Bush beforehand. According to Bush's
account.[16] Reagan's manager, John Sears, was reported to have
invited candidates Bob Dole, Howard Baker, John Anderson,
and Phil Crane to show up.

As they walked on to the stage before the debate began, the
audience grew unruly. Some shouted out that the other candidates should be included even though the event had been
advertised as a two-man contest.

When Reagan started to explain where he stood on the issue,
Jon Breen, the moderator, ordered that his mike be shut off.
Reagan then declared sternly, "I paid for this microphone, Mr.

Green."[17] He got Breen's name wrong, but he hit such a commanding note that George Bush and everyone else shrank in comparison. When the stage was cleared of all candidates except Reagan and Bush, it was obvious who had grabbed the "Big Mo." Reagan proceeded into the debate calm and assured; Bush was as uneasy as a whiny, disgruntled schoolmaster.

It's a measure of Bush's character that his recollection of that evening allows no excuses for himself. He lost the New Hampshire primary 20 percent to Reagan's 50 percent, with other aspirants trailing behind. He admitted the loss and moved on to the next primary. He looked at the bright side: The field had narrowed to two viable men, Reagan and Bush. With only one opponent to worry about in the remaining primaries, it would be easier for Bush to target his attacks.

Bush found his slogan "Voodoo Economics" a useful weapon with which to beat Reagan. Reagan appeared to be stating that a tax reduction without a commensurate reduction in government spending would boost the economy. Bush said this idea was nonsense—Voodoo Economics.

After what Bush himself termed the "debacle of New Hampshire," he did more than just survive. He remained a powerful opponent, outscoring Reagan in the key industrial states of Massachusetts, Connecticut, Pennsylvania and Michigan. Nevertheless, Bush never recovered enough to stop the grass-roots surge for Reagan that followed New Hampshire.

In fact, his May 20 primary win in Michigan coincided with Reagan's taking Nebraska, which gave the latter virtually enough delegates to guarantee nomination.

Campaign executive David Keene explains now that Bush's base in the party by 1980 comprised only about 35 percent of its registered voters; Reagan had most of the rest. He believes that Reagan's New Hampshire victory wasn't really due to Bush's failure to stand up to Reagan at Nashua. His analysis is that two things happened that night: First, Reagan's performance showed that he certainly still had the stamina to be president; second, despite his upset of Reagan in Iowa and his temporary "Big Mo," Bush was not eight feet tall.

With that rationale in mind, one could see Bush's ultimate

downfall since Reagan had the majority of Republicans on his side to begin with. Evidently, Keene was open with this opinion, and therefore was thought by some people in Bush's camp to be pro-Reagan.

After Nebraska, Keene was not alone in the campaign organization in calling for a halt. Since the end now was preordained, Bush's continuation would reduce him to a hate figure in the party. In other words, since Reagan was effectively the nominee, Bush would be attacking the standard-bearer for what could only be hurtful results to both Reagan and himself. For this offense, Keene felt that Bush would be "consigned to outer darkness forever" in the minds of Republicans.[18]

Immediately after Nebraska, the press were aware that Bush would have to decide whether to stop or continue against Reagan. In Ohio they asked him if he would withdraw from the California primary. He replied no. Oh, but Jim Baker has already said you have, taunted the reporters. This turned out to be true. Baker was out there negotiating with the Reagan forces to assure that Bush delegates could appear at the Detroit National Republican (nominating) Convention.

Baker and Bush agreed to discuss the matter over the weekend in Houston. Jim Oberwetter, Bush's former aide then working for Ray L. Hunt in Dallas, mentioned that he and Baker ran into each other at Washington's National Airport the day before the Houston meeting. He said Baker told him he would recommend that Bush step out of the race.

Bush, meanwhile, had gone to New Jersey. There he was unable to get plane reservations to Texas since it was a three-day holiday. He called Oberwetter, who arranged for the Hunt plane to take him. The trip would be paid for by Bush campaign funds. Oberwetter flew all the way back to New Jersey so he could accompany his old boss on the late-night flight to the Houston reckoning.

Oberwetter remembers that in the ten-seat plane there were, besides the Secret Service personnel, only Bush, his traveling assistant, David Bates, and himself. He sensed that Bush still was grimly firm on staying the course.

Next day, the discussions in Houston were heated. Bush

believed that there was always the chance Reagan might slip or that he might pick up last-minute strength through his own hard work. At last his team turned him around. Keene said that Vic Gold, speechwriter and longtime associate, became the decisive voice for withdrawal. A week later Bush officially ended his candidacy.

His campaign expenditures had put Bush $400,000 in debt. Although he had given up the race, he determined to pay his creditors. He promptly scheduled a series of receptions to attract additional donations. He managed to wipe the slate clean before the national convention in Detroit that summer.

What had gone wrong in Bush's campaign? From the beginning, public perception of the two had it that Reagan was the "Man with a Plan," and Bush, the "Man Who Can." After all, Bush could boast numerous accomplishments.

Perhaps Bush failed to produce a ringing, hard-hitting, easy-to-grasp theme. He had made a commendable effort to master the issues. In the Kennebunkport study seminars, he had boned up on America's problems and the positions he should take on them. Yet these thoughts had never coalesced into a compelling, saleable vision of what he would do as president.

Facing him was Reagan, also a Man Who Can, whose considerable successes as a governor put him in good stead. Additionally, Reagan could trot out a market-tested spiel that he had been airing for years, first in the institutional advertising for General Electric and then as a local, regional, and national political personality. He had been calling for a renewal of faith in America, strong defense, better morality among the citizens, and confidence in the private enterprise system.

The Republicans' conservative wing adopted him as their hero. This set speech was enhanced by his ability to project it with a professional actor's polish.

George Bush had built a powerful organization from the nationwide clan of friends and associates he had collected since boyhood. He had lived and worked in so many places and organizations in and out of government, and been so popular along the way, that he could virtually command an army to rise and march with him.

The number and dedication of his adherents beggared the much-touted legions of family and friends behind Jack Kennedy in his day. In all fairness Bush made his run when he was more than 20 years older than Kennedy and had more children plus grandchildren.

So how did Reagan overcome Bush's great advantages of money and friends and Republican regulars from his tour as chairman of the national committee? There were probably two main reasons: First, Reagan already had mounted a formidable assault group in 1976 and also was nationally known through his films; second, Reagan cracked Bush's armor at the Nashua debate, and he never recovered.

It was not a complete failure. Bush had made his mark as the undisputed runner-up. He had lined up many pledged delegates, and so had to be counted a likely candidate for the second spot on the Republican ticket. But, once more, Bush's destiny lay in the hands of others.

In June a national survey by Republican pollster Richard Wirthlin indicated that Reagan's most-promising picks (in order) would be Ford, Bush, and Howard Baker, with Paul Laxalt and Jack Kemp distant possibilities. But until the mid-July Republican convention in Detroit, Reagan forces kept mum as to their leader's preference. James Baker, who had served as Bush's manager, figured that Ford would not deign to play second fiddle in a band he once had conducted. So, said Baker, Bush would be the number-one choice.

Baker was a former Democrat and a graduate of Princeton whom Bush met in his early days in Houston. They had played tennis together and grown closer when Baker's wife had succumbed to cancer. Bush, already having lost his daughter to the same disease, offered deeply felt solace. Baker was a well-heeled lawyer and kept an eye on political currents and dynamics. Some would say in years ahead that some day he would like to be president. Meanwhile, he eventually switched to the Republican party.

Baker had proved to be a skillful political henchman in Bush's 1970 try for the Senate by helping him win 61 percent of Houston's vote. In 1976 he managed Gerald Ford's failed re-election bid. In 1978 Baker ran for attorney general of Texas and was beaten.

As the years passed Baker and Bush often chucked politics for the joys of fishing and wild turkey hunting on Baker's ranch. Another friend of Bush's, a Texas construction executive named Jack Fitch, introduced me to Baker in the spring of 1979. This was in a Houston men's lunch club. Baker struck me as a genial, alert businessman who might be a corporate CEO. We talked about Bush and he took my name to be on a fund-raising letterhead of some kind.

Bush's selection of Baker as manager shortly thereafter showed excellent judgment; Baker's acceptance was a tribute to Bush. Their professional alliance would flourish, as had their friendship of nearly 20 years. For one thing, they were honest with each other whether or not they agreed with each other's views. The stress of the situation leading up to Bush's departure from the 1980 primaries seemed to leave no distaste. Rather, the two worked closely right up to the convention itself.

As the great meeting drew nigh, there was little that Bush and his numerous fellow campaigners—like Baker, Dean Burch and dozens of others—could do except collect intelligence concerning the Reagan camp. What they soon discerned, along with sharp media observers, was the first outline of the "Dream Ticket": Reagan and Ford. Negotiators for the two already had met to hammer out the nitty-gritty of an association, and they continued to propose, promise and compromise until hours before the decision was to be announced.

Bush was selected to make one of the convention's opening addresses, and when he did so in Detroit, the "Dream Ticket" still was percolating. In an interview with Walter Cronkite, Ford delineated his wishes and revealed that he envisioned himself as a sort of co-president with Reagan. Reagan would handle domestic issues and Ford would deal with foreign affairs and defense. He didn't go so far as to specify who actually would be in charge or who would sit in the Oval Office.

Political cognoscenti knew immediately that Ford had

cooked his own goose. Anyone who knew Reagan couldn't imagine him agreeing to cede 50 percent of his power to Ford just to lever him onto the ticket.

A news blackout followed. Bush and his gang of friends, supporters, and family milled about gloomily in their convention suite at the Hotel Ponchartrain. They were fairly sure that Ford had talked himself out of the vice presidency, but they had no clue that Reagan might shift to Bush.

Bush's speech had gained a warm reception, but on his way to the podium one of the convention staffers greeted him with the words, "I'm sorry, Mr. Bush, I was pulling for you." He explained that Reagan had picked Ford. When Bush spoke, he rallied his own delegates to get behind Reagan.

Bush was telling himself not to stew over matters he couldn't control, when two telephone calls broke his concentration. First, an agent of the Secret Service called to report they had just installed themselves two floors below him, and that he should let them know if he needed anything.

As he puzzled over the significance of that statement, Bush took the next call and heard, "Hello, George, this is Ron Reagan. I'd like to go over to the convention and announce that you're my choice for vice president . . . if that's all right with you." Bush didn't hesitate. "I'd be honored, Governor."[19]

As this bulletin hit the scores of loyalists gathered in Bush's hotel quarters, they erupted, I am told, into a bedlam of exultation.

After this reaction calmed into a semblance of order, Bush shared with his cohorts the details of his conversation with Reagan. The governor had given Bush the opening to express any reservations he might have in becoming his partner. Bush assured him there were no reservations and said he was comfortable with the ticket. They agreed to meet in the morning with their wives.

The switch was nearly instantaneous. The fierce rivalry dissolved and ripened into a jovial and trusting partnership. Both men from that moment assiduously guarded their commitment to the ticket and its platform.

These two had been at each other's political throats for over a year. Reagan reportedly had sneered that George hadn't displayed much courage on the night of the Nashua confrontation. George and his team had expressed doubts that a glitzy Hollywood star could be a serious contender for the presidency. Now, they automatically put these slights behind them, demonstrating anew the dictum that one should never get so angry at someone that one can't some day be his friend.

Although Bush journeyed, worked, and spoke across the nation with prodigious vigor, the burden of the next three months of campaigning fell on Reagan. It was his act, and he gloried in it. Every time Jimmy Carter tried to gain some altitude, Reagan shot him on the rise. "There you go again!" was Reagan's affable putdown as Carter attempted to attack him in their national debate.

On election day in November 1980, the Reagan-Bush ticket sailed to an easy victory.

Bush's 25 years of activism in pro bono works, hard-fought electoral campaigns, high-level executive leadership in government, business achievement, wartime heroism, personal decency and genuine gregariousness had brought him to within a heartbeat of the highest office in the land.

CHAPTER 14

Vice President

IF VIGOROUS ACTIVISTS LIKE TEDDY ROOSEVELT, Richard Nixon and Lyndon Johnson rose to high office by virtue of extraordinary energy, they also realized that as vice presidents they had to curb their drives and allow their presidents to reign supreme.

The vice president who fails to keep his own agenda under wraps fails as vice president. George Bush understood this truth well when he became vice president in 1981. He instantly stored away even the merest hint of competition with the president.

Bush faced more perils than most vice presidents. The Reagan White House was held by two groups, and both were as suspicious as guard dogs. First, the "Reaganauts," as some called them, were long-time California henchmen who occupied key posts around the president. They dated back to Reagan's days as governor. The second group were the arch-conservatives who grumbled at Bush's selection in the first place. Both types questioned Bush's bona fides. In him they saw a moderate and a menace to the purity of their ideology.

They circled him like sharks. Bush came to believe that his

salvation lay in convincing the president of his total loyalty. If
he could win Reagan's confidence, Bush reasoned, the Reagan
faithful would follow.

Bush assiduously pursued this policy for a year. He selected
a politically neutral staff. He made certain his office kept a low
profile. As for himself, he kept mum with the press, studied
hard to comprehend the wide-ranging issues before the presidency and just listened in cabinet meetings. He discovered
this last tactic was essential when a comment he offered in the
supposed security of the cabinet room quickly surfaced in a
newspaper.

Gradually his circumspection bore fruit; the president grew
to like and trust him. The sharks soon swam off to circle other
meat in the White House tank. Content with Bush's sincerity,
the president grew to enjoy their weekly private lunches together and soon no topic was taboo between them as long as it
remained confidential.

Apparently, what was for public consumption were the jokes
they told each other. The president liked to use Bush as a
source for his own ever-growing repertoire, according to cabinet members. "Tell them that latest one, George," Reagan often
would say at cabinet meetings. Or, if Bush called Reagan when
he was with the cabinet or whomever, Reagan would say, "Put
him through, I want to hear the latest."

From the outset of his vice presidency, Bush had the benefit
of Mondale's experience. Despite their tangling with each
other in the slam-bang campaign of 1980, Mondale was coop-
erative and open about telling Bush what had worked for him
as Carter's vice president.

Three points impressed Bush in particular and he adopted
them. First, Mondale suggested that he have an office in the
West Wing of the White House, near the Oval Office, so that he
would be easily accessible to the president.

Second, like Mondale, Bush asked that he receive all the
communications that went to the president, including the classified ones.

Finally, Mondale advised that Bush not let himself be so

burdened with small assignments that he would not be free to handle the important jobs that the president asked him to undertake. This is a real danger, since most cabinet members' perception is that the vice president has no constitutional responsibilities except to be president of the Senate. Hence, odd jobs that don't fall automatically in any one department often fall on the shoulders of the vice president.

Bush surveyed the vice presidency. He and Barbara moved into an airy, large-roomed Victorian structure on the grounds of the Naval Observatory. It stands free amid twelve acres of lawns, gardens and trees just above the corner of Massachusetts Avenue and 34th Street in northwest Washington.

The Bushes soon were comfortably ensconced. They were fated to stay here longer in one stretch that in any previous dwelling place during their marriage. As in their previous 27 houses, they shared their table, their space and their family warmth. When friends appeared on their doorstep they could see right away the little boy whose nickname had been "Have Half."

George Bush wanted his friends to enjoy the kingly mansion and its pleasures. He would bound upstairs to show off his mechanical running machine, Barbara's floor-wide needlepoint rug that she created in China, or the near-empty but extensive greenhouse nearby.

Both he and Barbara welcomed people at the house generously for a drink before dinner, at a simple dinner party with old friends, for a brunch with former neighbors from Texas, or for receptions and formal dinners for 500 under a monstrous tent.

Barbara's candor was delivered with kindness, George's spontaneity was complemented by his remarkable knack for name recall. Not much escaped the vice president. One friend he didn't see very often appeared at two crowded receptions with the same lady. Although the parties occurred a year apart, when the pair filed through the receiving line along with a thousand other people, Bush perked up instantly. "Ha," he exclaimed, "You two are becoming an item!"

But what does the vice president do besides entertain? The answer is twofold: First, interact with his boss, the president; and second, everything else.

Bush began the first function shortly after the nominating convention. The two took off from Detroit in Reagan's campaign plane, a Boeing 727, on July 18. They landed in Houston to launch their joint venture for the nation's two top offices.

To demonstrate their unity they lunched together at Bush's house there. Houston staged a VIP motorcade, and the modest Bush was impressed by the large crowds wherever he and Reagan traveled that day. This is "a shade more ostentatious, I told Barbara, than my first arrival in Texas as an Ideco trainee just out of college, some thirty-two years before."[1]

His prime responsibility to the president was re-emphasized the day after the two were elected. It was November 5, 1988, and he was flying to Calfornia to huddle with his ex-rival and new chief. While airborne, he called four-star Admiral Daniel Murphy and asked him to be his chief of staff and kick off his other duties. Namely, he wanted Murphy to recruit the staff he would need to operate his four offices as vice president. Murphy had served under him at the CIA as deputy director for Administration. The admiral is a nattily dressed, alert veteran of numerous command posts in the navy. His sky-blue eyes under a thatch of gray reflect the steadiness of a commander and the fierce honesty characteristic of admirable political leaders.

Four offices. Only dentists, doctors, prostitutes and vice presidents, it seems, need multiple places of work. One office, as already stated, was close to the president's Oval Office. Nearby in the White House were the triumvirate that shouldered the chief of staff duties at the beginning of Reagan's first term: James A. Baker, III, Michael Deaver and Edward Meese.

Then there was a large, elegant suite at the Executive Office Building adjacent to the White House. Here, Murphy would sit and run the total staff of 68 people, two-thirds of which handled the clerical load. Twenty others tracked the major government issues. Then there was the office in the Capitol where Bush served as president of the Senate. The fourth office was located in a senate office building and gave Bush a base for lobbying senators and congressmen on administration matters. Finally, he maintained a fifth office in Houston for dealing with constituents of his home state. For the man who would be away from Washington 1,475 days out of the 2,677 on the job by April 30, 1988, Air Force 2 became a key office as well. Bush's trips as vice president included stops in 50 states, four territories, and 68 foreign countries.[2]

On Walker's Point in Kennebunkport, Bush set up still another informal den equipped for office work. This one is located in the building where his security personnel are stationed, some two hundred yards from the main house. This was unmanned except when he was in residence. So there were a total of seven offices in all for this peripatetic vice president. Only someone of exceptional energy could get around to this many places, much less use them fruitfully. Given Bush's penchant for endless personal note writing plus the constant load of briefing papers, it would appear that he needed every one of these work stations.

In recent years, certainly reflecting the plethora of press in Washington, vice presidents have been the subject and often the butt of more publicity than ever before. They have for the most part welcomed the attention, since the post is a way station to the highest political office.

Bush was no exception. But he came within inches of promotion on March 3, 1981. There was an eerie déjà vu about the day President Reagan was shot as he emerged from the Capitol Hilton Hotel. The seriously wounded president was rushed to George Washington Hospital for emergency treatment. The vice president was in Dallas, just as Johnson had been on November 22, 1963. At noon Bush had just dedicated the Old Texas Hotel in Fort Worth as a national historic site. Its new name was the Hyatt Regency Hotel; Kennedy had spent the night there on November 21, 1963—his last alive. Now Bush was headed for Austin in a plane Johnson had used as president. This was a Boeing 707 with lots of James Bond gimmicky gadgets that Johnson liked to play with including furniture and doors that magically appeared and disappeared.

En route, Bush was alerted of the shooting by Secretary of State Alexander M. Haig, Jr., who cautiously withheld details. Ever since Lincoln's assassination, attempts to kill a president have been evaluated as parts of a larger plot.

After the standard cautionary steps were pursued, Admiral Murphy verified the news, and at last specifics of the whole terrifying story were teletyped into the plane. Characteristically, Bush excused himself from his numerous fellow travelers—seven guests, twelve reporters, cameramen and the Secret Service detail—closed the door to his private cabin, and said prayers for the president.

In Washington key officials had gathered in the Situation Room at the White House awaiting Bush's return. Larry Speakes was answering press questions on live television. Secretary Haig, watching him, decided to clarify what he was saying. Haig rushed up to the press room, grabbed the microphone and declared "I am in control here (meaning the White House) until the vice president returns."

The scene was beamed nationwide. Unfortunately the secretary's manner struck most viewers as bizarre and nervous. Even worse, it was seen as an indication that he gratuitously was seeking power for himself. Haig's apologists argued that he was trying to act properly to let it be known that there was a constitutionally appointed man at the helm until the vice president arrived back at the Capitol. After the vice president, the secretary of state is the senior officer of the Executive Branch.

But the Constitution has been amended to designate the speaker of the House of Representatives, not the secretary of state, as the third in line for the presidency.

Many abhorred Haig's behavior. It seemed in keeping with the turf consciousness displayed in his request to be known as the "Vicar of Foreign Policy" and his fruitless fight to be named head of "Crisis Management" in Reagan's government. The president had chosen Bush instead, frustrating Haig.

Haig had presidential hopes himself up until this emergency. His "I'm in control here" lingered for years to haunt him. It appeared to be the prime reason he thereafter was rejected as a viable candidate for the White House. A four-star general acting uptight under pressure was simply out of character. His nervous system had doubtless lost some elasticity.

Meanwhile, on March 3, Bush ordered his plane to return to Washington after refueling at Austin. On arrival at Andrews Air Force Base, he rejected the suggestion of aides that he be flown to the White House by helicopter. They mentioned that it was rush hour: if he were helicoptered to the vice president's residence and then took the limousine, as was usual, he would be delayed in traffic. It was an emergency. He was urged to meet with the cabinet as soon as possible.

Bush was kind but firm. Quietly he reminded his advisors, "Only the president lands on the South Lawn (of the White House)."[3] He visualized the reaction of Americans and foreigners alike if he were to seem too eager to grab the reins. Either he would create fear that the president indeed was dying, he would be exhibiting unseemly ambition or both. He also wanted to spare Nancy Reagan the clatter of a helicopter descending outside her windows during what had become a stressful time for her.

Sometime after 7 P.M. Bush arrived at the White House and called the cabinet together. He was careful to sit in his normal seat at the cabinet table.

At 8:20 he and Larry Speakes went to the press briefing room. White House spokesman Jim Brady had been shot in the head by Reagan's assailant, John W. Hinckley, Jr., and Speakes had stepped up as his deputy. He explained that Bush would make a statement, but would not take questions. Bush declared confidently: "I can reassure this nation and the watching world that the American government is functioning fully and effectively."[4]

He paid particular attention to the CIA's daily reports while the president recuperated in the hospital, so that he would not be caught off guard by events elsewhere in the world.

Throughout the crisis Bush handled himself with grace and restraint. His firm and modest demeanor was not lost on Americans who watched him in action, including the cabinet, other government leaders, the public and even the hard-eyed Washington press corps.

When the president recovered, he realized along with everyone else that the vice president had acquitted himself well. Bush had proven himself under duress, and this time in a role floating on political quicksand. One Reagan aide reportedly said, "He had a perfect touch. In the moments after the shooting, you knew that the situation was not exactly harmonious among some of the rest of the people in the administration. But Bush came through like a star."[5]

Bush was exhibiting backbone in other quarters. At fundraisers his speeches drew $3.5 million for Republican candidates in 1981. Before Labor Secretary Raymond J. Donovan's proposal for a job safety regulation was considered, Bush reportedly insisted that he do some more homework. Additionally, the president felt the thrust of Bush's recommendation to let the sale of AWAC planes and equipment be approved and saw Bush's persistent lobbying to persuade the Senate not to block it.[6]

Bush was a bit too hearty in a toast he delivered in the Philippines to President Ferdinand Marcos, who had kept his country under martial law for many years. He spoke of the love that Americans have for your "adherence to democratic principles and to the democratic processes."[7]

Bush worked diligently on a dozen fronts, and conservative Republicans sometimes were uneasy about his moderate ways. He was often the featured speaker at black colleges and publicly conferred with black leaders and entertainers. Without fanfare, he spent a weekend in 1982 with a diplomat from the Cameroons who had recently had a cross burned on his lawn in nearby Silver Spring, Maryland.

The right-wing people could not have been pleased with one particular event I witnessed in Newport early in the Reagan-Bush term. The vice president had just arrived at a large guest subscription dinner for perhaps 1,000 people. The affair was given under a tent outside the mansion where the movie of Fitzgerald's *The Great Gatsby* had been filmed. A hundred yards or so offshore, a Coast Guard cutter provided security for the vice president.

When I greeted him on the dais, he asked me to introduce him to key Republicans present from around the state. I agreed to do that, but before I did, I told him about a black diplomat from a small African country who was in town for the weekend and who wanted to meet the vice president. Sure, he said, and spent several minutes with the African, who had neither votes nor money, but went away vastly flattered.

As in his first race in Texas, Bush continued to reach out beyond traditional limits to attract more blacks into Republicanism. He wanted the party to be one of inclusion rather than exclusion, as he would put it in the campaign of 1988.

As 1984 approached the president made it clear he wanted to keep Bush on the ticket. He already had several merit badges. One was for keeping the peace in a turf battle that repeatedly had appeared in previous administrations. This was the tug-of-war between the national security advisor and the White House versus the secretary of state. The national security advisor, as established under President Eisenhower, was to coordinate views and information of the National Security Council for the president. The members of the Security Council are the secretaries of defense, state, vice president and president. Normally the director of the CIA and the chairman of the Joint Chiefs of Staff attend the meetings as advisors.

After the smooth performance of Gordon Gray* as national security advisor under President Eisenhower, subsequent incumbents of that office began to take advantage of the physical proximity to the White House and actually compete with the secretary of state in establishing foreign policy. Strong personalities like McGeorge Bundy, Walter Rostow, Henry Kissinger—who at one time was both national security advisor and secretary of state—and Zbigniew Brzezynski often operated closely with the president. This situation clearly imperiled the influence of the secretary of state.

*Gordon Gray's son, C. Boyden Gray, is George Bush's long-time áide.

At the beginning of Reagan's first term, this scenario was set
to repeat itself. Richard Allen, who possessed a forceful personality, and Secretary of State Alexander Haig faced each
other from opposite corners. Like their predecessors these two
were positioned for confrontation. Haig moved first and inti-
mated he would brook no interference. To avoid confusion in
case of emergency, the president decided to appoint someone
to head crisis management. He ignored the vying between
Allen and Haig and picked George Bush.

Shortly thereafter Bush kept the peace between these two
factions. He came up with a recommendation, which they
accepted and the president adopted, to deal with a crisis in
Poland over the Solidarity labor union.

Bush's heaviest specific assignment in Reagan's first term
began in February 1981. That was when the president told
Bush to make good his campaign pledge to reduce needless
federal regulations. Reagan's victory had stemmed, at least in
part, from a belief in his ability to help both large and small
businesses. There certainly was much waste in the mere filling
out of forms and the exercise of restrictions that bureaucrats
were requiring.

For the next two-and-a-half years, Bush chaired the task
force to attempt deregulation. He and Reagan soon discovered
that Americans did not object to environmental regulations
fashioned to cut pollution.

The administration's first chief of the Environmental Protection Agency did not understand this distinction. Administrator Anne Gorsuch of Denver, Colorado, tried to back away
from some of the controls that the EPA had established. Additionally, there was evidence that at least one of her assistant
administrators was influenced by polluters. Together, the two
developments infuriated the ecologically conscious. They initiated legal action and launched a broad counterattack.

Mrs. Gorsuch tried to argue that she was only cutting costs,
deregulating and doing the new president's will. There was
indication that she had been encouraged by some in the White
House, but when the suits and prosecutions and widespread

complaints combined to drive her from office, the president let her go.

While she still was there, the vice president did side with her in the reduction of the lead in gasoline standards. For technical reasons, leading environmentalists grumbled that he was legally out of order in interjecting himself into the process.

But before Bush's name could be tarnished, Anne Gorsuch was rolled in the giant combers of citizen outrage. The president appointed a sort of bureaucratic SWAT team under White House operative Lee Verstandig to assume temporary charge of the beleaguered agency. Former EPA people, myself included, provided free counsel to Verstandig until a replacement could be found for the administrator. It was now the spring of 1983.

Soon a consensus was reached both in and out of government to bring in William D. Ruckelshaus. Like Bush, a noble stalwart of the Nixon years, he had started EPA in the first place, later bailed out the FBI from its troubles and eventually sacrificed his attorney general position rather than fire Watergate Special Prosecutor Archibald Cox. Ruckelshaus left the vice presidency of the Weyerhaeuser Lumber Company and reluctantly headed back into battle.

The president promised Ruckelshaus that he could have the people he wanted and the money and freedom of action he required to restore the agency's morale and effectiveness. Reagan honored his commitment and thus put out the fire. From that moment in 1983 until the end of his term, Reagan suffered no more serious flak from the environmentalists, although they had branded him as an implacable enemy on this issue. Bush also would be marked in campaigns to come as an anti-environmentalist, in part because of his success in running the deregulation task force.

A report of the Reagan administration's regulatory achievements was released on August 11, 1983. Bush could point proudly to solid results in reversing the slowdowns due to needless regulatory practices. In fact, the White House claimed that its reform of federal regulations had brought the creation of new jobs, reduction of inflation and increased competitiveness with foreign producers.

Some specific boasts were that $100 billion in regulatory costs in the 1980s had been eliminated that would otherwise have been paid by consumers, businesses and governments. Also, 600 million man hours of annual paperwork had been cut out. Finally, there was a dramatic reduction in the growth of the regulatory bureaucracy (as measured by Washington University's Center for the Study of American Business.)[8]

CHAPTER 15

Reaching Out of the Vice Presidency

A PROMINENT COLLEGE DEAN IN WASHINGTON WHO admires George Bush concurred with the critics in mid-campaign 1988 in saying that you can't define the man. Bush is like water; he takes the shape of his container. Another former neighbor from Midland, Texas days described him similarly. Bush must have his parameters set for him; that done, he operates well within them. Of course, what these people referred to is his ability or lack of ability to create public policy and lay out a vision for how he would govern the United States.

By 1985 Bush had logged sixty years on planet Earth. Until then he had never lacked for a goal. The many goals he sought required varying tactics, and he was innovative and persistent in developing them.

A tennis partner, Tony Thompson, gives a droll example of how the vice president's mind works. One can assume that if he has tactics like this for sport, he will think up analogous

197

moves in politics. Naturally, he is not going to talk about them as he did in this tennis story.

Thompson's example: "He loves to hit a little backhand thing which he calls the Falling Leaf. It is sort of a drop volley. Sort of an angle drop volley. And he'll say, 'Oh jeepers, I mean, that is awesome.'" Thompson was a handler before the debate with 1984 Democratic vice-presidential candidate Geraldine Ferraro. He recalls that with the group who were giving him a run-through of likely questions and answers, he asked, "Mr. Vice President, do you regard the Falling Leaf as a strategic or tactical, offensive or defensive weapon?"[1]

Bush promptly declared that it was an offensive weapon and that was the difference between the Mondale-Ferraro and Reagan-Bush teams. The Democratic ticket always was defensive, the Republicans offensive. After the debate Bush pencilled a note to Thompson on the evening's printed program. It read, "Dear Tony, the leaf has fallen."

Once Bush had analyzed the realities of his vice presidency, he set his own limits and tactics for the first four years. Admiral Daniel J. Murphy, his chief of staff for that period, talks about how Bush fashioned his habits to meet his aims.[2]

To begin with, Murphy found the vice president's self-discipline outstanding. When I quoted Bush's legal counsel, C. Boyden Gray, as saying that Bush arrived in his offices at 7 or 7:30 every morning, the admiral corrected me.

"He arrived at exactly 7:20. I know exactly how his day went," the admiral added. "Boyden wouldn't know, because he never got in that early. But I had to get in ahead of him— can't have a chief of staff get in after the boss. So I had to get in about 7:15." This aside, coming with no rancor, furnished a fleeting insight in the lifestyle difference between lawyers and naval officers.

The admiral continued, "He would often have an appointment, perhaps a photo op, because for the rest of the day you don't have time to get these people in. So there would be early, quick things, not more than ten minutes each. One of his buddies is in town. Come on in. Have breakfast. He would have breakfast at his desk, if he was alone. Usually a little cereal and melon. I can't remember coffee or tea. Probably tea. He was great for tea. And we had a steward."

"A Filipino from the navy?" I asked, since it has long been traditional for the navy to detail Filipino-born mess stewards to the White House mess.

"Yes. He's retired, a civilian, but ex-navy. Or he might have the press in for breakfast."

Then Murphy would be off to James A. Baker's (Reagan's chief of staff for the first term) early meeting. At first it was 8:00, then it was pushed back to 7:30. Murphy would carry Baker any messages or questions from the vice president.

Then Bush's intense formal schedule commenced at 8:00 with a CIA briefing (identical to the president's, but delivered separately to Bush). Don Gregg, Bush's national security advisor, would sit in.

Somehow Bush would squeeze in a perusal of the daily newspapers and be at Chief of Staff Baker's 9:00 briefing of the president. Following that, he attended the president's national security briefing.

The admiral sketched the tableau of those meetings in the Oval Office: "The president sits in front of the fireplace in the big white-backed chair, and Bush sits in the other chair. The national security guy sits on the couch."

Other meetings followed, continuing for the rest of the day. They might involve Bush's task forces on drug interdiction or deregulation. Or Bush might attend a gathering of the NSPG (National Security Policy Group) that handled covert activities—"sensitive stuff, use of military forces, that kind of thing," the admiral explained.

He also spelled out why Bush was apt to remain quiet in cabinet sessions. "He does not want his position to be compromised in front of the whole cabinet, where he's going to show that he is agreeing with Haig and disagreeing with Weinberger or vice versa. Because, in his mind, for him to run afoul of one of the department heads undermines his own ability to go in and talk to the president openly. So he doesn't. He talks to the president either before a meeting like that or after the meeting."[2]

Bush generally took an hour for lunch, often sharing it at his desk in the EOB (Executive Office Building) with a guest or group of guests. The admiral emphasized that Bush called his office in the West Wing of the White House his headquarters. He didn't want to risk losing that symbol of tight proximity to the president. He added that Bush would split his time about 50/50 between the White House and the EOB. That didn't leave much time for his two other offices on Capitol Hill. Since he was away from Washington at least a third of his tour, he divided his attention among three more offices—in Houston, Kennebunkport and Air Force II.

By 6 P.M. on an average Washington day, Bush would quit his office world for home or his many official social functions. If office work held him past 6, he would take a break at that hour to try to sandwich in a tennis game or a run before returning to finish the evening's tasks. The admiral's final comment on the vice president's day: "He's very, very good at doing homework. You give him a paper at 4, you will have it back the next morning with his views on it."

When Bush appointed Craig Fuller to replace Murphy as chief of staff in 1985, he began to redirect his thoughts and schedules toward his political goal: He was now reaching out from the vice presidency toward the presidency.

It is relevant to remember that the president and vice president must give the political dimension priority in every policy formation or action. They were elected by the people to serve the people, and to do that properly requires staying abreast of what people are thinking and how they react to their government's moves. The president never acts in a vacuum, even when he's trying to be statesmanlike, for ultimately he depends on the people's approval.

Moreover, the president is the titular head of his party and therefore has the duty of encouraging good candidates to succeed him. Although the president had not yet committed himself publicly to Bush in 1985, he only could approve his positioning himself toward the nomination in 1988.

Part of this positioning was to identify issues that had voter appeal and take a stand that could both help the country and his own popularity.

One such issue was the idea of promoting alternate fuels to cut down on the air pollution from gasoline. Through advisor C. Boyden Gray he steadfastly pursued the possibilities of using methanol or ethanol, for example, to replace or blend with gasoline. Gray, a lawyer with a brilliant academic record, embraced this issue with enthusiasm. The vice president saw it as a positive matter for Gray to concentrate on, because it potentially carried both an environmental and economic benefit to the country.

Methanol is a methane gas that is given off by rotting animal or vegetable matter. It is found in combination with crude oil or in isolation as a "natural" gas. It can power automobiles if they are modified somewhat to burn it. Its great advantage is that a car's exhausts will contain considerably less pollution than from purely gasoline-driven engines.

Ethanol is derived from corn and other grains in a rather expensive conversion; it can be combined with ordinary gasoline in varying percentages, and the resulting exhaust emissions will also carry reduced pollution.

Vice President Bush promoted increased use of these compounds because each aided the fight for cleaner air, but he particularly pushed ethanol because he saw it as a way to whittle down the grain surpluses—the eight billion bushels of corn in particular. Every barrel of ethanol would lower the nation's need to import oil and thereby assist in lessening the trade deficit.

At the same time that barrel would provide an outlet for the surplus grains. With less surplus grains the farmers would be drawing less agricultural price supports and hence draining fewer tax dollars from the public. However, the vice president did not have an easy time with this issue.

Actual figures on exactly how ethanol manufacture impacts the bulging grain elevators are not readily found. Critics of ethanol argue that the substance is too expensive to produce both in dollars and in the quantities of fuel required for the conversion from grain. They say there is a net loss both in money and energy in the final product.

Boyden Gray often lobbied the Environmental Protection Agency to pursue these alternate fuels as part of their strategy for implementing the Clean Air Act. For a time he met with a rather small hello. Finally the vice president's regulatory task force required the EPA to issue industry guidelines for the use of alternate fuels. It was a bureaucratic victory, but Bush could also claim some effect on industry as well. The Archer, Daniel, Midland company, in particular, has built a sizeable market for ethanol.

In 1982 President Reagan responded to the Miami cries for help in curtailing the rampant drug trafficking and associated crimes in the area by creating the South Florida Task Force. Its purpose was to interdict the flow of drugs into the United States. He put George Bush in charge. Bush promptly studied the situation and promised remedial action, which was accomplished within a month: specifically, he succeeded in providing more jail space, more judges, more courtrooms, a permanent U.S. Attorney, more prosecutors, more law enforcement people—including the FBI, Customs, the IRS, DEA and an increase in military assistance from Coast Guard cutters and planes, Navy ships and planes—and help from the Army, Air Force and Marines. Whereupon President Reagan, using the South Florida Task Force as a model, expanded these efforts to the rest of the nation. He converted the task force into the National Narcotics Border Interdiction System (NNBIS). Bush, as chairman of NNBIS, set about melding and coordinating the existing government programs. This meant persuading such agencies as the Drug Enforcement Administration, the Customs Service, the Coast Guard, the FBI, the U.S. Border Patrol and the Department of Defense to put aside turf battles and concentrate on the target: an illegal drug trade that threatens America's moral and physical health.

In assessing the effect of the vice president's war on drugs, his chief of staff, Admiral Daniel J. Murphy, pointed out that NNBIS was only responsible for the interdiction program. It was not responsible for the measures necessary in the source countries, the effectiveness of law enforcement in the United States and the curbing of drug users in the United States. The admiral counts the vice president's record on this specific front in the drug war as highly successful. But the administration didn't put enough money into the job. It would take a fulltime flotilla of ships and planes to stop the inflow over the vast U.S. border.

Most vice presidents are free to go wherever and virtually whenever they choose. George Bush's regular duties on the regulatory and drug task forces were completed in his second term. Except for specific surprises, like the president's bouts with cancer, George Bush could schedule himself as he saw fit for both political purposes and recreation.

He planned his time to include fairly frequent forays to Kennebunkport between 1985 and 1988. Such weekends replenished his own reservoir of energy and refreshed his spirit.

Early in his first term, he sold his house in Houston and took the payment to acquire the big house on Walker's Point from his relatives. There is an irony to this move. He had spent over thirty years trying to take on the coloration of a Texan. Now he had unloaded his house in Texas and was trying to reduce his taxes on the argument that his main dwelling was in Maine. This was the same George Bush who could call a half-dozen states home during his career. He might fairly be judged an ersatz Texan, but he is 100-percent American.

Meanwhile, the IRS refused to grant him a tax reduction on this transaction. They ruled that his official vice-presidential residence was his home and therefore Walker's Point would count as a home away from home. In short, Bush now owed the government more than $200,000 in taxes. He was incensed at what he considered an inequity, but with customary self-control, he didn't allow himself the luxury of lashing back at the IRS. He paid up, just as would be expected of any other citizen.

The salubrious breezes of Kennebunkport soon cooled him and the friendly attitude of the year-rounders cheered him.

Among these was Kenneth Raynor, the local pro at Kennebunkport's Cape Arundel Golf Club. The husky, blond, mustachioed six-footer had a lot to say in the spring of 1988, but it was not about the upcoming hard-knuckled campaign for the presidency. He wanted to talk about his golfing and fishing pal, George Bush—"The Vice"—as he called him.

"The Vice loves to look for balls. We'll be playing along, and all of a sudden he disappears. We find him reaching down into the water to rescue a golf ball." The club rises off the banks of the tidal Kennebunkport River. Balls often get lost in the nine-foot tides. Come ebb tide, a player can find balls that others knocked in at high tide.

"He's also a great mudder," Raynor continues, speaking in his private room behind the pro shop of the club. On one wall hangs "The Vice's" fishing rod, which Raynor says sadly hadn't seen much use for the past year due to politics.

"It rains a lot up here," Raynor says, "and about half the time it will rain torrents right in the middle of his game. Everyone else heads for shelter, but not the Vice. To the discomfort of the Secret Service, he'll insist on finishing the match."

Former Senator and Secretary of State Edmund Muskie tells about the game he and Bush had with their respective pros, Raynor and the man from Muskie's club in the next town. At the end the game was tied. "Aw shucks," said Bush, "that was about as exciting as kissing your sister."

Raynor laughs at that account of Bush's competitive nature. "He never gives up. For example, he put a shot in the water once, and to get it out he had to stand with one foot in the mud and the other on the grass. It was about the third hole and he hit it very well, but he scooped up so much mud he was covered with it. He said that when he got home, Barbara was furious.

"He definitely doesn't want to waste time on the golf course. We accuse him of playing cart polo. He never goes around in longer than two-and-a-half hours; his record, with a foursome playing, is two hours and five minutes.

"If you haven't played with him before, you have to get used to playing George Bush golf. He wants to hit and move, not wait around like so many golfers. I have had to learn to walk fast and then slow down for the shot. He writes left-handed but plays golf right-handed.

"He thoroughly enjoys seeing other players and is concerned about interrupting them. Other players are astounded by his flamboyance. He goes through, shakes hands with everybody, throws them a couple of bags of tees with his name on them or other memorabilia. The Vice may be playing with his son, or whomever, and, when he leaves, the group he's going through has grins stretching from here to here. Innumerable times he'll kid with them: 'Sit back and watch if you want to see a perfect shot. You'll see golf history made here.'

"He does *not* want to putt or hit pitches or come out of traps. He's good from tee to green, but when he gets near the green he can't seem to loosen his wrists and he hits awkwardly from there on in.

"The Vice has told me that he likes to play here, because it gives him an opportunity to share some family time with his sons and son-in-law." With that, Raynor showed me a golf card, filled out by Bush, of the scores made in a game with his son-in-law Richard LeBlond, Ken Raynor and tennis champion Ivan Lendl. Lendl shot an 85, one under Bush.

Much of what Bush does seems to reflect a desire to emulate his father, but to eliminate his mistakes. Golf was one area in which Prescott Bush might have been a bit kinder to those on the course with him. Fellow members of the Chevy Chase Club in Washington remember the senator and his wife carrying their own bags and hurrying through all the other players. One victim of this practice, Mrs. Hamilton Robinson of Washington, grins as she remembers one day when she encountered Prescott Bush at Chevy Chase.

"We were pitching up to the fifteenth green when a golf ball rolled swiftly between my feet," she recounts. "I looked behind and saw that it was Senator Bush who had barely missed me. Well, I had a nine iron in my hands, so I just smacked that ball off into the woods. Last I saw the senator, he still was hunting for his ball."

"Did he ever say anything to you?" I asked her.

"No."

Democrat Harry McPherson, the political writer with a literary touch, deftly describes Bush from his point of view: "Pres Bush was fashionable and decent, a contemporary money aristocrat whom a John Cheever hero would have met at a party, but in whose pool he would not have swum."[3]

Some who knew the senator at Kennebunkport found that he was a bit stand-offish with local tradespeople and year-round neighbors—"Mainers" they call themselves. Not so George. He talks to everyone regardless of station. Anyone who lives there and has dealings with the Bushes is apt to find himself invited for food or drink at Walker's Point.

These people seem not to be impressed by the glitz, glitter and glamor of Bush, the international celebrity—though these elements can enhance the love and affection that one human may feel for another. With Bush, however, there appears to be a reason for each individual "Mainer's" fondness, gratitude or admiration.

For example, one of the numerous Hutchins in town lost her husband and Bush called her in Florida until he finally got through to her at midnight, interrupting his own high-level meetings in order to do so.

Another Hutchins, a lobster wholesaler named Sonny, spoke to me about Bush in clipped, even New England sentences while convalescing from a hurt back. Bush and the locals deal with each other in a relaxed way, he said. After all, "We've always had famous people come here in the summer—like Booth Tarkington, Kenneth Roberts; we talk with them and that's the end of it." The message is clear: There is no fanfare. You either fit in or you don't.

"Last week, Bush was here. He and Mrs. Bush were walking over the bridge in town and I tooted and waved and kept right on going. He's just one of the people when he's around here. He goes to church with all the people in town who go to the church up there; he's one of the natives."

A year or two earlier, one Kennebunkport parent asked Bush to speak at the local high school graduation. He not only spoke but also stayed and handed out several hundred diplomas.

In interviews with storekeepers and tradespeople, the story was the same: All expressed affection and pleasure to have the man in their midst.

All seem to concur that what distinguishes Bush is his loyalty, his commitment to friends and family. Early in his vice presidency, this quality was tested when his older brother, Pres Jr., announced that he would make a try for the U.S. Senate from his Greenwich, Connecticut, home base. The older Bush was a respected insurance executive who like his father had done more than his share of civic duty. In the family tradition he now was ready to sip the seductive brew of appointive politics.

George's reaction was straightforward. He said fine, you've always supported me, and I'll do everything possible to help you. When George informed President Reagan that his brother was seeking office, Reagan allegedly told him "not to worry about it; I've got my own problems with Maureen." At that time his politically active daughter was laying the groundwork to become co-chairman of the Republican National Committee.

There was no conflict of loyalty in either case. Pres Jr. appealed to friends like myself who had contributed to George over the years, and we happily responded. He ran a good effort but the competition was too stiff. Although he spent about a million dollars and developed a small army of backers, he was wiped out before the primary election. Politics can be an unforgiving mistress for those of us who fail to win her favors.

By 1987 George had to begin to dust off his own laurels as his presidential campaign began to take shape. Boyden Gray cites Bush's little-known accomplishments in moving the administration toward concrete goals.

According to Gray, when the crunch came as to how to deal with the U.S.-Japan trade imbalance, for example, Bush was able to head off a disastrous trend toward protectionism. The vice president occasionally was willing to speak up on issues that would advance the nation's cause, although speaking up might be politically perilous. But having achieved some forward movement, he would be wise enough to resist grabbing credit. He was so modest about affecting the car imports com-

promise with the Japanese, suggests Gray, that Secretary of
State Haig took the bows himself.

One kind of bow-taking George never indulged in was the
sort of commercialization one of his predecessors displayed in
1954. It was Sam Huff Day at Griffith Stadium in honor of the
great linebacker of the Washington Redskins. At halftime Sam
Huff stood on the 50-yard line as the tributes were spoken. The
cheers for each succeeding bit of praise rose to a crescendo
until a brand new sedan was driven slowly out on the field to
be presented to Huff. The door opened and out stepped the
vice president of the United States, Richard M. Nixon.

The stands erupted with boos, whistles and catcalls. Although I was in the stands, I could not determine whether the
reaction was one of anger, disdain or just irritation that the VP
had the poor taste to try to cash in on Sam Huff's glory.

Bush earned some glory for himself for his stop in El Salvador, although the American public knew little of what he
had done there. He had gone in December of 1983 to deliver
the United States' message against that country's death squads.
He was received amid excessive security to protect him and
the militaristic hierarchy surrounding President Alvaro
Magana.

This group included Jose Napoleon Duarte, who would succeed Magana and the commandantes who operated the death
squads to crush enemies of the regime. Tanks, missile carriers
and soldiers accompanied Bush to a rough-hewn dinner where
he delivered his undisguised rebuke. The regime feared attack
from either the Nicaraguan-funded rebels or perhaps their own
right-wing death squads.

Bush came to the point in a formal toast he was invited to
make. First, he blew them a few compliments like "Mr. President, you and many other Salvadorans have demonstrated
extraordinary personal courage in the struggle against tyranny
and extremism."

Then he unloaded, "But your cause is being undermined by
the murderous violence of reactionary minorities. These right-
wing fanatics are the best friends the Soviets, the Cubans, the
Sandinistas, and the Salvadoran guerillas have. Every mur-

derous act they commit poisons the well of friendship between our two countries and helps impose an alien dictatorship on the people of El Salvador. These cowardly death-squad terrorists are just as repugnant to me . . . President Reagan . . . and the American people . . . as the terrorists of the left."[4] This from the vice president who was soon to encounter the "wimp" epithet from his detractors at home.

While being tough as necessary, Bush had exhibited his "kinder, gentler" side. Boyden Gray recounts how deeply he would get involved with various handicapped groups. Gray quotes Dr. Henry B. Betts of the Betts Rehabilitation Institute of Chicago: "I just don't know where your boss learned these issues. How did he learn to deal with these people?"[5]

Gray thinks it may have to do with his daughter's death from leukemia and son Neil's dyslexia. Others with disabilities insist, Gray adds, that Bush is "one of only two modern-day politicians who can make instant rapport with the disabled. The other one is Jesse Jackson."

Gray also mentions a report from the Twentieth-Century Fund, which credits the vice president with the maintenance of civil rights statutes for the benefit of the disabled. "We're talking about 36 million Americans, one helluva large minority group, for whom the vice president has set the policy," concluded Gray."

Certainly a root reason for Bush's solicitude for others' physical vicissitudes is the full plate of suffering among his own brood. The latest incidence centered on Marvin (29) in 1986. He began to experience symptoms similar to those of President Reagan when he had cancer of the colon. He kept the condition quiet, thinking that whatever ailed him would not threaten his healthy athletic physique. But his secret illness persisted, and after a dramatic attack on an airline, he deplaned in Denver, where his brother Neil lives and works in the oil business. With Neil's help, he returned home to Alexandria, Virginia.

When his father learned of Marvin's condition, he remembered his own struggles with an ulcer and urged Marvin to lighten up on his schedule.

Shortly thereafter, Marvin entered Georgetown University Hospital in Washington, D.C., and a terrifying, six-week ordeal commenced. The doctors' examination found a severe, chronic irritation of the lower colon. They ordered a colostomy. This reroutes body wastes to a permanent, artificial opening in the abdomen.

Marvin grew extremely sick. Although his wife Margaret was at his side, Barbara would join her during some of the day and George would stop on his way to and from the White House. The severity of Marvin's malady registered on him when he saw his dad spend entire days at the edge of his bed, silently pencilling his way through piles of government papers.

But Barbara and George were ready to will Marvin through his crisis if they could. They were determined not to lose another child to disease. Once he was headed for recovery, they encouraged him to accept the permanent reminder of his disability. George let the former star place kicker of the San Diego Chargers, Ron Benirschke, know what had happened. Having undergone the same surgery, Benirschke assured Marvin that life could go on normally despite the little sack by his abdomen.

Much has been said about George the politician. Privately, friends of the Bushes have been heard to say that Barbara could get elected to most any office she might seek. This is a woman who possesses a keen analytic intellect. I learned of her levelheadedness firsthand when I made a political suggestion in 1981, during the early months of Reagan's administration.

Our exchange occurred at a lunch the Bushes were giving for some Texas pals. It concerned the annual meeting of the Planned Parenthood Federation of America scheduled for the following week in Washington.

Many of the members were wealthy Republicans who normally would be pro-Reagan, but they were vexed at his stance against abortion. As a courtesy, and in an effort to keep those people in the Republican ranks, I asked Barbara if perhaps the vice president or his designate would appear at the convention, at least to listen to the arguments. Her reply was immediate, incisive and persuasive.

George had sympathy for Planned Parenthood, she said, but even if he favored an action, he should not press it just then because the president was trying to concentrate on one thing at a time, and remedying the economy was his current priority. Second, she pointed out, Carter's presidency had faltered precisely because he had tried to take on too much at once, and Reagan was consciously avoiding that pattern. Third, whatever George might *want* to do, it was important to bear in mind that Reagan was president.

Her statement on the front page of a newspaper, of course, might well have caused controversy on that explosive issue. Most Americans have come down firmly on one side or the other. I felt she had negotiated the mine field safely at that time. Like peace in the Middle East, however, that subject will continue to elude answers that satisfy everyone. Barbara Bush has on that and on countless other occasions proved herself a thoughtful, savvy diplomat. Her candor and grasp of reality impresses reporters throughout the country.

Even if George Bush hadn't married Barbara Pierce, she would have reached the top rung, whatever the field of her choice. I realized this one day as we talked at the vice president's house in May of 1988. The Republican convention was still three months off.[6] Some national polls counted George as trailing Michael Dukakis by as much as 17 points. Dukakis was already the acknowledged, if not the official, Democratic presidential nominee. Tension City, as George might put it.

I have known Barbara off and on since we were children, but she suddenly appeared before me that day as a new presence. Here was the wife of the vice president of the world's most powerful country. Her husband was also in a political pinch. In this situation she would want to be strong and alert as well as her usual dignified and human self.

She entered the library precisely on schedule and found me perusing its numerous books about the presidency and vice

presidency. I had gleaned from her assistant, Susan Porter
Rose, that the titles had been chosen by a three-person committee, and, presumably, were the best on their subject. It was a
touch of the professional care on which Barbara insists.

She seemed wary. No wonder. In place of a childhood pal sat
a probing reporter. She and others in the family had been stung
before by sloppy, sometimes hostile stories in the media. We
faced each other almost as strangers. I was humbled by the task
ahead of me.

She gently voiced concern that we not waste our scant thirty
minutes together. She ducked no questions, but she tailored
each reply to boost her husband and his quest. She kept it light
and was self-effacing and funny as always. We began by recalling how long we have known each other. I said, "I am much
older; though you are more mature." "That's true!" she replied
with a twinkle.

"Jack Kennedy was at one time slated to enter my class at
Princeton." I said. "There are so many similarities of background with George. Did the two ever meet?"

"George's father got an honorary degree at Yale at the same
time JFK did. I think George came up to New Haven from Texas
and saw him get the degree. I believe that's it."

Barbara discussed the relative influence of George's father
and mother.

"His father had enormous influence on him, and his mother
had ten times more.

"They held him [Prescott Sr.] in enormous awe as young
children. I believe that even when I married into the family, we
tip-toed around his dad because he was full of energy and
business. As he got older he got gentler. His older grandchildren thought of him as sort of scaryish, but our older
grandchildren thought he was a sweet, wonderful, funny, hug-
gable man. Time does that.

"But their mother had the most influence, and not in a bossy
way. As a young woman, [she was] just a great athlete, even-
tempered, fair, loving. But I'm sure that her sisters-in-law
heard their husbands asking, 'Why can't you be like Dottie?'

"You know, when Mrs. Bush comes to your house and uses

your telephone, she would leave 47 cents. Or if she took a stamp, she'd leave three cents.

"She brought those kids up under just the most extraordinary values. I never write a thank-you letter when I don't think of Mrs. Bush."

My mind wandered to what one of George's tennis companions told me: "He has a sort of crablike serve, and I asked him why he didn't straighten it out. 'Well,' he answered, 'you know I am naturally a southpaw, but my mother insisted that I play tennis right-handed.' "

He also plays golf right-handed, and has trouble with his wrists being limber enough approaching the green, as his golfing friend and pro Ken Raynor has pointed out. Mrs. Bush had power over her children; perhaps in this matter she used it unwisely.

"When do you think going for the big prize [the White House] began to form in his head?" I asked Barbara.

"Of course everybody's got a different picture of when these things happen. First, in 1968 or so at that convention in Miami, there was some discussion of George as vice president. Then again it happened when Ford looked at George. On TV we saw him [Ford], and they said, he's just gone into his room. While in his room he called George to say, "I've just picked Nelson Rockefeller.'

"The timing was right for us then [the campaign of 1979– 1980]. The children were all out of school, we had no crises, he was doing jobs that really helped it. He traveled around the country on boards and did a lot of speaking. It just was right."

We finished our chat at exactly the appointed time. I left convinced that this devoted wife, partner and mother could easily and gracefully take the helm of any large organization.

George recognized the type of person Barbara was when they first met. He had seen the same characteristics in his mother: a woman of strong character and personality, direct and honest; one who cares about the outdoors and people, especially children and is oriented to home life. He's not given to making statements about such matters, but anyone who has met both mother and wife can see they belong in the same category. As a husband it's clear he's done his part. He is loyal, enthusiastic about his home and his children, and meshes family with all other interests. No one is left out.

Remarkably, throughout their jumping from domicile to domicile in different states and different jobs, although George has sustained his share of political attacks, no one, to this day, ever has publicly maligned Barbara.

Having escaped direct personal insult doesn't screen her from suffering, however. Criticisms of her husband infuriate her. Tactless remarks that she looks more aged than he bother her. At least once before she became so widely recognized, she had to put up with the embarrassment of a news cameraman barking, "Will the lady in the red dress please get out of the picture!"

Over the years there has been the inevitable political ploy to paint adultery into the picture. The most persistent targets of George's accusers have been a member of his staff and the wife of a friend. In isolated locations during the 1988 campaign, supporters of Dukakis reportedly waved posters challenging Bush to concede that one of the women was his mistress. When the furor began to rise that year, young George Bush quelled it. He stood before the newsmen one day and declared there was no "Big A." After that, the story never caused much stir and Governor Dukakis even fired one of his campaign staff for trying to raise it once more.

Some of her friends say that despite her easygoing manner, Barbara Bush never relaxes. She agonizes over slips of the tongue that give the press a chance to skewer George. She was deeply remorseful when she said one day that her husband's opponent for the vice presidency in 1984, Geraldine Ferraro, was something that rhymed with "rich." Barbara apologized, quipping that the poet laureate had retired, and Geraldine Ferraro forgave her.

Barbara has embraced life with a full grasp. She gives of herself to all her constituencies: children belonging to her and others, friends both new and old, and her husband and his vast interests. Simultaneously, she takes care of herself by walking several miles per week, gardening when possible and playing tennis with a small circle of ladies. Among them are Supreme Court Justice Sandra Day O'Connor; Peggy Lord of New York and Washington; Meredith Dale, who is a Republican activist and the wife of Edwin Dale; Aileen Train, wife of environmentalist Russell Train; and Andy Stewart, widow of Supreme Court Justice Potter Stewart.

1988 was like any other political year for George, only more so. Steadily he was adding an ever-growing group of admirers and friends through his never-ending stream of personal notes. This correspondence with thousands created a bank of support that increased daily as he met and dealt with new individuals whose names and significance he would record in his remarkable memory.

Like countless numbers of other Americans, I, too, have been startled and gratified numerous times while sitting or walking in some large crowd—often of thousands—and suddenly have George Bush grin in my direction and call out my name. This gift that he exercises so gracefully endears him more firmly than millions of dollars of TV time.

Despite Bush's impressive federal assignments, including the vice presidency, he faced many obstacles in the struggle for the presidential nomination. Much of his challenge was snide, gossipy commentary which was impossible to address.

A "common wisdom" about Bush began to emerge, and it was passed along by political commentators. The press poured out such statements as

He is the logical man to be president, but he's unelectable.

He's a nice fellow, but what does he stand for?

He's got a good resume, he's been into a lot of jobs, but he never gets anything done. He never lets you know what he thinks. He's been everywhere but his footprints are nowhere.

He's had a lot of high positions, but he never runs anything. He's no leader.

He's done nothing for eight years as VP; how can he suddenly be president?

He's boring. He and Dukakis are about as exciting as a box of
Sominex (this was said after the national conventions).

He's so preppy. He doesn't relate to people, especially to
women. They're defecting in droves.

One woman, a long-time colleague and friend, commented
to me, "The publisher asked you to write 60,000 words about
George Bush? What will you find to say after you've copied his
resume?" She is a life-long Democrat.

Columnist Mike Royko wrote a piece for the *Chicago Times*
entitled "Why Bush Leaves Women Cold."[7] He said, "Women
are not turned on by George Bush. All the polls show that
while he is about even with Michael Dukakis among male
voters, he's far behind among those of the female persuasion."

Arnold Beichman, a commentator for the *Washington Times*
said, in part: "Bush is too chatty; an idiot. His suggestion of
sending Russian mechanics to Detroit; his fake bonhomie—a
guy who wants to be loved by everybody ends up being loved
by no one; also his silly remark to Andropov, Soviet Chariman
and former KGB head, 'We've been in the same business. . . .' "[8]

This kind of chatter gave aid and comfort to the mounting
number of primary candidates who tackled Bush. The most
noteworthy were Senator Robert Dole, the Reverend Pat
Robertson, Congressman Jack Kemp, former Governor Pete Du-
pont and former Secretary of State Al Haig.

The biggest plus for this group came in a bonanza dubbed
the Iran-Contra affair. U.S. officials had sold Tow missiles to
Iran and channeled proceeds from the sale to Contras, guer-
rillas who were trying to unseat Nicaraguan President Daniel
Ortega's Sandinista regime.

As the tale came out in small bits, Bush's competitors fed on
them, rising to grab them like fish in an aquarium. Now,
several years later, the bits still don't add up to a complete
whole even after the Tower Commission report ordered by
President Reagan and the extensive House of Representatives
hearings with the dramatic testimony of Lt. Colonel Oliver

North and the North trial in 1989. The public never has learned a great deal more than the original disclosures of Attorney General Edwin Meese in his 1986 announcement.

Despite energetic efforts of the press and Democrats to pin culpability on George Bush, he escaped major political hurt. Bush has acknowledged knowing something of the affair and admitted the administration was at fault. He denies any direct management of the operation, pointing out that it never was officially brought to the attention of the National Security Council, of which he was a member. It was handled at a staff level, some say with the tacit connivance of CIA Director William Casey.

Reportedly, Secretary of State George Shultz kept Bush out of the loop to protect his presidential candidacy. Shultz himself is on record as having advised against the actions taken. Similarly, Bush's staff members have stated that they didn't clue him in on whatever specific details to which they might have been privy.

Bush responded repeatedly to questions on the issue, conceding some responsibility as a member of the administration. In December 1986 he stated to reporters, "I wish it hadn't happened. I think everybody, to the degree there were mistakes, should share in the blame."[9]

A more complete delineation of Bush's views can be found in Bush's autobiography *Looking Forward*. He spells out two warnings: "Rule one is that in planning and carrying out a covert operation,, the law has to be followed. Rule two is never try to strike a bargain with terrorists."[10]

He also offers some hindsight.

"In retrospect there were signals along the way that gave fair warning that the Iran initiative was headed for trouble. As it turned out, George Shultz and Cap Weinberger had serious doubts, too. If I'd known that and asked the president to call a meeting of the NSC, he might have seen the project in a different light, as a gamble doomed to fail."[11]

As the 1988 primary season opened, surveys indicated that a high percentage of the public thought that Bush was in on the scandal, that he at least knew all about it. It was doubtless a contributing factor to his defeat in Iowa, where he came in third after Dole and Pat Robertson. After months of leading in the polls, this was a devastating setback. He took the news stoically, and in a calm voice rallied his followers to hang in there, that his record should encourage them to remember that he always did better as the underdog.

The New Hampshire primary did not find Bush with the easy confidence he had brought into the 1980 race. This time scores of his workers canvassed the state, and he walked, rode, and flew everywhere. He was the man who was down but fighting fiercely. Then the breaks went his way: Dole lost the primary to Bush by looking surly and calling Bush a liar.

Bush never was behind again. Super Tuesday's primaries in the South made him unstoppable. Three months before the convention, he had the nomination locked up. That was the good news. The bad news was that the Democrats were still scrapping and getting all the headlines, while in terms of news Bush's candidacy was quiescent. Before the Democratic convention opened in July, Bush's poll ranking against Democratic Governor of Massachusetts and likely nominee Michael Dukakis had fallen some 17 percentage points behind.

What went sour? The *Washington Post* provided their assessment.

"Wimp, wasp, weenie. Every woman's first husband. Bland conformist.

"These now shop-worn pejoratives are the essence of George Bush's 'image problem'—the vague but powerful suspicion of many citizens that the vice president may be too feckless and insubstantial to be the leader of the Free World. It is the GOP's worst strategic nightmare and the single most absorbing aspect of the 1988 presidential race.

"I have to be better at projecting my passions, my concerns, my strengths . . . and if I can't do better at it—why, who knows what will happen?" Bush said to *Washington Post* editors.[12]

The darkest hour is before the dawn.

CHAPTER 16

New Orleans Conventioneer

FIFTEEN THOUSAND JOURNALISTS FILED STORIES ON the 1988 Republican National Convention in New Orleans. Like the convention itself, their views are recorded in bits and pieces, the way war correspondents present military actions. In the mind of anyone who was there, the event loomed far larger. Tolstoy himself would be extended by the challenge: How to paint the broad panorama of skirmishes and principal battles that it took to launch George Bush into his campaign for the presidency of the United States.

The city of New Orleans was a palpable player in the two-week drama. This hot-blooded, exotic mix of cultures is unlike any other town in America. Its million inhabitants, diverse in language, color, and mores, worked together to welcome, entertain and serve the throng of Republicans and their camp followers.

From restaurants and hotels to topless bars, from the city's notables to street musicians, taxi drivers and shoeshine men, visitors rode a river of friendliness throughout their stay.

The first week was quiet as the Republicans built their campaign platform. A battle did rage behind closed doors as the moderate and conservative factions pushed their ideological wares. The result was characterized by the press and those present as "all George Bush." Since the platform suited him, the prognosis for his ability to overcome any last minute convention rebels was excellent. He had come personally to work with the platform committee in New Orleans. He had his first experience on this task in the 1950s. His father had brought him along to similar meetings when he chaired the Republican platform committee in San Francisco.

On this platform that had an anti-abortion plank, a pro-SDI plank, a no-new-taxes plank and many more that he favored, Bush had made peace with the conservatives. He was hoping to reach nomination without any last-minute fireworks. It now bid fair for the convention to be his in a way that Atlanta could not be for Michael Dukakis, given the impact of Jesse Jackson's brilliant theatrics. The Reverend Jackson had made such a dramatic speech in the Democratic convention that nominee Governor Michael Dukakis's address, sound as it was, seemed drab in comparison.

By the weekend of August 13–14, George Bush had excused himself from New Orleans. He returned to Washington to prepare his speech for the coming week and don his warpaint. He would reappear shortly for the final phase of the political battle of his life.

Already on hand and functioning in New Orleans were hundreds of the paid and volunteer members of the Bush for President campaign committee. Their offices and rooms for the candidate and his family and friends occupied several floors of the Marriott Hotel on Canal Street, the main thoroughfare.

When Bush returned, some fifty relatives and one hundred friends thronged together into a kind of Southern house party. One large "hospitality suite" became the common room where, whenever time permitted, refreshments abounded and numerous chums and relations mingled. Bush is no loner, although he likes his privacy. New Orleans was something wonderful to celebrate.

The press, too, had landed. They set about filing pictures, texts and video images by the thousands. Familiar faces, such as CBS's Dan Rather and Bob Schieffer; John McLaughlin, host of "The McLaughlin Group" and husband of Secretary of Labor Ann Dorr McLaughlin; columnist Rowland Evans; TV commentator Nancy Dickerson; NBC's "Today Show" host Bryant Gumbel; *Washington Times* editor Arnaud de Borchgrave; Australian newspaper tycoon Rupert Murdoch and less-famous henchmen popped up all over town.

Senator Robert Dole and Congressman Jack Kemp had been in residence for days, along with their dutiful troops, conducting last-ditch pitches to be tapped for vice president.

The lobbyists swarmed in and took their positions. So did Republican financial backers. Their largesse accorded them entree to choice places in the convention hall and invitations to posh dinners in the country mansions of New Orleans. If you were an "Eagle"—a donor of $10,000—your handling was regal; for $1,000 you could be a member of the Republican Senatorial Inner Circle and entitled to comforts and access that still were superior to those of ordinary tourists.

Even the 85-or-so top foreign ambassadors on hand were well cared for. They shared in the fun while reporting to their governments on the odd configuration of American politics. Secretary of State George Shultz's assistants arrived to brief the diplomats, and he came later, too, as part of the vice-presidential retinue.

Meanwhile, city officials and Republican National Committee functionaries hurried to complete arrangements for the convention hall and all its complicated functions—from the sound system to facilities for print and electronic media.

Eventually the committee circulated an unbelievable schedule. It summarized the social get-togethers held throughout the city and explained who was and was not urged not to attend. The activities filled some ten pages daily.

The Bush committee issued the vice president's schedule. This, of course, was where everyone wanted to be.

Until President Reagan spoke on Monday night, the town stirred with anticipation. It felt like a college campus on Saturday before the big football game. Ronald Reagan was that big game, and, as usual, lived up to his advance notices.

He left his listeners in the hall with reassurance that the man was real, that his administration had done what it had promised, and that George Bush had earned the right to take over. Reagan's bravura vibrated with emotional purity. His taste and timing were true, his personality American, and his evident feelings moving to the audience.

Still, as the night came to a close, more than one of the thousands from his audience wondered if George Bush could proceed from Reagan's evident strength to his own strength. Wouldn't he suffer as Harry Truman had in the towering shadow of Franklin Roosevelt? Would he suffer as perhaps he always has suffered under the shadow of his own powerful father?

Ronald Reagan offered the answer. "The president of the United States," he said in his speech, is simply "given temporary custody of an institution called the presidency, which belongs only to the people and which has been for me a sacred trust." Like the captain of a ship, he cares for the vessel in his command and should turn her over to his successor in tip-top shape. That is what I have tried to do, he declared. The king is dead, long live the king.

A few miles upstream from New Orleans stands the Belle Chasse Naval Air Station. After breakfast the next morning, Air Force Two arrived there with the vice president aboard. The president greeted him, wished him well in the impending contest and flew off in Air Force One. It was a tidy changing of the guard. Light-hearted jokes by the two principals lent an air of informality to the ceremonial hail and farewell.

It was then the vice president touched off a cackle among his ready belittlers by singling out his half-Mexican grandchildren as those "little brown ones." These are George and Noelle, the two eldest children of Jeb and Columba Bush. They were present as Reagan and Bush said goodbye and Bush simply was mentioning them to the assembled press. His disparagers cited this as a racial slur. Bush angrily quashed the question at a press conference the following morning by stressing how much he "loved these kids."

As George Bush stepped aboard the antique paddle-wheeler *Natchez* to coast down the Mississippi to New Orleans, Dole and Kemp and their lieutenants stepped up their final maneuvers for the number-two spot. No one was aware yet which way Bush would lean, although it later was said that he had told Reagan in confidence that morning.

At two in the afternoon, journalist Rowland Evans could be found plying Boyden Gray, Bush's legal counselor, with the culinary artistry of Antoine's Restaurant, trying to scoop everybody on Bush's choice. Surely you can let me know now who it is, persisted Evans. I don't know, insisted Gray, and he meant it.

Minutes later, less than half-a-mile away, the *Natchez* approached the riverside Spanish Plaza, an area decorated like a Spanish town square and available for public events like this one. Fireboats pumping red, white and blue streams of water heralded her arrival. Red, white and blue bunting adorned her rails and upper decks. A throng of several thousand filled the plaza's various levels.

Upstream near the naval air base, two formations of old Grumman Avengers (the planes Bush piloted in WW II) had lumbered over the *Natchez* and dipped their wings in a salute to the vice president. The gesture brought tears to the faces of family members like Nancy Ellis, Bush's sister.

Another paddle-boat, the *Creole Queen*, carrying favored friends and Republican bigwigs, hovered nearby as the *Natchez* came dockside. The vice president, his family and Jim Baker descended the gangplank and mounted the wide podium awaiting them. Only a fraction of the crowd could see Bush and his entourage, and children and slender women had to be hoisted to the shoulders of helpful men. An unexplained pause of nearly ten minutes followed.

In the crowd some of us mused that we had gone back in time to a political rally for Abraham Lincoln. We were mesmerized by the white railed 250-foot river relics. Rising some

80 feet above their decks were black funnels, topped with jagged crowns to break up the soot from coal burning in the engine room.

People filled every available space on the ships and around the plaza. Their clothes painted the scene into a mosaic of color. They stood by patiently as the clouds bunched overhead and threatened a downpour. Watchful security men gazed out from the building tops. They eyed the thousands below and countless waving hands in open windows of other buildings.

Suddenly, a man in a dark blue suit was led through the packed crowds up to the platform beside the vice president. The hundreds of passengers on the *Natchez* moved to the rail to hear the vice president's announcement, and the ship listed perilously in his direction.

"I have made a decision," Bush said. "I have picked a candidate for the vice presidency. He is a vigorous, able senator. He is young enough to represent the future in my administration. He is the senator from Indiana, my friend, Dan Quayle."

The onlookers focused on Dan Quayle, a surprised and joyful face they perhaps never before had considered. The proceedings had been delayed a few minutes while a couple of Bush's lieutenants went to give Quayle word of his selection. They had found him lunching not far from where Rowland Evans was pumping Boyden Gray for information on the vice-presidential nominee.

Quayle removed his suitcoat. The vice president already had done this, revealing a short-sleeved white shirt. Quayle's hair showed red, his face pink. He radiated energy, as Bush had suggested in his brief introduction.

Quayle took the mike and shouted into it with staccato sentences to express his delight and honor at being designated as Bush's running mate. He ended with the exhortation: "Go get 'em, Mr. Vice President!" As he spoke these words, Quayle reached over with his left hand and grabbed the vice president's right shoulder. Bush stiffened visibly but smiled to paper over any embarrassment. Perceptive viewers didn't miss Quayle's undignified gaffe, slight as it was. How could Bush offer us someone so puerile?

But Bush's children and grandchildren soon paraded across the speakers' platform, some twenty of them, and the uncomfortable moment with Quayle passed. "You better get used to them," Bush laughed, "I've got hundreds of them and they're going with me all over the country."

Fireworks exploded above the ship. A calliope burst into music from the top deck. With each note a pink light glowed and smoke issued from the machine.

Bush and Quayle headed for their limousine beyond the plaza as the first questions about the senator from Indiana began to buzz through the city. TV and radio instantaneously had blared out the news. Many Republicans were thunderstruck by the choice.

The constant round of receptions took on new life as Dole and Kemp receded from public attention and conversations about them were replaced with speculation over Quayle.

At a salute to black Americans, I asked one South Carolinian delegate what he thought. "It's great," he replied. Why? "Because now Bush can be Bush. Bush is naturally moderate," he explained. With Quayle nailing down the right edge of the tent, Bush may follow his inclination to care for us ethnics. He didn't quite use those terms, but the meaning was unmistakable.

At a Wednesday morning press conference with Bush and Quayle, the questions grew querulous. Many were left unanswered. Quayle quickly was turning into a liability.

Although still reeling from the shock, Republicans repaired to the convention center on Wednesday and nominated George Bush according to plan. Each child spoke from their delegations, and George W., his eldest son, delivered the Texas vote to put him over the top.

The family theme continued next at the brunch given for Barbara Bush. A thousand women were there. Critics had carped that he didn't display enough tenderness, so the vice president popped in to give her a testimonial. The two clowned with kisses and compliments and called each other "Sweetie." But their forty-four-year-old affection for each other was so genuine that many guests found themselves moved.

The news story that dominated the morning, however, was Quayle's alleged draft-dodging during the Vietnam war. Bush's "G6," his six chieftains of advice, had huddled half the night on how to deflect negative reactions to Quayle's participation in the National Guard. By morning, more calumny was circulating, this time about a half-forgotten golf weekend in Florida Quayle had spent years earlier while he was a congressman. Quayle, three other congressmen and notorious lobbyist Paula Parkinson had been present and it was suggested that Quayle had enjoyed more than a golf game. He had risen above the smear attempt at the time and gone on to be elected to the Senate. But it was back again. The accusations were an ugly stain across the upbeat mood for which George Bush had striven.

Only an astonishing spectacle like the one that followed in the new riverside convention center could temporarily ease the tension. The $1,000-a-head program, underwritten by dozens of *Fortune* 500's luminaries, was labeled grandly the "1988 Republican National Convention Gala."

Standing at opposite ends of the arena were models of the White House and a Mississippi River paddle-steamer, each about a hundred-feet long with forty-foot stages in front. Singing and dancing troupes punctuated the speeches. Meandering through the hall was a carpet marked like a highway. On each side stood large street signs that read "The Road to Victory."

Suddenly doors opened at one end of the hall and an ancient fire engine entered, carrying the vice president, his running mate and their wives. Slowly it drove the length of the "road," as Bush stood and effortlessly smiled and accurately called the names of hundreds of admirers.

Finally, the fire engine disgorged its load and the principals ascended the dais, where there were more seats than in the audience of a customary large testimonial dinner. Included were Bob Michel, minority leader in the House of Representatives; Bob Dole, minority Senate leader; Secretary of State George Shultz and Leo Nadeau. The latter, a white-haired, lean man, stepped to the microphone. I had had breakfast with him the day before, but nearly no one else realized that Leo was

Bush's turret gunner from World War II. He had flown over 50 combat missions with the then-lieutenant (JG) Bush.

In manly, well-delivered phrases, Nadeau introduced his former pilot and friend of forty-five years. The effect was electric. The four thousand listeners were transfixed and then wild with applause. What could have been a disjointed, overly ornate staging was off to a good start. Only the convention's final act, the critical acceptance speech, lay ahead for the vice president.

That evening George Bush made a masterful address. Many agreed that it was the best of his career, certainly the finest of his long campaign for the nomination. With humor, humility and high purpose, he told why he was a candidate and what he would do when elected.

At the start he kept his tongue in cheek as he promised to keep his charisma in check. Then he declared simply that "I seek the presidency to build a better America."

He cited the peace and prosperity of the Reagan years. Giving the highlights, he pointed to the 17 million new jobs which paid, he said, an average of more than $22,000 a year. He stressed that women had filled more than two-thirds of these jobs. He said that the administration had arrested inflation and would not let it out on furlough. He added that the administration also would not let the Social Security trust fund get into the hands of the big spenders. After Bush mentioned each benefit, he intoned, "I'm not going to let them take it away from you."

For the future he predicted, "We will be able to produce 30 million jobs in the next eight years." Regarding the Soviets he warned that a "prudent skepticism" is in order, as well as hope.

As to the fact that after two terms of Reagan a switch would be made, Bush remarked wittily: "But when you have to change horses in midstream, doesn't it make sense to switch to one who's going the same way?"

He hammered on the campaign issues, in favor of the pledge of allegiance and voluntary prayer in school, the death penalty, and the right to bear a gun to protect the home; and against

prison furloughs for criminals who aren't yet eligible for pa-
role, abortion and tax increases. He promised he would tell
Congress, if they pushed him, "Read my lips: no new taxes."

He went on at length about his pet plans for first-rate schooling, a drug-free America, lifting the disabled to the main-
stream, no more ocean dumping, FBI check of medical wastes
on beaches, less acid rain, less dependence on foreign oil
through domestic energy incentives, more morality and "a
kinder, gentler nation."

He spoke against bigotry and for the collaboration of the
many communities that make up America—"the thousand
points of light."

Winding up, he said he knew he wasn't very eloquent, in fact
he sometimes was a little awkward, but this didn't interfere
with his love of country. Then he made a touching point. "I am
a quiet man, but I hear the quiet people others don't—the ones
who raise the families, pay the taxes, meet the mortgage."

He reminded everyone that he had worked with a great
president, seen how the job was done and what kind of a man
it takes. Then he said firmly, "I am that man."

At the end he persuaded the audience to join him in the
national pledge of allegiance. Clamorous approval erupted and
thousands of balloons rained down from the rafters where they
had been captive all week.

The Superdome proved adequate to the super demands of
the convention, at least for those sitting in the lower third of
the building illuminated for television coverage. Above them
sat those with less-favorable seats. The TV monitors were not
very sharp, the sound reproduction was faint and the result
was a tepid reception among the people seated there. People
talked among themselves, even unfavorably, as Bush labored,
out of reach, at that tiny podium we hardly could see. Those in
the lower third of the dome clapped deliriously and cheered,
unaware of the quiet in the upper two thirds.

On reflection perhaps the Democrats had it better at Atlanta,
where a strict selection cut down on those permitted to enter
the hall. There was a real shortage of seats, even for the party
faithful and some press people. At least those who got in could

laugh uproariously when Ted Kennedy needled Bush. He referred to the Iran-Contra scandal and chanted "Where was
George?" Later, Charlton Heston answered this jibe: "George
was at home, dry, sober, and with his wife."

The Republicans left their titanic conclave sailing proudly,
all passengers snug. But their vessel had struck an iceberg
named Quayle. Was the puncture fixable? Would they reach
their destination in November?

Their candidate had promised that his running mate would
be fully capable of replacing him as president. Yet he had
named a man some described as the youngest forty one year
old they had ever met. He had logged minimal management
time. He had failed to quell, so far, the furor over his past
inadequacies of judgment. Every slap at Quayle ricocheted
damningly at Bush.

CHAPTER 17

Nominee for President

Q UAYLE'S ENTRY ON THE REPUBLICAN TICKET GOT
the press's attention. To paraphrase Roger Ailes, it was
like putting a hot dog into a pool of piranhas. They accused
him of using his father's political clout to get him into the
National Guard. They exposed his mediocre scholastic record.
They wrote that he had been a fellow house-party guest in
Florida with a glamorous woman lobbyist.

For weeks after his nomination press people filed so many
column inches of newsprint and filled so many television
screens for so many hours that there was scant space or time
left in the media for Governor Dukakis.

In late August and early September, Dukakis was doing little
more than ride on his hope to remain about even with Bush.
Then he would start full campaigning after the traditional
hiatus between the national conventions and Labor Day. Indeed, to the extent he was active, he seemed to be focusing on
the problems of Massachusetts only. By the time he woke up to
the national situation, he had lost his lead. From then on he
had to play catchup all the way to November 8. Bush had not

rested on his oars after New Orleans. He campaigned almost daily.

Moreover, Bush himself had changed noticeably. He reduced his accessibility to the press. His convention acceptance speech gave a preview of his new style. He was speaking more slowly, pitching his voice lower, dropping the nasal whine that so often crept in, ceasing his inane asides and sticking to the script. The preppyisms and facetious quips made his friends laugh in private surroundings but gave his critics pleasure in public. *Newsweek* made a list of these remarks and expressions, labeling them "Bushspeak." That was all before Roger Ailes.

Until Ailes stepped in sometime before the convention, Bush had complained that his television and big speech style were the best he could do. He was getting irritated by all the criticism from opponents and the press and even from close associates.

It's a little like tap-dancing, he told his New York champion, Walter Curley. Curley, a man of universal charm who was former ambassador to Ireland and a long-time financier and public figure, would raise millions for Bush's campaign. Bush explained that even if he spent the rest of his life trying to learn to tap dance, he would never be better than proficient, and it was the same with speaking.

In the spring and summer of 1988, the young George Bush manager, Lee Atwater, and other Bush committee noteables had heard enough. They hired $25,000-a-month political wizard Roger Ailes. He had been consulting part-time but now the bearded, heavyset Ailes went into action and put a stop to all interviews. Until after the election Bush was going to be engaged eighteen hours a day.

The metamorphosis came gradually. By September 25, the day of the first debate with Dukakis, Bush was in the midst of his transformation. The goal basically was to present to the public the warm, intelligent, funny and attractive fellow his family and friends knew him to be. He was improving but still had a way to go.

Meanwhile, Bush's campaign management had undergone

radical adjustment. James Baker left his post as secretary of
Treasury and taken over the Bush-for-President Committee.
What had become a multiheaded monster fell comfortably into
his confident grip.

Baker rid the committee of some brewing trouble when he
leaned on Fred Malek to resign. Malek did so promptly. Bush
had designated Malek to run the convention, and he had done
a creditable job, but now some static from the past had arisen.
The *Washington Post* revealed that Malek, as White House
personnel director, had listed for Nixon the number of Jews at
the Bureau of Labor Statistics. Nixon was vexed that the B.L.S.
didn't accept his hopeful view of the economy. Malek denied
that he had had anything to do with the subsequent removal of
two B.L.S. employees. Later the Bush committee dropped
seven members of its group of ethnic advisors because of
accusations they were anti-Semitic.[1]

Soon the committee's strategy brought tough tactics. Before
the convention, Bush, as nice guy, had impressed the Republicans into a nomination by acclamation. But the polls told
the national story: Bush was between 10 and 20 points behind
Dukakis.

The Democratic convention at Atlanta in August provided a
kind of Roman orgy of Bush-bashing. Alluding to Bush's in-
volvement in the Iran-Contra Scandal, Senator Ted Kennedy
drew laughs by crying: "Where was George?" "A man born
with a silver foot in his mouth!" crowed Democratic keynote
speaker Ann Richardson, who hails from Bush's home state of
Texas. The polls showed Bush sinking lower.

The Bush force that emerged in September came out swinging its clubs. For television ads they picked themes that en-
raged the opposition: Dukakis is soft on crime—he furloughs
criminals, one of whom committed murder and rape while on
leave; Dukakis is weak on environmental protection—Boston
harbor is a slough of untreated sewage; Dukakis does not value
patriotism—he struck down the pledge of allegiance to the
flag. In short, Dukakis is liberal and incompetent.

These themes were interspersed with positive elements: the
fact that he had grandchildren; had come out in favor of money

for day care; ended the scourge of drugs; beat the budget deficit and ended the trade imbalance; was in favor of gun control, the Strategic Defense Initiative, the MX missile, the B-1 bomber and the Midgetman missile. In advance, he called himself the education president and an environmentalist. He had done that in Seattle in May and he did it again on the shore of Lake Erie in September.

But what got the news coverage and Dukakis's goat were the negative sound bites. As the two men approached the first presidential debate, the polls were wobbling. Bush was slightly in the lead, but real support was judged to be soft for both men. Neither was looking very presidential in the public eye. Perhaps the debate itself might reveal a true front runner.

Bush's followers, meanwhile, became restless. They were developing into a new category of castigators. Originally they had complained that the decent, well-mannered preppy might make a good president but he never would get elected. Now they were calling him a ruffian, a dealer of low blows. Worse, they lacked confidence that Bush could best the sturdy little liberal from Massachusetts. They believed that Dukakis was striking back effectively. It didn't matter who started it; the fight was on. Bush too had to accustom himself to the tough new style. In past campaigns he never had been happy taking the low road. The first presidential debate would be a proving ground.

The contenders stepped before the nation on September 25 in an auditorium at Wake Forest University in Winston-Salem, North Carolina. This debate was critical for there would be only two of these contests. Jim Baker had negotiated with the Dukakis team into agreeing to this limit; they had asked for at least four.

There was a sense of two boxers entering the prize ring as George Bush and Michael Dukakis walked to the stage and shook hands. Their bout was scheduled to last one-and-a-half hours.

Bush stood nervous and uneasy with a controlled smile trying to assert calmness. Facing him about three yards away, behind the ridiculous lectern fashioned to hide the different heights of the two men, was a grim Dukakis. The immediate question of any viewer must have been, "Does either of these tense men measure up to the awesome task for which they are striving?" The immediate answer had to be as tentative as the question at the end of the skirmish: Who won?

What follows are my own notes from watching the debate on television:

"From the outset both men show that they have been heavily briefed and packaged for this occasion. Each has a few one-liners to liven the exchange. Neither is very good at this; neither finds the punch that Reagan tossed against Carter with 'There you go again!'

"The match develops into a set of mere jabs. Neither contestant wants to swing so hard that he loses his own balance. Dukakis growls about having his patriotism bad-mouthed by the vice president: "I resent it." He hits him for dealing with the Iranian terrorists and Panamanian strongman Noriega; and sneers at his choice of Dan Quayle. He scores most heavily on Quayle by listing the merits of his own running mate, Lloyd Bentsen, and Bush is unable to parry effectively.

"Bush lashes at Dukakis's liberal leanings, citing his boast at being a "card-carrying member of the ACLU," and listing the leftist positions of that organization. He derides Dukakis's shifting views on defense, particularly SDI and alleges that Dukakis's health care plan (that is to be funded by corporations) will cost taxpayers their money and workers their jobs. He asserts that Dukakis's housing ideas if implemented will lead the country back to the high interest rates that the Reagan-Bush administration inherited from the Democrats and then halved.

"Gaffes are minor but telling in terms of defining the men. Bush makes several fluffs and manages to correct them or laugh them off. Dukakis lapses in comity by addressing the vice president as "George" at least three times and "Bush" once. One supposes that he does this to overcome the advantage of Bush's more senior rank.

Bush weakly defends his abortion stand. He leaves an opening for Dukakis to say, in effect, "You would call pro-choice women criminals," and doesn't have an answer on what the criminal penalties should be for women who undergo abortions.

Bush's summation is neither as smooth nor as convincing as Dukakis's, who evidently has memorized his pitch. Each echoes themes from his nomination acceptance speech. Bush's overall performance, though marred by error and small slips of the tongue, is more lively, humorous and warm. Dukakis seems to glare, bore in like a street fighter and talk with the metallic speed of a professional auctioneer. Though tougher than Bush and effective in making debating points, his icy demeanor leaves a bitter aftertaste.

All in all the spectacle must leave the nation's voters nostalgic for the simplistic but vivid impact of Ronald Reagan. Neither of these two is gifted naturally as a politician. But time marches on.

Now, like parents with two children and only enough money to send one to college, Americans are left to make the only choice available to them. Most likely they will not let tonight's mundane discussion influence them decisively. My guess is that the debate will furnish fodder to feed all the prejudices pro and con viewers formed in advance. Naturally, then, I believe Bush successfully blocked more thrusts and scored more often than his too-feisty challenger.

The polls recorded a contrary result, with Dukakis winning by a small margin. But George Will expressed the disappointment of many Americans on September 27:

"The winner? Are you kidding? Do we give a trophy for being a millimeter less tiresome than the other guy?

"It was a national embarrassment. Michael Dukakis was marginally less embarrassing than George Bush was, if only because his canned thoughts were ladled out in understandable syntax. However, the small-mindedness and tactical overtuning were so oppressive on both sides that Bush may benefit. Boredom and disgust may drive down voter turnout so much that Bush (Republicans are more reliable voters) may benefit from the ennui."[2]

In the days that followed, Bush and his ad program reinforced each other as well-planned scheduling should ensure. Dukakis's speeches and his ads often reached the public at the same time with different messages. He was shifting from topic to topic too often, so that his themes never rose in tandem as did Bush's.

Shrewd observers believed Dukakis and his inner group suffered from inexperience. They never had organized more than a statewide race before. Whereas some of Bush's people, like Baker, Teetor, Teeley and others were on their third national campaign together.

Within a few days after the September debate, Dukakis had fallen to seven points behind. But he was anticipating help: Senators Lloyd Bentsen and J. Danforth Quayle were scheduled to square off on October 5 for their one and only debate.

Quayle still was encountering ugly situations on the road. He was asked about the Holocaust at a press conference and replied, "It was an obscene period in our nation's history." In flailing to get out of that mess, "Quayle looked rattled and terrified. The Bush campaign strategy was to have Quayle target Dukakis, but he was apt to hurt himself in the attempt. For example, he joked that Dukakis had "lost his top naval advisor. His rubber duck had drowned in the bath tub."[3]

If Dukakis had been asked how to spell "relief" that autumn, he might well have said, "Q-U-A-Y-L-E." In his contest with Quayle, Bentsen didn't waste much time. First, he was helped by the question one moderator asked Quayle, "What would you do if the president died?" Quayle did his best, which was to say he would pray and then call in the cabinet members. He resembled a deer at night, caught in the headlights of a car.

He struggled to profit from his extensive briefing and stated, quite acceptably it seemed, that he had the same amount of public service in Congress that Jack Kennedy had when he ran for the presidency. Like a bandit ready for ambush, Bentsen turned on Quayle and made his lethal slash: "Senator, I served with Jack Kennedy. Jack Kennedy was a friend of mine. And Senator, you're no Jack Kennedy."

Quayle retorted calmly, "That was uncalled for, Senator." He controlled himself, was able to get many valid opinions and facts before the audience after that blow, but the damage was done.

The curious fact about Bentsen's subsequent popularity was that it emphasized to many that he seemed more presidential than Dukakis. He demonstrated in his conduct during the debate that he was familiar with the issues and comfortable with himself, more so than either Dukakis, Quayle or Bush. Most extraordinary, he appeared to have more trouble extolling the virtues of Dukakis than other subjects on his agenda. These were two odd couples. In the Democratic pair, the number-two man loomed stronger than the number one. Of the Republicans, the number two was deemed by many as unqualified to step in if the president should die.

The following day a delighted Dukakis reran an ad that said, "This is the first presidential decision that George Bush and I had to make. Judge us by how we made it and who we chose."

Dukakis's brief afterglow from the confrontation of the two vice presidential candidates was short-lived. He had to meet Bush once more. This time he found that Bush, leading in the polls by increasing numbers, was comfortable and articulate compared to their first matchup.

Dukakis was thrown a curve on the first question and flubbed it as seriously as Quayle had when asked what he would do if the president died. Dukakis was given the chance to react to the query, "Would you call for the death penalty if someone raped and murdered Kitty Dukakis?" Dukakis avoided any emotion in replying to this tasteless, outrageous idea. He said pedantically that he would not invoke the death penalty.

Now many viewers saw an example of what they suspected all along: Mike Dukakis was acting cold and dull. For the moment, at least, he lacked gallantry or imagination to respond like a normal fellow when even theoretically his wife was threatened.

Three weeks remained before the election. There was time now to examine the candidates carefully before making a choice. This was the quadrennial season when Americans start to hunt seriously for their national leader. How do they decide? What kind of person do they want?

Traditionally Americans have voted for the father figure if there is one on the ticket. Second, they prefer a father figure with a plan. With Eisenhower they got the father figure. With Kennedy they got the plan, or at least they thought they did. With Reagan they had both. Now, with Bush and Dukakis, they didn't perceive either.

So how would they judge? One measure might be which man had best stood the test of time. As the older of the two, Bush had had more experience and had come through without seriously blotting his copy book. Another test would be who had the finer ideals, morality, probity and physical courage. Both men were trustworthy, loyal, helpful, friendly, courteous, kind, obedient, cheerful, thrifty, brave, clean and reverent. As to who was the better scout, it was a standoff.

How about vision for the country? Bush long had been faulted for not offering a shining holy grail before the electorate. People all over the world seek a raison d'etre and when a leader appears to "show them the way" he usually gets their allegiance.

But Dukakis, too, had failed to dish up a "vision." True, he had predicted that "The best of America is yet to come." Yet this vague concept never grew more precise with his references to it.

So there were two visionless candidates. How were voters to differentiate between them?

The candidates tried to guide the voters to the "right" decision. For the whole campaign, perhaps $100 million had been spent to educate and persuade citizens as to the better man. During the final three weeks, a kind of focus finally was achieved.

On Dukakis the sharp lines showed a rather glum, grim personality who was exhibiting energy and pluck as he tried to reduce his opponent's lead of some ten percent in the polls. Rather than panic he was grasping at a few techniques that were pleasing the crowds. To the poor people and the middle-income groups, he repeated that Bush's proposal for reducing the capital gains tax would hurt them and enrich the rich. Therefore, he intoned, "I am on your side." He said the furlough of murderers was a bad thing and he had corrected the practice. He said he was for a strong defense to be achieved through a build-up of conventional forces. As the man who had balanced the state budget many times, he was the fellow who could fix both the national and international financial deficits. He promised to protect the environment and enhance the education system. Furthermore, he was a "liberal" and proud of it.

These were good themes and they were applauded by the people who listened to the governor as he chugged feverishly around the country just once more before election day.

If Bush had stayed in his tent for those three weeks, Dukakis might have won. But with the skilled guidance of Jim Baker, Roger Ailes and manager Lee Atwater, the Bush juggernaut was rolling surely and powerfully. It had found its direction and its pace, and with Peggy Noonan the words, that Bush needed to win. Perhaps most important of all, he had Reagan's record to run on: Near-full employment, a healthy economy, low interest rates, low inflation, strong defense establishment and increasing signs of peace in the world. All the negatives Dukakis could conjure up—big deficit, drugs, trade imbalance, Iran-Contra and Quayle—paled against the robust attractions of peace and prosperity.

Additionally, the Bush onslaught against Dukakis the liberal never stopped. Dukakis was the man who let Willie Horton loose to terrorize innocent victims—and two victims, Clifford and Angela Barnes, actually were given a four-state tour to share their anguish with anyone who would listen. Dukakis was pounded again and again for the filth in Boston Harbor, the financial problems of Massachusetts and his wishy-washy stand on SDI and national defense. Bush ads used the photograph that Dukakis's campaign had generated and made him look foolish. This recorded Dukakis's ride in a tank while wearing a bulbous helmet. Unfortunately for Dukakis, the picture resembled a child playing soldier.

Bush and his entourage knew full well that their negative approach not only was enraging the opponents but also disquieting the faithful. In fact, vociferous objections were being raised. Name calling was replacing what should be a states-manlike exchange of issue-oriented volleys.

So Bush alternated the hard blows with feathery exhortations for a kinder, gentler America whose needs might be met with generous contributions from a thousand points of light.

Those who know Bush well recognized that he was far more content breathing sweetness and light than fire and brimstone. Being mean simply was not his nature or style.

Bush's close friends also kept their own counsel when the Willie Horton story was carried to extremes in certain state campaigns. It was becoming apparent that he wasn't just a criminal let out to roam, he was a black criminal. To the extent this fact was understood, Bush's outreach to the black community was nullified. He and the committee, of course, denied that Willie Horton was a symbol for anything more than Dukakis's stance on crime.

Dukakis put on his final spurt in the last three days. Virtually sleepless and hoarse, he said he could sense a victory; he could smell it, feel it. Bush whipped his team to ignore the encouraging polls and softened his tough rhetoric a bit but kept plugging hard to the very end.

November 8 at last brought armistice to this endless war, this campaign that seemed to have lasted forever. The results came quickly, cleanly and painlessly that evening.

George Herbert Walker Bush was elected to be the 41st president of the United States. The popular vote was 47,917,341 for Bush to 41,013,030 for Dukakis. This translated into an electoral college count of 426 to 112. In percentages it was Bush 54 percent to Dukakis 46 percent. Dukakis announced the next day, as he returned to his governor's office in Boston, that this was no mandate.

Also on the debit side of Bush's crowning personal fulfillment lay one inescapable obstacle: The Democratic majority in both houses of Congress. In this respect Americans had spoken with forked tongues.

Bush had triumphed handily. At last he could engage in the actual job of governing. He never really had cottoned to the campaign demands that he change his personality to get votes.

He always preferred to be himself. As president he could put his skills and vast experience to good use without having to be theatrical about it. The rest would be relatively simple. All he had ahead of him were the world's intractable problems. But he would be in the driver's seat of the world's strongest and most idealistic nation.

CHAPTER 18

President-Elect

*The fault dear Brutus lies not in our stars but in our-
selves that we are underlings.*

—William Shakespeare,
Julius Caesar

G EORGE BUSH IS NO UNDERLING NOW, AND HE
never gives much value to guiding his life by the stars.
After eight years of alleged White House reliance on the star-
gazers, for a change of pace let's hear what they see in George
Bush's immediate future. A popular professional astrologer in
Washington has offered some readings from her heavenly
charts.

First, she concedes that most astrologers were surprised
when George Bush beat Michael Dukakis. They saw the race as
between a mongoose and a cobra. Bush was the versatile and
agile Gemini facing Dukakis, an intense, secretive Scorpio.
They admit they were wrong, but say that's no more proof

against their credibility than an occasional misreading by a doctor or a business analyst.

Our expert plunges right ahead with assessments on Bush's character and likely future as president: Bush is anxious to please and be part of a harmonious team (Moon in Libra), but he clearly wants to be the boss (Sun in the tenth). With Virgo rising and Mercury in Taurus, he is practical and pragmatic.

Daniel Quayle is more of an ideologue (and under much stress until late 1990). Bush's chart shows periodic sudden changes. He is naturally loyal, but people are startled when his sharp mind looses a sharp tongue.

Some astrologists have been fearful of a warlike juxtaposition which ties Bush to the U.S. chart, but say this connection was triggered in 1987 and should not repeat soon. They reassure us that Bush rather would build consensus and coalition.

One politician with whom Bush is dynamically related is the Reverend Jesse Jackson. Both like the Rainbow Coalition concept and are willing to work toward it.

There is a chance that Bush and Gorbachev will get along and help each other. The Russian chart exhibits continuing major transformation, at least through Bush's first term.

The summary of future potential conflict points to fairly specific areas which will not be cited here. Predictions of danger ahead, no matter how limited, are too likely to be self-fulfilling to merit mention.

Regardless of where the reader stands on astrology, its earnest practitioners are busy producing a detailed forecast for George Bush's first White House tour. Let the scoffers scoff and the believers believe!

Returning to earth, Houston to be exact, George Bush began his heady months as president-elect by meeting with friends, exercising with a jog and beginning to telephone and write the usual hundreds of personal notes to thank supporters all over the country.

Michael Dukakis had signed off with a graceful concession speech the night before, which revealed that this hard-fighting opponent was not a sore loser. It was odd to find him at his desk the very next morning. One wondered if his wife might not have appreciated a few days in the sun somewhere. She had campaigned almost as fiercely as he and had been sidelined in the hospital with a high fever and virus just days before the election. Their disappointment did not affect the Dukakises' public demeanor, which could be rated in the highest tradition of American good sportsmanship.

Some weeks later Kitty Dukakis checked into the Edgehill Sanitarium in Newport, Rhode Island, for a month's treatment for alcoholism. She maintained her courageous attitude afterward, saying to the press that her malady did not stem from her husband's defeat.

Other Democrats, both officially and privately, were quiet. Bush, Lincolnlike, began immediately to bind up the wounds from the bitter contests of the past two years. Before the month was out, he reached out not only to Dukakis, with whom he met on December 1, but also to Robert Dole, his chief foe of the primaries. He lunched with Dole and buried the hatchet in preparation for collaboration ahead.

His most spectacular move toward peace was to the Reverend Jesse Jackson. He called Jackson to say it was time Jackson stopped "kicking my butt."

Their lunch meeting came off well. Both men openly joshed each other as they exited together from the Executive Office Building to face reporters outside. Only months before Bush had referred to Jackson as "that Chicago Hustler," and Jackson had hinted strongly that Bush lacked the moral fiber needed to be president. They answered questions amicably, and allowed that although they had considerable political differences, they shared much on which they could agree and cooperate.

After the shouting was done, the average American had a chance to examine what kind of president they had just voted into office. What they saw was a basically homespun fellow who truly was oriented toward family and friends. They saw a man of innate courtesy; one who cared about people of all social and economic levels, colors and credos. They saw a man who kept physically and morally fit. They saw a disciplined person who always did his work first. Right or wrong, he lived up to his commitments.

They saw someone who, despite the reckless rumors spread by the occasional political arsonist, was not busy in the extra-curricular romance department. On that point a female friend of both Bushes sums up what seems apparent to all who know him. He is so involved in his home life and work that he never would endanger either with outside adventures. "Endanger" is no exaggeration when one considers that in 1988 the New York Stock Market dropped 43 points one day over a rumored Bush infidelity. The *Washington Post* supposedly had a news account on the subject. The *Post* denied the allegation and the market promptly bounced back.

The informant mentioned above recalled an incident to underscore her point. She and Bush encountered each other after an absence. She admits that she looked more attractive than usual, having just returned from a sea vacation. He obviously thought so too, and wanted to express his reaction. But, exercising his common caution on this subject, he said merely "Gee, gosh, uh, you look so . . . outdoorsy!"

Unlike many men who have risen high in both business and politics, Bush never has worn the attire of a dandy. At least until he entered the White House, he never appeared any better dressed than a farmer duded up for Saturday night on the town.

His buying habits are modest, and he finds his suits mostly "off the rack" at the ready-made house of Arthur Adler. According to his sister Nancy Ellis, in early 1988 Bush owned only three suits—one on his back, one in the closet and one at the cleaners. He supplemented these basics with one or two old tweed jackets, a few pairs of slacks, plus a leather jacket given him by the Astros. He was very proud of that, she mentioned.

The only elegant note in his sartorial getup has been his shirts, which occasionally are custom-made. By chance I discovered one day that I use the same firm and asked them to comment on his tastes. They prudently were reluctant to give away any secrets. Still, they did confirm what I already had heard. He vetoes button-down oxfords. They suggest that is because he has tried to shed the Eastern preppy image while in

Texas. The only other fact they let slip was that he never wears green shirts.

But these are tidbits on the way we see the man. What about the way he sees the future of America? Along the many campaign years he often was assailed for lacking a shiny chart with a fresh new course plotted on it. People have insisted that he has no ideas. He'll simply get into office and let America drift.

During his eight long years in the vice presidency, some wondered why he was not busy laying out a scenario for the post-Reagan era, the Bush administration. The Rockefeller Brothers Fund had conferred with experts from around the country to present their "Prospect for America." This special studies program gave Nelson Rockefeller some sound foundation for his own road to the presidency—which never materialized. Bush, in his own style, had done just that long before in his study seminars at Kennebunkport in the summer of 1979.

While vice president he also was assiduous in tracking the affairs of the world and America, reading everything and absorbing thousands of written and oral briefings. In his other years as diplomat and CIA chief in the executive branch, he was admired as a quick study who could retain what he read and heard. Furthermore, he displayed a probing curiosity beyond what was merely proffered officially.

For instance, when he headed the U.S. mission to the United Nations, he frequently would call Washington for extra information on topics about which he didn't feel sure enough.

But Bush doesn't pontificate on where he wants the nation or anyone else to go. Although the public sees him mostly in a speaking mode, he is a prodigious listener. As an executive he has learned the simple device for command of a meeting: Hear out all the participants before letting his own views be known; even then the skilled leader may defer making a decision.

In the midst of the 1988 pre-convention campaign, I pressed Nancy Ellis to tell me about her brother's attitude toward the presidency. Let's say the nation is a trolley car operated by the president, I suggested. When George steps into the driver's seat, would he want to lay new tracks in different directions or would he be content to grab the controls and guide it perfectly along the tracks already in place? She thought he would choose the latter course.

In the campaign and the months that followed, Bush said as much himself. The country is moving in the right direction, he would point out. We made fine progress during the Reagan years. Let's build on those accomplishments. We don't need to start all over again.

As inauguration day neared, he began to repeat the themes of his winning race: No new taxes; a kinder, gentler nation; better environmental protection; improvements in education; cautious forward movement toward more extensive arms accommodation with the Soviets; continuing humanitarian aid for the Nicaraguan Contras; flexible freeze on federal spending to bring down the budget deficit; more productivity through a capital gains tax to stimulate more jobs and cut the trade imbalance and a war on drugs and homelessness. Skeptics already demanded to be shown how one could spend more and cut the deficit without raising taxes. Bush vowed to show them.

Since Franklin Roosevelt, most of the presidents have had to learn how to operate the executive branch almost from scratch. Of course, Eisenhower, Kennedy and Johnson had relevant knowledge when elected, but not as chief executives. Nixon had the fullest training or at least contiguity to the job. But usually it was taking more and more time just to find out what there was and how to operate it as president. It was getting so that perhaps two years would transpire before the new chief fully understood the machinery at his command; not to mention the two thousand and more presidential appointees he was privileged to bring into his vast domain. Paul Volcker's commission on the bureaucracy has just announced the number has topped three thousand and should be reduced to two thousand.

Yet here was George Bush and his seasoned entourage, who could step into their traces and start pulling the load almost immediately. The haunting question remained, as it does for every new administration. What lay down the road for Bush and the country, and where would he and his team take that load?

Despite the Reagan legacy of peace and prosperity, which eased the way for Bush's electoral triumph, the United States of 1989 carried some heavy burdens at home and challenges abroad.

Domestically there was a soaring crime rate in many cities and a growing underclass in the urban ghettos of apparently uneducable and unemployable people, not to mention drugs and AIDS.

Overseas there was the Third World debt, which involved many American lending banks. The borrowers, particularly in Latin America, were finding it impossible to keep up their interest payments yet wanted to borrow more. This situation threatened the stability of the U.S. institutions.

Additionally, there was the spectacle of Japan's economic supremacy over the United States, even to the extent of what some considered intrusive buying into American real estate and industry.

In Europe, President of the Commission of European Communities Jack Delors had launched a dynamic economic policy for the Common Market, one which some analysts estimated would toss a challenge to American business very soon.

Mikhail Gorbachev, with his vision for the Soviet Union, had become a commanding political presence on the global stage despite the pitiful weaknesses of Russia's economy. Could George Bush maintain America's role as the world's last best hope for mankind, with an economically strong country, but without a comparable vision?

CHAPTER 19

The Vision of President Bush

THE CYNICS WHO HEARD GEORGE BUSH LAY OUT HIS priorities on the campaign trail rejected them as exaggerations at best and pure political lies at worst. They didn't know their target. As Bush believers have been aware since he was a little boy, Bush doesn't dissemble. He means what he says and will plough through walls to keep his word. Although light-hearted in manner he is dogged in redeeming pledges whether they be familial, social, commercial or political.

Consider the twenty years or so he spent aiming at the presidency. During that period of weighty executive and political responsibility, he made thousands of promises and day-to-day assurances to employees, presidents, constituents and supporters. He meant to honor them all, and to this writing I've been unable to discover an omission.

As this and other personal characteristics began to be written and talked about, Bush friends could say, it's not that he is evolving into this nice guy, it's only your perception of him that is evolving.

When Bush began to apply himself to the presidency, he met his campaign pledges one by one. Let's examine what in the minds of many is a paramount promise. True environmentalists treat their passion profoundly, even metaphysically. They are not to be put off with palliatives. Did the candidate really intend, if elected, to translate rhetoric into conscientious implementation as president?

Russell E. Train, former administrator of the Environmental Protection Agency (EPA), was suspicious of the term "balance" during the Reagan period. According to that administration, balance meant a fair consideration of both environmental and industry needs. Train felt that it was code for "screw the environment."[1]

Bush personally was programmed to be different. Look at his tastes as an individual: He has chosen a house that meets the open sea and sky on the Maine coast. He revels in fishing, swimming, camping and all the fresh-air games including horseshoe pitching. He would quickly have a pit dug for horseshoes at the White House.

At the same time he is hooked on his power boat and "treats," if that is the word, visitors to high-speed rampages—and that is the word—through the choppy blue waters off Kennebunkport. Lyndon Johnson gave his guests similar thrills by driving them at 75 miles per hour through the dust of Pedernales. As an oil man Bush was more enthralled by promoting an innovative offshore drilling rig than simply making money.

These competing predilections suggest a balance in Bush's mind between unblemished environment and industrial activity. When elected, Bush progressed into full-fledged commitment to save the biosphere. He thought for several weeks before assigning an EPA administrator. At last he came to William Reilly, who with Russell Train headed the U.S. World Wildlife Fund and the Conservation Foundation. He would be the first career environmentalist to head the agency. Bush wasn't just flirting with the issue, as Reilly's account of his appointment bears out.[2]

"The week of December 19, Bob Teeter of the transition team

called and asked me to see the vice president on December 21, which I did. He and Craig Fuller (VP's chief of staff) and I talked for 35 minutes. Fuller said, 'Mr. Vice President, we advisors are leaving the decision to you.' The VP then said 'Will you give me another 48 hours? I won't keep you hanging; there are just a couple of things I want to check out.'

"On December 22 the VP called and asked, 'Will you do it?' I replied 'Yes, I'd like to work for you to be the environmental president.' The vice president replied, 'That's what I want you to do.'

"On December 23, the VP invited me and my wife, Libby, to a lunch he and Barbara were giving at the White House mess. Barbara told the guests, 'Since this is Christmas I guess no one has to worry about calories.' George Bush said, 'Not everyone can forget about them.' Barbara replied, 'Listen, all my mail says the people like me fat and wrinkled and white haired.'

"He is so spontaneous and warm as a person [The slender, youthful Reillys hadn't really known the Bushes before]; they both are so terribly courteous. They took me and Libby on a tour of the White House. We went into the Lincoln bedroom and he showed me a copy under glass [one of five extant] of the Gettysburg Address. Then we went out on Truman's balcony and looked at the south lawn. Then we saw Reagan's exercise equipment—mostly weightlifting gear, plus the automatic running machine that Bush had in the VP's house."

Later, Governor John H. Sununu, now White House chief of staff, called Reilly to read the environmental part of the budget message and find out whether he had any problems with any part or wanted anything out of the message. He told Reilly that Bush's instructions were that anything on the environment must be cleared with Reilly.

Furthermore, said Reilly, the word had gone out that our foreign policy must be sensitive to environmental considerations. Comparing George Bush to his predecessor, said Reilly, "He is personally engaged, aware and reading things."

The indications are that Bush made similar personal effort to know the issues of each department and the people whom he had selected to run them. He would appear for the swearing in

of the new chief in each case, even at the EPA, where he was
the first president ever to go near the agency. In his acceptance
speech Reilly, making sport of the difficulties his predecessors
had with access to the president, told Bush he "should feel
free to drop by any time."

At the first meeting of the cabinet, in Blair House before the
inaugural, Bush said, "This is going to be an open presidency. I
want you all to feel free to call me at any time; I'm going to call
you." Whereupon Sununu looked at the cabinet people and
said that when they did, he hoped they'd let him know. Bush
answered for them, "Well, okay, if we remember to do so."
Bush wanted no shield from his direct contact with his cabinet
officers. It would become evident that he wanted no shield
from contact with anyone with whom he chose to communi-
cate. Sununu himself would clarify the point that the president would sift information and opinion himself, but still
would want those on his team to speak up even when they
differed with him.

On January 13 the *Washington Post* published a list of
"Marching Orders" that Bush had prepared for the cabinet.
Some of the points were Think big, challenge the system and
adhere to the highest ethical standards. I don't like "kiss and
tell" books. Don't leak; put your name on the record if you have
something to say. Air your differences to me before the decision; afterward support the decision. Work with the Congress;
whatever the problems, remember we're not dealing with the
enemy. I don't expect a lot of my children or their children to
be on the payroll.[3]

He also initiated a new approach to the press. He would be
much more available; didn't want questions shouted at him as
he mounted his helicopter; and soon made it clear that he
preferred small, informal get-togethers with newsmen to the
large, formalized pomp-and-circumstance affairs of the Reagan
days. Marlin Fitzwater, who once had been spokesman at the
EPA and had served as Bush's press aide during his vice
presidency, would stay on. Fitzwater is calm, honest, funny
and well liked by his demanding clientele. When twitted by
the press about the dearth of new faces in Bush's burgeoning

group of nominees, the chubby-visaged, balding Fitzwater said he'd be happy to have a new face.

What would Fitzwater say when the "Vision Thing," as Bush had come to refer to this recurrent question, came up? Kenneth Tomlinson, editor of *Reader's Digest*, raised this point with a quote from Proverbs: "Where there is no vision, the people perish." Tomlinson declared that it's the same in federal agencies. "Where people are not working toward specific goals, stagnation or mayhem is inevitable."[4] This question, if valid, must have a response in some form from the chief executive. What is it?

By "vision" most people seem to mean the ability to foresee what lies ahead and the imagination to overcome it if it is a problem, the wit to take advantage of it if it is a windfall, or to achieve an objective if it seems possible and desirable.

George Washington exercised vision by warning the young United States against foreign entanglements. Woodrow Wilson and Franklin Roosevelt exhibited the same kind of vision when they saw the European wars of 1914 and 1939 as threats to the United States. They each tried first to avoid the conflict and later to engage the American people in it victoriously. Dwight Eisenhower showed vision when he counseled Americans to be wary of the ominously growing military-industrial complex in the United States. John Kennedy frequently gave the impression of having vision, for example, when he saw the potential of a U.S. mission to the moon and pledged that there be one within ten years. Ronald Reagan filled the air waves with his visionary shining city upon a hill where all Americans could be happy.

George Bush tries for vision as he talks about a thousand points of light where all Americans can work together to help the unfortunate. Mostly his vision is expressed in practical terms. In keeping with his belief in the Declaration of Independence and other shibboleths of democracy and the worship of God, he wants for all humans to enjoy peace, prosperity and the pursuit of happiness.

So far he has offered no specific vision of what he wants the country to do and be under his presidency. Yet he is an idealist. He views the world as susceptible to the principles by which he has guided his own career, by which he clearly intends to run this country. In his inaugural address he had the opportunity to set goals for those principles.

Bush would be well-served to promulgate a "vision" or two. As president he has writers and thinkers available in any quantity or quality he chooses. He should call for them to dish up visions to catch the country's fancy. From his "bully pulpit," as Teddy Roosevelt called the presidency, he would have no difficulty sharing them with his countrymen. He is sound enough in judgment to pick only the visions that are consonant with the welfare of the nation.

There are citizens who deem Bush to be a shallow man. He seems to many simply a nice fellow who knows how to fight for what he believes. He sticks to the covenants he makes, such as loyalty to friends, adherence to his marital and commercial contracts and trustworthy service to government and business commitments. His background demonstrates over and over again that what you see is what you get. He is a disciplined, experienced public servant who never forgets the feelings and concerns of the individual. Does that make a shallow man?

He's not an intellectual, others cavil, How can he understand enough to run the most diverse and important country on the globe? How can he compete with the savants heading other governments?

His words and actions on January 20, 1989, provide the necessary clues, as this story reaches its end. George Bush's swearing in before a throng of 300,000 on the West Side of the Capitol was a fitting finale to his quest of so many years.

He began his address with simple language and pronounced some soaring thoughts, but kept this most important talk of his life, clear, caring and direct. He spoke of the "new breeze" that would sweep the nation as the 30-knot wind blew his forelock across his forehead. Pushing it away several times, even as he repeated the phrase "new breeze," his tone was cheerful and firm. There was no hint of the whiny schoolmaster personality that had once dismayed his loyalists and irritated his opponents.

There were no unnecessary generalities. He ticked off the way he would govern and the issues on which he would focus. He turned toward Speaker of the House James Wright and Senate Majority Leader George J. Mitchell and held out his large open fist, matching words to that gesture. America has sent us to Washington to work together, not to bicker, he stressed. For twenty minutes his ideas came, brief and unelaborate, yet electric with meaning.

Possibly the only marring note was his allusion to pregnant women who had chosen life for their unborn children. This jarred the pro-choice factions, but not enough to invite an uproar.

Did a thought fly through his head, as he saw his eighty-seven-year-old mother sitting close by? Was he wishing that the man who started him in this direction, whose influence has been so strong, whose record he tried first to emulate and then to exceed could be here today? How would Prescott Bush feel about his son ascending to the highest office in the land?

George finished speaking, and below him, spread along the Capitol Mall and around its huge new reflecting pool, hundreds of thousands clapped. Surely many millions more in the United States and around the world applauded in different settings and in different languages at that very instant.

George Bush had won the greatest contest of his career. His fight for the ultimate goal was done. Yet the hardest test of his life was just beginning.

Notes

CHAPTER 2

[1] John Davies, *The Legend of Hobey Baker* (Boston: Little Brown & Co., 1966), p. 52.
[2] August Heckscher, *St Paul's, The Life of a New England School* (New York: Charles Scribner's Sons, 1980), p. 360.
[3] Davies, *op. cit.*, p. 6.
[4] Heckscher, *op. cit.*, p. 155.

CHAPTER 3

[1] U.S. Navy Memorial Museum records in Washington, D.C.
[2] *Ibid.*
[3] *Ibid.*
[4] Ibid.
[5] *Ibid.*

CHAPTER 4

[1] *Omaha World Herald* article on George Bush by Jack Cavanaugh, 1988.
[2] George Bush, *Looking Forward* (New York: Doubleday, 1987), p. 43.
[3] John H. Chafee, senior senator from Rhode Island. All the quotes come from an interview with the author in 1988.
[4] Robert Ireland of Brown Brother, Harriman, interview with author in 1989.

[5] George deF. Lord, interview with the author in 1989.
[6] Nancy Bush Ellis, interview with the author in 1988.
[7] Darwin Payne, *Initiative in Energy, The Story of Dresser Industries* New York: Simon and Schuster, 1979), pp. 110–111.
[8] *Ibid.*, p. 115.

CHAPTER 5

[1] Werner Erhard, notable founder and administrator of the EST training program.
[2] George Bush, *Looking Forward* (New York: Doubleday, 1987), pp. 50–51.
[3] *Ibid.*, p. 58.
[4] John Ashmun, interview with the author in 1988.
[5] George Bush, with Doug Wead, *George Bush, Man of Integrity* (Eugene, Oregon: Harvest House Publishers, 1988), p. 26.
[6] "Midland Scrapbook," special issue of the *Midland Reporter Telegram*, Midland, Texas, p. 2.
[7] *Ibid.*, p. 11.
[8] *Ibid.*, p. 8.
[9] *Ibid.*, p. 11.
[10] *Ibid.*, p. 5.
[11] Article by David Hoffman in the Washington Post, October 30, 1988, p. A1.
[12] Bush, Prescott S., Oral History Research office of Columbia University interview by John T. Mason, Jr., Greenwich, Connecticut, 1966.
[13] George Bush, *op. cit.*, pp. 70–71.
[14] Hugh Liedtke, interview with the author in 1988.
[15] C. Fred Chambers, interview with the author in 1988.
[16] Charles R. Powell, interview with the author in 1988.
[17] William T. Bush, interview with the author in 1988.

CHAPTER 6

[1] George Bush, *Looking Forward* (New York: Doubleday, 1987), p. 82.
[2] *Ibid.*
[3] Prescott S. Bush, Oral History Research office of Columbia University interview with John T. Mason, Jr., Greenwich, Connecticut, 1966, pp. 293–294.
[4] George Bush, *op. cit.*, p. 83.
[5] *Ibid.*, p. 85.
[6] *Ibid.*, p. 86.
[7] Ralph Yarborough, interview with the author in 1988.

CHAPTER 7

[1] John Ashmun, interview with the author in 1988.
[2] Public Broadcasting System (PBS), "Campaign: The Choice," a 90-minute "Frontline" documentary, November 24, 1988.
[3] *Ibid.*
[4] George Bush, *Looking Forward* (New York: Doubleday, 1987), p. 84.

[5] *Wall Street Journal* commentary "Politics and People" by Allan L. Otten, September 21, 1966.
[6] George Bush, *op. cit.*, p. 91.
[7] "The First Family That Just Won't Quit," *People* magazine, (date?), p. 56.
[8] *Ibid.*, p. 63.
[9] *Ibid.*, p. 61.

CHAPTER 8

[1] Rose Zamaria interview with the author in 1988.
[2] *Ibid.*
[3] Marvin Bush interview with the author in 1988.
[4] *Ibid.*
[5] *Christian Science Monitor* series of three articles by Lyn Shepard, last article, January 6, 1968.
[6] George Bush, *Looking Forward* (New York: Doubleday, 1987), pp. 94–95.
[7] *Ibid.*, p. 92.
[8] *Ibid.*, pp. 92–93.
[9] *Ibid.*, p. 101.
[10] *Ibid.*
[11] Gail Sheehy, *Character, America's Search for Leadership* (New York: William Morrow & Co., 1988), p. 174.
[12] *Washington Post*, October 27, 1970, article by William Greider.
[13] *Ibid.*
[14] The *New York Times*, November 11, 1970, "Washington Notes" by James M. Naughton.
[15] The *New York Times*, November 5, 1970, article by Martin Waldron.
[16] *Ibid.*

CHAPTER 9

[1] Charles W. Yost, *History and Memory* (New York: W. W. Norton & Co.), p. 242.
[2] George Bush, *Looking Forward* (New York: Doubleday, 1987), p. 110.
[3] Bush, *op. cit.*, p. 112.
[4] Christopher Phillips interview with the author May 24, 1988.
[5] *Ibid.*
[6] *Ibid.*
[7] Bush, *op. cit.*, p. 114.
[8] Brian Urquhart, *A Life in Peace and War* (New York: Harper and Row, Publishers Inc., 1987), p. 266.
[9] Bush, *op. cit.*, p. 114.
[10] *Ibid.*
[11] Jacob D. Beam, *Multiple Exposure* (New York: W. W. Norton & Co., 1977), pp. 224–225.
[12] Walter Ganzi interview with the author on February 17, 1989.
[13] Urquhart, *op. cit.*, p. 263.
[14] Bush, *op. cit.*, p. 119.
[15] The *New York Times*, "Man in the News" article by Kathleen Teltsch,

headlined "A Diplomatic Exalter of Politics, George Herbert Walker Bush," December 12, 1972.
16 The Hon. Seymour M. Finger interview with the author on March 10, 1989.
17 John Stevenson interview with the author in Washington, D.C., May 12, 1988.

CHAPTER 10

1 George Bush, *Looking Forward* (New York: Doubleday, 1987), p. 121.
2 Nancy Thawley interview with the author at the RNC, June 6, 1988.
3 *Ibid.*
4 *Ibid.*
5 Mary Louise Smith interviews with the author in 1988 and 1989 ending February 19, 1989.
6 The lady does not wish to have her name used.
7 The *Washington Post*, August 9, 1988, part of a series on George Bush by Walter Pincus and Bob Woodward, p. A10.
8 The *New York Times Magazine*, March 6, 1988, article by Randall Rothenberg, "In Search of George Bush," p. 46.
9 Bush, *op. cit.*, p. 124.
10 Ibid., p. 122.
11 *Washington Post*, *op. cit.*, p. A10.
12 Bush, *op. cit.*, p. 6.

CHAPTER 11

1 Dean Burch interview with the author in 1988.
2 Charles H. Percy interview with the author in 1988.
3 George Bush, *Looking Forward* (New York: Doubleday, 1987), p. 134.
4 *Ibid.*, p. 135.
5 *Ibid.*, p. 153.
6 William Colby, *Honorable Men, My Life in the CIA*, (New York: Simon and Schuster, 1978), p. 340.
7 *Ibid.*
8 John Vandeleur article from Hong Kong for *London's Sunday Telegraph*, February 26, 1989.
9 David Maraniss article for the *Washington Post Magazine*, January 22, 1989, "All the President's Kids," p. 18.

CHAPTER 12

1 George Bush, *Looking Forward* (New York: Doubleday, 1987), p. 156.
2 Nomination of George Bush to be director of Central Intelligence Agency hearing record of Senate Armed Services Committee, December 15 and 16, 1976, p. 2.
3 *Ibid.*, p. 10.
4 *Ibid.*, p. 9.
5 *Ibid.*

[6] Bush, *op. cit.*, p. 164.

[7] *Ibid.*, p. 169.

[8] L. Dean Brown, interview with the author in 1988.

[9] George Bush, *op. cit.*, p. 172.

[10] Bob Woodward and Walter Pincus, fourth article in a series, "George Bush: Man and Politician," *Washington Post*, August 1988, p. A8.

[11] *Ibid.*, p. A1.

[12] *Ibid.*

[13] *Ibid.*

[14] Cord Meyer, *Facing Reality, From World Federalism to the CIA*, (New York: Harper and Row, Publisher, Inc., 1980), pp. 225–226.

[15] James L. Holloway III, interviews with the author in 1988 and 1989.

[16] William Colby interview with the author in 1988.

[17] Richard Helms address at the Veterans of the OSS Dinner, Washington, D.C., May 24, 1983.

CHAPTER 13

[1] George Clifford, article for *People* magazine, November 21, 1988, p. 58.

[2] Bob Woodward and Walter Pincus, fifth article in a series, "George Bush: Man and Politician," *Washington Post*, August 1, 1988, p. A16.

[3] Roswell B. Perkins, who served in the Rockefeller Brothers Fund studies project, interview with the author in March 1989.

[4] Jing Xianfa interview with the author in 1989.

[5] C. Fred Bush, *C. Fred's Story*, slightly edited by Barbara Bush, (Garden City, New York: Doubleday, 1984), p. 42.

[6] Jim Oberwetter interview with the author in 1989.

[7] Andrew Falkiewicz interview with the author in 1989.

[8] M. Charles Bakst article for the *Providence Journal*, September 8, 1979, p. A-7.

[9] *Ibid.*

[10] George Bush, *Looking Forward* (New York: Doubleday, 1987), p. 191.

[11] *Ibid.*, p. 197.

[12] David Keene, interview with the author in 1989.

[13] *Ibid.*

[14] *Ibid.*

[15] George Bush, *op. cit.*, p. 201.

[16] *Ibid.*, p. 15.

[17] *Ibid.*

[18] Keene, *op. cit.*

[19] Bush, *op. cit.*, p. 15.

CHAPTER 14

[1] George Bush, *Looking Forward* (New York: Doubleday, 1987), p. 16.

[2] These numbers furnished by Barbara Bush's office, April 30, 1988.

[3] George Bush, *op. cit.*, p. 223.

[4] Larry Speakes, *Speaking Out* (New York: Charles Scribners' Sons), p. 11.

[5] *New York Times*, February 28, 1982, article by Steven R. Weisman.

[6] *Ibid.*

[7] *Ibid.*

[8] Report of Reagan administration's regulatory achievements, August 11, 1983.

CHAPTER 15

[1] Anthony Thompson interview with the author in 1988.

[2] Direct quotes and other references to Admiral Daniel Murphy are drawn from an interview by the author with him on August 8, 1988.

[3] Harry McPherson, *A Political Education* (Boston: Little Brown & Co., 1972), p. 70.

[4] George Bush, *Looking Forward* (New York: Doubleday, 1987), pp. 238–239).

[5] Comments made by Boyden Gray during an interview with the author in May 1988 and other short exchanges that year.

[6] Barbara Bush, interview with author on May 9, 1988.

[7] Mike Royko, "Why Bush Leaves Women Cold," *Chicago Times,*

[8] Arnold Beichman, interview with the author on July 11, 1988.

[9] *Washington Post,* December 21, 1988, article by David Hoffman.

[10] Bush, *op. cit.,* p. 244.

[11] *Washington Post,* Outlook section, article by Curt Surplee, July 10, 1988.

[12] *Ibid.*

CHAPTER 17

[1] Elizabeth Drew, "Letter from Washington" article in *New Yorker* magazine, October 10, 1988, p. 100.

[2] George Will, column in *Washington Post,* September 27, 1988, p. A21.

[3] Drew, *op. cit.,* p. 102.

CHAPTER 19

[1] This point based on author's observation of his friend Train's reaction to the first two years of the Reagan administration's handling of environmental issues.

[2] William Reilly, in an interview with the author in February 1989.

[3] The *Washington Post,* January 13, 1989, p. A13.

[4] Kenneth W. Tomlinson, Advice to Incoming Appointees,*Washington Post,* March 7, 1989, pF1.

Index

Ailes, Roger, 231, 232, 240
Allison, Jim, 93, 94, 100
Andover *see* Phillips Academy
Ashley, Ludlow, 72, 107, 129
Ashmun, John, 59–60, 89
Atwater, Lee, 232, 240
Avenger Torpedo Bomber (TBM), 29–31, 33, 34–36, 223

Baker, Hobey, 21
Baker, Howard, 173, 175, 176, 178, 180
Baker, James, 180–181
Baker, James III, 170, 188, 199, 233, 240
Barrett, Joyce, 6–7, 8
Barrett, Richard, 6–7, 8
Bemiss, Fitzgerald, 14, 40
Bennett, W. Tapley, 120, 124
Bentsen, Lloyd, 86, 112, 113, 114, 235; 1988 campaign debate with Quayle, 237–238
Briscoe, Frank, 93, 94, 95
Brown Brothers, Harriman, 3, 4–5, 6, 44, 52
Bruce, David, 140, 144
Bush, Barbara Pierce, 30, 44, 95, 118, 168, 211–215; and Robin, 72; at Yale, 45; characteristics of, 102, 131, 165, 187, 211–215; community service, 61; courtship of, 24–26; in China, 144, 146, 150–151, 152; in Texas, 56–57, 60, 61; marriage of, 25, 40–41, 95–96, 213–214, 225; on George, 213–214; on George's family, 212–213; relationship with children, 96–97, 102–103, 151, 210; *see also* Bush, George
Bush, C. Fred, 145, 150–151, 152
Bush, Columba, 151, 222
Bush, Dorothy, 2, 3, 7, 13, 51, 151; characteristics of, 212–213; influence on George, 212; relationship with children, 15–16, 17
Bush, Dorothy ("Doro"), 72, 93, 96, 97, 152, 166
Bush, George, and assassination attempt on Reagan, 189–190, 191–192; and Iran-Contra scandal, 216–218, 233; and Lyndon Johnson, 108, 109; and Nixon, 93, 112, 115, 116, 122, 134–136, 149; and Quayle controversies, 225–226, 229, 231, 235; and Robin,

265